WAR MORTAL GODS (Book One)

Kipjo K. Ewers

For Sophia...

OTHER WORKS

ACKNOWLEDGMENTS

I would like to take a minute to thank everyone who brought me to the dance. My mother and father for having me and giving me the best life a kid and his two brothers could have. My brothers are not just my siblings but my best friends. Mrs. Greene, my second-grade teacher who taught me and made me believe at a young age that I could be a writer. My wife, who is also my business partner in EVO Universe, both got me into New York ComicCon and paid out of her pocket for me to attend the event, among other things. She's the woman that stands next to the man, not behind him.

Finally, I would like to thank you, the person reading this book. Without you, this would not be possible for me. So thank you from the bottom of my heart.

And I hope you enjoy reading this as much as I did writing it.

CHAPTER 1

Planet Volori, several billion light-years from Earth, a world ruled by a single iron-fisted monarchy, its citizens, a species of humanoid hairless felines with feathers growing mostly on their heads and backs, were judged by a class and gender system. Where being male and of nobility got one a seat at the table.

An industrialized planet once covered in foliage, was now seventy percent covered in harden metal.

~ ~

On the surface of the planet, an intense battle teetering on all-out war erupted throughout the capital city as the massive Volorion War Machine faced off against three Anunnaki emissaries known as the Eye of Set, the Eye of Osiris, and the Eye of Ra.

A peaceful diplomatic meeting with the High Prime Vbzarma to discuss putting an end to his citizens partaking in piracy against ships under the protection of the Dominion Council in exchange for the Council not levying sanctions against his empire and barricading their trade routes, turned into an ambush in the throne room with the intention of beheading and mutilating Laurence and his cousin Anubis's bodies while enacting vile sexual atrocities upon their cousin Bastet.

Needless to say, the trio decided not to partake in the High Prime's plan, and to leave the planet by force if necessary.

The battle-torn capital littered with destroyed Volorion war machines and dead or injured soldiers was a clear indication that prior negotiations had fallen through.

~ ~

Armed with their familiars and powerful Anunnaki armor, the trio currently in their Celestial mode conversions, Laurence Danjuma, and his cousins continued to wreak havoc on the Volorion military forces attempting to bring them down.

The mouth of Anubis's helm, shaped similar to a jackal creature, opened up, and fired an intense sheering blue beam that tore through three Dominator tanks. Red and black gargantuan thirty feet tall crab-like four-legged vehicles with two plasma beam cannons on the side of the main body along with other armaments. The main body rotated and elevated on the arm attached to its underbelly and base legs allowing it to execute three hundred and sixty-degree attacks.

The beam cut each of the tanks' arms in half, sending the central bodies crashing down on top of their bases, causing explosions to shake the ground.

Not to be outdone by her cousin, Bastet, also in Celestial mode, had the appearance of a metallic humanoid lioness as she leaped into the air going aerial with her familiar Mafdet in its bow configuration. She took skillful aim firing an arrow-shaped energy projectile punching a fatal hole straight through a flat metallic gunmetal grey hammer-shaped Volorion warship.

Smoke spewed from its new orifice as it went into a stalled drift before falling from the sky. The ship first became a fireball as it clipped a small building breaking in half. Its two parts came down, crushing any soldier or vehicle unlucky enough to evade it while scattering the ground forces in the vicinity.

As she descended back down into the capital, her familiar transformed into its bolo whip mode. With a lashing motion, she latched onto the hammer-shaped bow of another warship. As her familiar channeled raw Awakening energy through its tail converted whip, Bastet gave a simple pull cutting the ship into several pieces.

She landed shaking the ground while bringing destruction from the sky onto more of the Volorion War Machine.

Mirroring his cousins, Laurence, the Eye of Ra with his armor in Celestial mode, which gave him the shape of a metallic golden humanoid eagle, tore through the sky with sound barrier-breaking speed barreling through a squadron of Birds of Preys. They were one-person black fighters with a mix of speeder bike and a headless metallic hunting bird with razor-sharp wings and tail feathers housing three powerful anti-gravity engines.

The sky became crackling fireworks as Volorion soldiers and fragments of detonating Birds of Prey fell from the firmament due to the Eye of Ra's raw planetary brute force tearing them apart.

Those that survived the attack spun their ships in mid-air, regrouping to chase Laurence down and kill him.

Laurence quickly decreased his acceleration and hovered in mid-air, aiming with Sol in staff mode. Sol widened his mouth, firing a cosmic beam of Awakening energy obliterating another large portion of the advancing squadron, leaving just a couple that scattered avoiding the attack.

There was no opportunity to celebrate as he created a golden energy shield construct to block a powerful primary cannon blast from a Volorion warship.

Although the shielding prevented any damage, the force of the blast smacked the Eye of Ra out of the sky, launching him through two buildings. Inches away from plowing into a boutique store, Laurence got his bearings and slowed his momentum coming to a full stop.

"Well, that was embarrassing." He muttered to himself.

"Yes, it was."

Laurence sneered to the sound of the playful gloating voice of Bastet ringing in his helm as a visual of her face showed up on his inside display.

Before he could respond, the Eye of Ra came under fire again. Laurence rocketed back into the sky skillfully, flying through the tunnels his crash landing created within the two buildings for a bit of cover. As he exited the second building, Laurence mentally punched his armor to hypersonic speeds plowing into the hull of the warship that shot him out of the sky.

Stunned Volorion soldiers froze in their tracks as the Eye of Ra, now inside the vessel itself, aimed his staff firing another cosmic energy blast, which blew off the front of the ship while vaporizing anyone within its path. Laurence exited the remains of the burning craft, joining the overall battle with his cousins as it fell from the sky, detonating from the impact of it striking the ground.

"We cannot continue this battle," Laurence announced while landing next to Anubis, swatting away energy attacks with his familiar transformed khopeshes.

"Who says we can't?" Bastet asked with a scoffing tone. "I still wait for these Volorion scum to draw sweat from me."

"The longer we stay here fighting, the faster this turns from a diplomatic incident to an act of war in favor of the Volorions." Laurence summated.

"Our cousin speaks painful truth," Anubis answered in agreement.

"Agreed," Bastet snarled in disgust. "However, we're not the ones drawing out this conflict. Further bloodshed would come to an end if they dropped their shielding and let us go about our business."

"Sol, how do we break through this barrier?" Laurence asked.

"Given the energy sources that are powering it, any counter-power source used to bring down the barrier would tear the planet apart. The shielding is also currently preventing me from tapping into any external power source."

"Killing billions of innocent inhabitants just to escape is not an option," Laurence growled. "There has to be some form of generator or series of satellites focusing this barrier!"

"Detecting a combination of both being used to generate this field." Sol analyzed. "A total of two hundred satellites focusing the power of their sun, along with twenty strategically placed power plants across the planet connected to the planet's core."

"What about commanding their systems to shut down the field?" Laurence asked.

"I, Ska, Azkra, and Mafdet have already attempted that. The Volorions have educated themselves on how to deal with a hostile cyber-attack. Their system is guarded by ten independent artificially intelligent programs that are quite efficient in keeping us out."

"How many of those stations need to fall for the shielding to fail?" Laurence asked.

"I calculate at least half."

"Tactical change then," Laurence determined. "We need to split our resources to bring down the shielding ourselves so that we can leave this planet."

"Well, what delays you?" Bastet snorted. "Be off then. Anubis and I shall continue to play with the Volorion War Machine."

Laurence glared at her as he sidestepped the primary cannon blast from a War Chariot and returned fire with Sol blowing it to bits.

"This is an age thing …isn't it? I'm forty years old woman."

"And fifty human years is weaning age on Anu."

"Bastet gives valid point, cousin," Anubis answered.

"Fine! I'll do it my damn self!" Laurence barked.

With a thought, the Eye of Ra took flight shaking the sky of Volori, heading for the first power plant he had to bring down.

Sure enough, several squadrons of Birds of Prey and some power suits that had flight capability gave chase to hunt him down.

"Think he'll be alright?" Bastet asked while bringing down another Dominator.

"You raze him every opportunity afford to you, and then act as a mother whose child no longer craves the tit when he leaves," Anubis mocked. "Our cousin is more than capable of the task at hand."

"I act no such ways toward him!"

"Aye, you do."

~ ~

The Eye of Ra skillfully maneuvered out of the array of energy cannon fire from Volorion warriors chasing him as the first shield power plant came into range. As expected, heavy defenses were in place to repel him. Several Dominators, soldiers in heavy-duty power suits, and stationary cannons opened fire with scorching air volleys to blow Laurence out of the sky.

His speed did not decrease as he weaved through the hostile attack, while the squadrons behind him were torn apart by friendly fire. The remainder that followed him broke off their chase two miles from the plant as ports opened up and fired missiles and the Dominators protecting it.

"Identifying projectiles as energy seekers," Sol relayed.

"Tankable?" Laurence asked.

"If by 'tankable' you're asking if you can survive two hundred fifty projectiles, each with ten times the destructive force of an Earth Soviet RDS-220 hydrogen bomb. The answer is yes; however, it will not feel pleasant."

"No pain, no gain," Laurence smirked.

"I highly doubt the phrase popularized by Jane Fonda originating from a second century Hebrew text pertained to this."

Laurence ignored his familiar's retort changing his trajectory, shooting upward heading toward the stratosphere of Volori. As the missiles tracking his immense energy signature switched course chasing after him, the Eye of Ra evaded them for a second time, going into a dive bomb.

"Based on your evasive flight pattern, course, and unwillingness to destroy the missiles, you are leading the armaments back to their origin point."

"Killing two birds with one big stone," the Eye of Ra confirmed. "And no, I wish not to learn the origin story of that phrase."

As Laurence suspected, the stationary cannons protecting the plant were prepared to suppress any incoming attack except for one directly above. Before the Dominators and Volorion soldiers in power suits could get into position to shoot him down, the Eye of Ra increased his speed punching a sizable hole through the ceiling of the power plant.

Laurence quickly flipped in mid-fall, landing into a crouched position cratering the metal floor while startling the technicians and soldiers inside the plant.

"I would run if I were all of you," he advised.

At the sound of incoming missiles, they all scattered, screaming for the exits.

None would escape the impact of all two hundred fifty energy seekers detonating at once combined with the explosive destruction of the plant itself, taking out anything within a radius of several thousand miles.

Standing in the center of ground zero, surrounded by smoldering rubble of what was left of the plant, was the Eye of Ra protected by a gold dome energy shield constructed by Sol.

"You're right," Laurence admitted. "That was very unpleasant."

"Planetary shield strength has deteriorated by five percent," Sol confirmed.

"Off to the next target then."

With a thought, the Eye of Ra took off rattling the sky to bring down the next power plant.

~ ~

Back at the capital, the battle was turning into a stalemate. The Volorion War Machine could not fell the combined might of the Eye of Set and Osiris, while on the other side, the forces quickly replenished what the dual of cousins destroyed.

Eventually, it would come down to whether Anubis or Bastet would either tire or make a mistake, or if the War Machine would be brutally decimated to no longer become a threat.

"You have to commend them for their bravery," Bastet jeered.

She said it while skillfully side spinning and sidestepping a barrage of Dominator cannon fire, before returning fire with two energy arrow blasts popping the massive four-legged vehicle's turret similar to that of an egg, while her second arrow obliterated a War Chariot before it could get a shot off.

"Most of the Dominators and War Chariots are drones," Anubis informed her amid his battle. "Volorion soldiers who fail to fight, or desert are punished by drawn and quartering of all six of their appendages."

His cousin paused, thinking about what he said.

"I assume the fifth rope is for the head, what is the sixth rope …?"

Her eyes widened as it dawned on her from Anubis's dull expression on her display.

"Oooooh!"

"It is said they use a hook for that appendage."

"No wonder we're winning, warriors driven by fear never …"

Bastet's sentence was interrupted as she barely evaded a destructive missile attack from a Warhammer ship that knocked her off her feet. She cursed in the language of her homeworld while using the momentum of the blast to tuck and flip backward, landing in an upright crouched position. She slid at least two feet back before coming to a stop.

Before she could retaliate, Anubis, already airborne, landed in front of her. He unleashed an Awakening sword slice projectile splitting everything in its path in half, including the offending Warhammer ship that attacked his cousin.

"Mafdet, I will need you to even our odds," Bastet commanded her familiar.

"As you command Mistress Bastet."

Mafdet converted back into its cat form, detaching itself from its tail, which Bastet held. The tail transformed into a long double polearm weapon with massive blades on each side, similar to a Japanese naginata radiating with Awakening energy.

As its tail transformed, Mafdet changed as well, growing in both size and mass, similar to that of the Volorion War Chariots, ground vehicles with the characteristics of an Earth tank only more heavily armored. They hovered via anti-gravity propulsion systems, while the main gun on their turrets was shorter due to firing metal melting plasma rounds.

With a mighty leap, the feline-shaped familiar went on the attack pouncing on a War Chariot caving it in with its weight. Mafdet then opened its mouth, unleashing a powerful beam of Awakening energy demolishing the base of a Dominator bringing it down on top of itself. Mafdet then went about the battlefield on a calm, calculated rampage attacking anyone and anything within its path.

"Ska, join Mafdet," Anubis commanded his familiar.

"As you command."

Upon his release, the Eye of Set's familiar transformed into its scorpion mode, landing on its six metallic legs. As it scurried away, it also increased in size and mass, becoming slightly more massive than Mafdet. The stinger in its tail retracted as it turned into a cannon. Its first victim was a Warhammer ship that it brought down with one shot.

The mammoth-sized rampaging cybernetic Scorpion slammed straight into an inbound Dominator tearing it apart, starting first by blowing the main turret off at close range with its tail and then ripping its base in half with its massive claws.

It tossed apart the two destroyed halves searching for more targets to bring down.

Ska's twin Azkra still in Anubis's hand, also transformed, growing in size, becoming a khopesh sized two-handed great sword. The Eye of Set temporarily raised a blue protective dome shield around himself and his cousin to communicate with Laurence without interruption.

"Cousin, what is your status?"

"Within the range of the next plant," Laurence confirmed.

"Do bolster your efforts, little cousin," Bastet jumped in. "I tire of the Volorion's hospitality."

"On it."

Anubis turned to his cousin with a dull, boring glare.

"Care to entertain our hosts once more?"

Bastet answered first with fluttered eyes of disgust.

"If we must."

Both went aerial splitting up the second the Eye of Set dropped his shielding. With one swing from her dual bladed polearm, Bastet removed the head of a Volorion soldier on top of a Bird of Prey, sending his body and ship crashing into a nearby building. She descended back into the streets, landing into a nest of armor powered warriors. She used close combat techniques to cut down whoever was unfortunate enough to come into range of her weapon.

Anubis hunted larger prey as he cleaved through two Dominators severing their rotating arms, bringing the massive turrets down on top of their bodies, causing them to detonate. On the way down, he used a one-arm swing with his khopesh to split a War Chariot in half before landing.

~ ~

Time is no longer on our side to get fancy. Sol, pinpoint the location of the main reactor."

"Reactor has been located."

With a thought, Laurence's armor simulated speeds equivalent to a lightning bolt. The attack was similar to the firing of a railgun, only several times more devastating. The Eye of Ra, using his body as a missile, blitzed through the plant's defenses while punching a crater-sized hole right through it, which ruptured the reactor as he came out on the other side.

He decelerated, coming to a hover several miles away as the plant became the devastating equivalent of a lit Blockbuster firecracker tossed into a birdhouse, with falling debris reaching the distance Laurence covered.

"Planetary shield strength has now deteriorated by ten percent," Sol confirmed.

"On to the next one," Laurence sighed.

The Eye of Ra took to the skies again, going semi-orbital skimming the boundaries of the planetary shield to cover more ground.

~ ~

From a safe distance away, High Prime Vbzarma, in his battle armor, stood within the confines of a War Chariot flanked to his right by his eldest son Prince Volker also adorned in his armor. They watched on two holographic displays as the Anunnaki warriors wreaked havoc within his capital and across his planet.

"Our forces are taking a heavy toll from these bloody Anunnaki scum, father."

"Remember your history boy, there is a reason why our military is known throughout the universe as the War Machine," High Prime Vbzarma reprimanded his son. "The Volorion Empire has spent eons amassing, and perfecting weapons of war that has made us a profitable militaristic presence."

"Then it is abundantly clear those three are not educated in our 'glorious' history."

High Prime Vbzarma slowly turned to his son, intending, to backhand him for his snarky remark when one of the holographic images in front of him changed without his command.

Both Vbzarma and his son's eyes widened to the image of Horus projected before them.

"Lord …Horus?" Vbzarma addressed him with concerned bewilderment.

"I see the Eyes are holding their own relatively well against your infamous War Machine."

An unnerved Vbzarma glanced at his son, who shrugged his shoulders utterly oblivious to how Horus could have any insight into the battle raging on in the capital.

"How …?"

"The same way I am able to communicate with you, I am currently viewing the battle through your warships and surveillance systems within the capital."

"Then you should also know with our planetary shielding up, the Eyes have nowhere to go. We shall overcome them in moments, and ..."

"About that," Horus dryly interrupted him.

"Plans have changed. The Eyes must venture here to Earth. Raise your shielding and allow them to depart."

A scowl of confusion fell upon High Prime Vbzarma's face as he narrowed his eyes a bit, attempting to comprehend what was demanded of him.

"Did you just order me to release them?"

"Is there a problem?" Horus asked with visible impatience growing on his face.

"You devise plan which causes Council to give notice to my homeworld, which is the last thing I wanted. A plan that delivers three Eyes from Anu to my soil. Eyes who are currently tearing up my planet, which includes the financial toll of the massive amount of damage done to my War Machine, and you want me to 'release them'?"

"Yes, immediately."

High Prime Vbzarma answered Horus's blank careless gaze with a face of rage and exposed feline teeth.

"Just who in the covuck do you think you are?"

The High Prime found his answer as he lost his voice, gasping for air, while his body began to rattle from his bones vibrating as Horus's eyes beamed brighter, revealing his power that could be felt light-years away.

"I am a living god promising you fortune, glory, and newly conquered worlds to claim as your own to expand your empire," he snarled. "Yours is not to question mortal; yours is to do as told. Unless I am to place your eldest son on the throne. Maybe he will be more obedient than you are after he witnesses your fall at my hands."

"No… Lord Horus," High Prime Vbzarma groaned. "I shall …comply."

Prince Volker nervously looked on as his father gasping for air was finally released by the Ancient whose eyes returned to their natural glow. A stumbling Vbzarma slowly raised his head, hiding his rage as he looked at Horus, staring back at him.

"Raise your planet's shielding and pull back your forces," Horus commanded. "They will come to me, and I shall deal with them in mine own way."

Horus, without another word, ended the transmission.

"Raise …the shields and pull the War Machine back," High Prime Vbzarma ordered.

"Father! You would take commands from a lowly …!"

High Prime Vbzarma violently grabbed the front collar of his eldest son's armor, draping him up as his son looked at him in disbelief.

"Silence thy miserable tongue and do as commanded! Give the order to raise the bloody shields and pull our War Machine back! Now!"

~ ~

"Detecting planetary shielding powering down," Sol relayed to Laurence.

Amid a dive bomb attack targeting a third generator plant, Laurence slammed on the brakes going into mid-hover.

"They dropped their shields. But we have only taken out two of their stations. Anubis. Bastet."

"Message has been confirmed by our own familiar's cousin," Anubis answered back. "The War Machine is also falling back to a defensive position."

"I guess the Volorions no longer wish to play with us anymore," Bastet snorted.

"I'm heading to Earth right now."

"We shall follow from our own portals and finally take leave of wretched planet," Anubis said, agreeing with his cousin. "Ska, send my ship home."

"As you command."

Ska communicated with his ship's artificial intelligence system. It did as it was instructed, taking off, leaving the planet back to Anu.

As his cousin's exited via their portal, Sol's eyes emitted a bright orange glow as he opened up a dimensional jump portal in front of Laurence, heading straight to Earth.

CHAPTER 2

Planet Earth, minutes before the lowering of the planetary shield on Volori, bordering the Democratic Republic of the Congo and Angola, was a stand-off on an intergalactic level. With almost a mile and a half between them, the Crown Prince and Princess of the Thracian Empire hovered in the air staring at a visibly distraught and enraged Freedom glaring back at them. She also hovered over a sinkhole she created from the force of the enormous energy reserves she unleashed within herself.

In her arms, she clutched the lifeless body of her only child.

As Freedom held Kimberly close to her bosom, bulging veins protruding from her exposed skin glowed bright blue, while the continuous tears that fell from her eyes became mist from the immense heat they generated.

Vengeance and hatred left her with little to no reason, save for what to do with her daughter's body.

On the other side, the royal dual each had their thoughts.

A brooding Attea interrogated herself as to how she allowed her elder brother to coax her into an insane plan of planetary appropriation that had gone wrong and now stood to threaten the very security of her homeworld that she was sworn to protect.

Merc's visage was one of irritation, while the wheels turned within his head on how to salvage their current situation.

"What is she waiting for?"

"She's deciding if she should drop her child's body knowing it will fall within the sinkhole she created and attack us," Attea bluntly answered her brother.

"So, why doesn't she just drop it?"

Attea slowly turned, glaring at her brother as her eyes blazed with the desire to remove his head from his body.

"You know I find that look vexing," Merc snarled. "Use your words."

"My words say you should be praying to the old gods that she does not drop that body," Attea snapped at him.

"So, what are our options?" Merc inquired with a mutter in Thracian.

Attea's eyes fluttered in disgust.

"First option, we attack her, she fights back, she detonates, and we lose the planet. Second option, she attacks us, we fight back, she detonates, and we lose the planet. Third option, we do nothing, the energies within her continue to build until she detonates, and we still lose the planet."

Her answer was met with awkward silence from her brother.

"So, very little options." Merc deduced.

"Yes, brother," Attea growled. "Very little options."

~ ~

Amid the portentous stand-off, the sky above them opened up to three portals, each expelling the Eyes of Ra, Set, and Osiris. A livid Merc locking onto Laurence prepared to hurl himself towards him, only to be stayed by his sister's hand.

"Remain where you bloody are," Attea whispered to him, "This is the last fight we wish to have given our current situation."

Merc muttered a curse in his native language as the Anunnaki warriors descended, hovering before them. Laurence wasted no time pulling up the faceplate to his helm and making his intentions felt.

"What the hell transpires here, Merc?"

Merc blatantly ignored him, turning his attention to his eldest cousin.

"Anubis inform that micro-breed relative of yours standing next to you that he is to address me as Prince Merc. Also, inform him that if he fails to learn his station and show me proper respect, I shall teach him final lesson by ripping his heart from his chest with my bare hands."

"I would like to see you try that," Laurence defiantly dared him.

Attea instinctively flew into the path of her brother, who unleashed a savage, animalistic growl as he attempted to rush the Eye of Ra.

Laurence hovered where he stood, unintimidated by Merc's aggressive action.

"What did I just tell you?" Attea admonished her brother in her native tongue. "Do not debase your station here of all places."

"Then reframe the micro-breed's tongue from wagging!" Merc howled.

"Find center and memory that we have more pressing matters than poisonous words between you and the Eye of Ra."

Merc forced himself to calm down. He remembered the human hovering several yards away whose power he could feel steadily rising to destructive levels soon to tear the planet apart with a slight movement.

"May we attempt conversation again?" Anubis asked, stepping in to mediate. "What transpires here between you and the human over there?"

"The human is wanted by the Council for recent attacks and assassinations on three diplomatic convoys," Attea answered. "We came to take her into custody for an inquiry."

"I don't believe it," Laurence said flatly.

"I care not what you believe, Laurence Danjuma," Attea coldly retorted. "The only reason I am extending you any professional courtesy is that we have a dire situation on our hands, which I can assure you all detect."

All five slowly turned to Freedom with a murderous catatonic look on her face clutching Kimberly's body. An enraged Laurence quickly turned to lock eyes with Merc as he gripped Sol tighter.

"What did you do?"

"Your gall knows no bounds, micro-breed," Merc answered with a sarcastic cackle. "I administered proper punishment to anyone who would dare lay a hand on a Thracian Prince. The question to be asked is, what did **you** do?"

"What are you accusing my cousin of, Thracian?" Bastet demanded to know as she stepped into the conversation.

"Infusing a human with Awakening energy!" Merc bellowed his accusation.

Anubis and Bastet slowly turned to Laurence with mirrored expressions praying that his next words were that what Merc spewed was a big fat lie.

His silence and visage told them that the Thracian Prince was telling the truth.

"Praise be to the old gods that I shuffled that little abomination from mortal coil before …"

"The child lives."

The notification from Sol wiped the sinister smirk from Merc's face and drew a surprising breath of relief from everyone else, including Attea.

"Detecting very faint pulmonary and cerebral activity. The child requires immediate medical attention so as not to expire."

Without a word, Laurence turned sailing over to where Freedom hovered.

"And where are you going?" Merc demanded to know.

"To defuse this debacle you created," he turned, snapping at Merc. "Unless you have formulated a plan in the past couple of minutes to stop her from going supernova?"

He rolled his eyes to the Crown Prince, rearing his fangs as he continued over to Sophia. At that moment, he wished it were anyone else other than him. As he got closer, Freedom's emotional state had a crushing effect he never felt before. Mainly because her eyes were filled with infinite rage, which was now all directed toward him.

"Dennison …"

"Are you with them?"

Laurence paused before he spoke, knowing that his words had to be chosen very carefully.

"No …I am not …with them," he answered while motioning to Merc and Attea. "I was informed of what happened, and came …"

"I need for you to take my daughter's body," Freedom cut him off with a cracked voice. "I don't want to drop her."

Laurence knew without asking what she was planning and how to stop her.

"Freedom, Kimberly still lives."

His words triggered her eyes to well with tears, as she gripped her daughter tighter.

"You're lying, she's gone, there's no heartbeat; no pulse."

"I assure you with my honor, there is activity, but it is the faintest. She needs immediate medical attention that she can receive from my homeworld. I need you to listen carefully to what I am about to say and not react, you've been accused of murder."

Freedom shook her head to focus.

"Murder? Who?"

"A total of seven-star ships, eight thousand four hundred and seventy-three dead, including three diplomats all from species under the Dominion Council."

"I haven't even made it to Mars!" Freedom screamed out as her eyes blazed.

"I believe you," Laurence said flatly. "The warrant for your arrest was sent by the Dominion Council. Prince Merc and Princess Attea were sent here to take you into custody."

"They tried to kill my baby and me!"

Her slight movement once again shook the entire planet as it did with her battle years ago with Peace.

"I assure you; they will answer for their actions. Right now, we have to get Kimberly to my homeworld for treatment immediately."

Freedom's body trembled as she looked at Kimberly, barely clinging to life.

"I'm not leaving her. I'm not leaving my daughter."

Laurence nodded, seeing in her eyes that she would not be moved on the issue.

"Bastet, switch places with me, please."

Bastet nodded as she flew over to his location to keep watch over Freedom, while he went to discuss terms between Anubis and the Thracian Royal family.

"You must allow her to come to Anu with us to seek treatment for her child."

"Out of the question!" Merc spat at him.

"You are not going to get her into custody any other way, Merc," Laurence told him flatly. "Especially if that child dies. Unless that was never your motive."

Merc's eyes blazed with rage at Laurence's accusation.

"What do you dare insinuate, you filthy micro-breed piece of …?"

"Enough, brother!" Attea cut Merc off with an admonishing tone.

"Yes, Merc, heed your sister's warning before you spill words that cannot be wiped clean," Anubis warned.

"The terms are that I will accompany you to Anu, with her and her child," Attea said, taking control of the conversation. "As soon as her child is stabilized, she is to be taken into custody by me for inquiry before the Council for her alleged crimes. She has my word as the Crown Princess of Thrace."

Attea glared at her brother, forcing him to speak.

"She also has my word as the Crown Prince of Thrace," Merc muttered. "But she must first quell the untamable power within her before she tears this bloody planet apart."

"Curious how you who has verbally expressed contempt for my species to my face all these years are now concerned for the well-being of my planet," Laurence said.

Merc answered Laurence's vocal observation with a sneer that expressed the desire to backhand him across the planet.

"The Thracian Empire is still the Warden of this Sector, and the current protector of your backwatered excrement slinging species, micro-breed. And as its Crown Prince, I take those duties seriously. And unless you intend to compensate me for damages done to my ship from a supernova blast, you will get her to power down immediately."

"Bastet, did you hear terms?" Anubis asked.

"Yes, cousin, we both are now privy to terms," Bastet answered while turning to Freedom, waiting for her response.

Freedom glanced down at her broken little girl before zeroing in on Merc.

"Do you understand what the word 'double-cross' means?" She asked Bastet.

"I know the meaning of the word."

"The second I smell one, I start again. If my baby dies …I start again, and I will not be stopped."

"They hear your warning and will ensure that it will not come to that."

"Then let them also hear this. On my life and everything I love, they will die for what they did here today."

An emotional Freedom finally powered down, returning control of the energies within her back to her independent cells. As she reverted to normal, Sophia gave Kimberly a trembling kiss on her forehead.

"On my life, they will die."

Merc's right eye began to twitch after hearing Freedom's promise of vengeance. Begrudgingly he kept his composure.

"Bastet, please escort Dennison to the homeworld," Laurence asked. "We shall follow."

Bastet nodded as the green Ember crystals on her armor emitted a brighter glow of Awakening energy opening a jump portal.

"Please follow me, Sophia Dennison," Bastet motioned.

Freedom's eyes briefly glanced at Laurence before following Bastet into the portal. It closed, leaving the Eye of Ra and Set with the royal siblings of the Thracian empire.

"Well, since that has been settled, I take my leave," Merc announced. "Breathing the same putrid air as your wretched species is slowly murdering my mental cells. Do expect a full report to the Council on what you have done, Eye of Ra. Anubis."

Merc rattled their location, launching himself upward, going hypersonic back to his ship. This time it was Laurence's right eye that twitched as he watched him leave.

"I too shall leave with my brother," Attea announced.

"I thought you were going to accompany us back to Anu?" Laurence asked.

"I have no desire to stand around playing sitter to a woman throwing me death glares over what my brother has done," the Thracian Princess said bluntly. "I will come with my own transport and acquire her at your homeworld. She should be more tolerable at that time. I can trust that neither of you will lose her before my arrival."

"Attea, you and I know your brother crossed the line here today. Why?"

Attea slapped him with a sarcastic smirk before she answered.

"Concern yourself with your own family affairs, Laurence Danjuma. Leave me to deal with mine. Do not have me waiting once my ship enters your home world's orbit."

Like her brother, the Thracian High General created a deafening sonic boom propelling herself into the sky, flying back to her brother's ship.

"She still despises you after all this time," Anubis gruffed.

"Yep," Laurence nodded as he watched her depart.

"Care to explain yourself before we depart to the homeworld?" Anubis inquired. "What in the name of the Ancients would possess you to do something both reckless and strictly forbidden against Dominion Council law?"

"My justification for my actions is not for your ears, cousin."

Anubis turned to Laurence with a visage of bewilderment and anger.

"Not for my ears? Have you any idea what will happen to you once the Council of Elders is privy to this? You fused a child with the Awakening! You created …!"

"I know what I have created," Laurence cut off Anubis's rant. "Know me, cousin. Would I have done something as you say, 'so reckless' with the knowledge of the full weight of the consequences, without a justification?"

A frustrated Anubis looked back at his cousin and knew the truth.

In the middle of their conversation, Sol, in Laurence's grip, became animated.

"Laurence, I detect an inbound ship. Belonging to the United Kingdom's superhuman unit Lions of Elizabeth."

"Send them back home, Sol. Now is not the time for any additional confrontations."

Sol's eyes glowed as he targeted the matted stealth black modified Concorde jet outfitted with military capabilities. He created a massive dimensional jump portal capable of fitting the plane. It strategically appeared in such proximity to the vehicle that the pilot could not evade it and entered.

~ ~

Seconds later, the ship exited the portal back over its home country.

Inside of the cabin, Lady of the Lake, the Lions of Elizabeth's new leader, marched into the pilot's cockpit.

"What the bloody hell happened?"

"I have…no idea," the pilot stammered. "Something just …swallowed us up. The navigational system went all screwy for a second, now systems indicate we're back in the UK."

"Son of a bitch!"

Her fist hammered the side of the ship's cabin, echoing her dismay and frustration. She turned to her team, which also mirrored her feelings.

~ ~

"I pray your actions have the purest merit, cousin," Anubis concluded with a headshake. "You will not be shown any leniency if it does not."

"If I have learned anything from being the second Eye of Ra and fighting by your side. Sometimes sacrifice is needed to accomplish the greatest good."

With a nod, Anubis reluctantly agreed with Laurence.

"Laurence, Erica Champion wishes to speak with you," Sol informed him.

"Relay to her that I shall return to speak with her. I must return to my homeworld so that Anubis and I can give a full report to the Council of Elders."

A sad smirk appeared on Anubis's face toward his cousin as Sol's eyes glowed brighter, opening a dimensional jump port for both of them to enter leading back to Anu.

If the Council had not been informed yet of what Laurence did from Merc's report, he knew Anubis would inform them even if he did not wish to. He also knew that Laurence expected him to do so.

It was one of the many things that forged his love and respect for his Earthly cousin over the decades they had known one another.

Anubis prayed to the Ancients that Laurence's reason that he kept from him was a just one. As the Eye of Set entered the portal, taking them home, Sol became animated for a second time, gazing up at the sky above.

"What is it, Sol?" Laurence inquired, looking up with him.

"My sensors for a brief moment detected a familiar anomaly."

"Can you pinpoint it?"

"Negative, it has passed."

"A Dominion probe?"

"Perhaps."

The Eye of Ra nodded, accepting his familiar's conclusion, and turned to enter the portal, which closed behind him.

~ ~

Grand Canyon National Park, Colorado,

Built underneath the canyon itself was the Project EVOlution base commandeered by Horus, the ancient superhuman self-proclaimed god. He watched on the main screen of the station through the eyes of his mechanized golden falcon familiar, Seker, as Laurence and Anubis departed Earth back to Anu.

Standing behind him, witnessing the events taking place were former Secretary of U.S. Defense Robert Graves, the newly appointed head of the EVOlution project, and Dr. Egan Alexander, the project and facility's lead scientist.

Both had been brought under the servitude of Horus against their will.

Both were afflicted with a whirlpool of emotions over what their mortal eyes witnessed. Images of alien species with immense physical and technological power and capabilities dwarfing anything the human race had ever created.

Species that their new master either intended to solidify deals with or wage all-out war against.

For Dr. Alexander, he experienced a mixture of fear and fascination. As terrified as he was, his eyes also beheld habitable worlds and technological advancements far beyond anything he could comprehend. Despite the fear of the immortal, that could snuff out his life with a thought, who introduced him to horrors that would haunt him until his possibly short end days; Dr. Alexander hungered for the knowledge he saw before him.

Graves, on the other hand, was afflicted with both fear and dread. A man once tasked with the security and defense of the United States knew the implications of Horus's actions even if it was on a universal scale.

If even a fraction of the Dominion Council possessed the power of technological advancements, he saw from the Thracian Royal Siblings, or the Eyes, the human race faced imminent extinction.

What unnerved him more was that Horus was unfazed by either party. His concern was more focused on getting Dennison off-planet while keeping his anonymity.

"Well now, as you mortals like to say, 'Disaster averted.'"

Horus chuckled, while Graves, who found nothing amusing about what just took place, fought to keep his emotions and thoughts in check.

"Lord Horus, Seker is asking if you wish him to return home," inquired the base's powerful new AI Meskhenet.

"Nay, instruct your brother to remain vigilant over the planet for the time being," Horus commanded. "I may instruct him to do some necessary dispatching on my behalf."

"As you wish, my lord."

Horus began to pace while running down his accomplishments.

"So, today we have given the inhabitants of Earth a glimpse of their new demon, removed the demi-god Dennison and her child from the planet, and are on schedule for the rebirth of my bride and children in the next six hours. I'd say I accomplished quite a bit in a day."

"Yes, Lord Horus," Dr. Alexander acknowledged.

"Yes, Lord Horus," Graves agreed.

"Then explain thy thoughts which have concerns for my actions."

A morbid chill fell upon the room as Horus's eyes slowly turned in their direction. A frightened Dr. Alexander shuddered for a second, believing it was him, only to realize he was addressing Graves. The fear remained as Dr. Alexander wondered what was going to transpire next.

Graves, with his head bowed timidly, stepped forward to answer for his transgressions.

"Lord Horus …you know my mind…and thoughts. As a mere human, I was once tasked with ensuring the safety of the very country we stand upon. I beg thee to please forgive my ignorance and lack of faith, comparing my feeble experience to your infinite knowledge and master plan, which I am not fully privy to."

Horus took his time walking over to Graves towering over him. He shuddered as the Ancient raised a hand intending to slap his head clean from his torso.

Horus instead placed a gentle hand on his left shoulder producing violent spasms inside Graves fighting to keep it together.

"You are forgiven."

"Thank you, Lord Horus," Graves gasped. "Thank you."

"Of course," Horus said with a sinister smile. "After all, I am a benevolent god, am I not?"

"Yes, you are."

"Very good, take this time, my child, to strengthen your faith in me, for the little time I allow you to exist in that frail shell you reside in."

The Ancient gave Graves a fatherly pat on the shoulder before walking away. His ominous reassuring words sucked the strength from his neck, keeping Grave's chin buried in his chest. His uncontrollable shaking became infectious as it passed on to Dr. Alexander standing next to him.

"Come, children!" Horus barked. "The day is still young, and there is much work to be done."

Both men found the strength to move and follow their master.

CHAPTER 3

Back on Merc's warship, the crown prince stormed the hall heading to his main bridge with frustration and a smidge of apprehension plastered on his face.

Attea followed behind him with a dull, emotionless glare.

"Bloody Anunnaki scum sticking their filthy noses into our affairs! And that wretched micro-breed shall pay dearly for his insolence if it is the last thing I do! What say you, Attea? Attea?"

Merc stopped in his tracks, turning to his disturbingly silent sister, who also halted where she stood. His eyebrow raised, finally witnessing her blank look that was directed toward him.

Attea calmly took a step toward her brother before bluntly asking him a question.

"Chin or ship?"

Merc's eyes became thin slits as he snarled at her.

"You wouldn't dare."

"Chin or ship?"

A frustrated Merc unleashed an animalistic roar toward his sister with eyes ablaze. An unfazed Attea folded her arms and tilted her head waiting for an answer.

Merc snorted and gruffed as he reverted to his calm demeanor before finally answering his sister.

"Chin."

With a finger, Attea gestured for him to assume the position. Merc cleared his throat, leaning forward while elongating his neck to expose his jaw.

Attea did not hesitate cocking and tagging her older brother square on the jaw blurring left cross. The punch lifted him off his feet, launching him into a nearby wall, which he savagely cratered on impact. The Thracian Prince groaned out his frustration as he gripped the damaged wall, gently pulling himself to his feet.

"Has satisfaction …been met …by striking your brother?"

Attea answered her brother with a dull gaze.

"For me to have satisfaction …I would have had to kill you with that single blow."

"When I become High Region, …you will reframe from laying hands upon me." Merc wagged a warning finger at his sister.

"I would love to hear how you will be High Region once father removes thy head from worthless body!

"This is still salvageable!"

Attea's eyes widened to the size of moons, while the energy emitting from them became blinding, emulating her rage.

She stepped into her brother's personal space, baring her fangs.

"This …is …salvageable? We have orchestrated the massacre of several Dominion Council diplomats and allies. Our staged accused still breathes air and will be under the additional watchful eye of the Anunnaki to ensure she makes it to hearing. Which means we are ended once she parts lips and speaks! How is this possibly salvageable?"

Merc held up both hands, pleading with his sister to allow him to think. His eyes expanded as he came up with an idea.

"Quite simple," he said with a nervous smirk. "We dispatch our assassin and return her body to sink vortex whence we found her. The human's words will have no strength for her defense."

A vexed Attea became slightly calm, getting behind the idea of finally killing Peace to cover their tracks.

"Tell me I am reserved the pleasure of ending the sow's life."

"Nay to that," Merc growled at her. "She must still appear as if she died via the vortex, not butchered by your hands. I shall be the one doing the dispatching. You must head to Anu and ensure the human is taken into custody by us and ferried to the inquiry. But not before I removed her counterpart from mortal coil."

"Show the warrior a sliver of respect," Attea sneered while folding her arms. "Your mongrel is nowhere on her tier."

Merc displaying his fangs with visible impatience, took a step while sticking a finger in his sister's direction.

"And you must cast your honor aside until the human is sentenced and executed! The fate and future of our species depend on you doing so!"

"All orchestrated by your actions!"

"You are not blameless in this either, Attea! Your hands aided me in composing this tune! We can either band together to write a song of victory or witness as this becomes our nation's death rattle!"

Attea folded her arms once again, narrowing her eyes before responding to Merc's grim ultimatum.

"I want the Life Hammer."

Her request produced a shocked and pouting visage on her brother's face.

"That's …that's not fair, Attea…the Life Hammer is mine. It has been handed down for eons from High Region to High Region; it is my turn to wield it."

"You will be allowed to wield it at your coronation," Attea nodded. "Afterwards, you will hand it over to me."

"But, you're already getting mother's ax!"

"And I desire father's sword. Accept terms, and you shall have my aid and support. Refuse, and you shall fend for yourself, and I shall allow the old gods to decide the fate of our empire."

A frustrated Merc let out a whining roar while stomping around like an infant. He threw three savage blows putting holes in one of the walls of his ship. Attea calmly waited for him to end his tantrum, expecting an answer.

"Fine," Merc muttered while wiping away tears of frustration. "The Life Hammer is yours."

"Tis as you said, brother," Attea coldly reminded him. "All things eventually change, and we must change with the times. Father's sword would fair better attached to my hip instead of gathering additional dust in the throne room."

"You knew how much I coveted that sword," Merc seethed while leaning forward.

Attea fearlessly got nose to nose with her brother, looking him dead in his eyes.

"Not more than becoming High Region. So, end thy infantile moaning, so that we can ensure there is a throne for you to ascend to!"

A reluctant Merc sadly nodded in agreement.

CHAPTER 4

Regulator Base, the Ranch, the facility was officially on high alert as all active members stood within the central command center. Sergeant Abe Rogers, the team leader, stood with his arms folded as Erica Champion, also known as Lady Tech, navigated through holographic screens with taps and hand swipes while giving commands executed by Maxine, the primary artificial intelligence system for the base.

Agnes Shareef, also known as Sister Sledge, along with the rest of the team, stood anxiously waiting for updates. The silver-haired senior Titan powerhouse of the unit was Rogers's current girlfriend and longtime close friend of Freedom. Standing next to her was Adrian Esposito, who went by the call-sign Heavy Element. The Elemental EVO possessed the power to transform into almost any inorganic material he touched.

Standing next to him was Teuila Kalani, who went by the call-sign Cyclone, one of the newest members of the team, with the ability to manipulate air pressure to create powerful tornados and cyclones.

Next to her was Adrian's twin sister Rosann known by her call-sign Merge. She was also an Elemental EVO capable of taking the appearance and abilities of any human or animal she touched. Merge stood mirroring Cyclone's visage of concerned sprinkled with the frustration that she was not out on the battlefield when the action took place.

Her sentiment and expression were championed by her boyfriend Oliver, the powerful electrical manipulating Apollo EVO of the group known as Blitz, and Aashif Salek, the resident Apollo class EVO thermo-kinetic energy wielder who went by the call-sign Nitro.

A semi-exhausted Lady Tech turned to them with updates after witnessing Earth's first alien invasion, which consisted of Freedom doing fierce battle with a female alien from the invading ship. The situation became critical when Freedom's energy spiked to World Buster level.

Power, if not subsided, would have either detonated or ripped the world apart.

Eventually, Freedom's energy levels dropped, preventing a planetary catastrophe.

Minutes later, Freedom's energy pattern disappeared from the planet altogether, before that Lady Tech detected the Eye of Ra on the Earth and attempted to contact him only to be told by his familiar Sol that he would speak to her the next time he returned to the Earth.

This left the Regulators where they were when all hell broke loose, still in the dark.

"The alien ship is now leaving our orbit," Lady Tech indicated, turning to the team. "Communication is being slowly restored all over the planet."

"If one ship can take down our entire network in one shot," Heavy Element interjected. "We're in a lot of trouble."

"And we have no idea who they are or what they want," Cyclone added in frustration.

"I think it's pretty clear who they came for," Lady Tech said while pointing to her screen. "The first attack happened on Dennison's island. The whole battle across the planet was between Freedom and that female alien. Now she's gone."

"That still doesn't answer the questions, 'what and why?'" Merge shrugged. "What was their objective for coming after Freedom, and why the hell did the Eye of Ra allow this to happen?"

"Because he knew who they were," Rogers dryly answered.

Everyone turned to their leader as Lady Tech reluctantly nodded in agreement.

"What about Kimberly?"

A nervous Sister Sledge inquired of Lady Tech. The look on her face told Shareef she was not going to get a happy answer.

"Kimberly's energy levels went through a massive spike nearing her mother's base levels approximately eight to five minutes before dropping close to flatline."

"What does that mean?" Sister Sledge pressed with a high pitch in her voice.

"I don't know," Lady Tech earnestly shook her head. "Based on my readings, she disappeared the same time Dennison did, which means wherever they went, they're both together."

Rogers's eyes shifted, glancing at the nervous expressions each of his team members tried desperately to hide. For Shareef, she wanted to know where her friend and her daughter, her second family, were taken. For everyone else, it was the fact that Earth's primary and secondary powerhouses were gone leaving them vulnerable to the unknown.

"Alright," Rogers elevated his voice, getting everyone's attention. "Now's not the time to be sitting in a corner sucking on our thumbs. We still have a job to do. Judging by what went down, it is safe to say that these hostile forces will return."

"He's right about that, folks," Lady Tech acknowledged.

"Which means as of now, we will remain on official high alert," Rogers announced. "Maxine, get me a meeting with the Pentagon and the White House. We need to discuss coordinating with our allies, and if necessary, our enemies in case these hostiles return for round two."

"You think you can convince the brass to work with the Russians, North Korea, and Iran?" An uncertain Blitz inquired.

"They will because the survival of the human race as a whole will depend on it," Rogers bluntly answered. "We can go back to hating each other if and when we survive this. Everyone dismissed except for Merge."

The rest of the team save for Merge, Sister Sledge, and Lady Tech exited the command center.

Merge approached Rogers standing at attention, waiting for orders.

"Sir."

"I need all hands on deck," Rogers got to the point. "This means your suspension is officially put on hold until then. Can I count on you?"

"One hundred and fifty percent, sir."

"I will hold you to that, and then some, dismissed."

With a nod, Merge turned on her heel, leaving. Rogers turned his attention to Sister Sledge, who approached to have an audience with him.

"Permission to leave the base for a while," Sister Sledge requested.

"To go where?" Rogers asked with concern.

"I want to go to Sanctuary," she swallowed. "Make sure everything is okay there."

Rogers knowing, he was not going to stop her even if he ordered her not to go, gave a reluctant nod.

"Take one of the Tornados, be back here in three hours, no more than that."

"Thank you." Sister Sledge gratefully nodded.

"You should take Vincent with you." Lady Tech advised.

Sister Sledge turned to her, unsure what she meant with her statement.

"Take Vincent with me? He's not with Sophia?"

"I'm afraid not," she shook her head. "She never got a chance to put on her armbands during the battle. Vincent wasn't able to upload and was left behind."

"So, how do I take him with me?"

"He can upload himself into one of the tactical Replicator bodies and provide assistance and support after you come back." Lady Tech explained. "Maxine?"

"He is here with us."

"Hello Miss, how may I assist?" Vincent inquired vocally, projecting himself over the Central Command audio system.

"Maxine is going to upload you into a Replicator body," Lady Tech ordered. "While you're at it, take a Sentinel body for additional back up. You will go with Sister Sledge to Sanctuary, and when she leaves, it will be your responsibility to aide, defend, and protect the people there at all costs until Sophia Dennison returns."

"I shall execute your commands without fail," Vincent confirmed.

"Thank you," Sister Sledge answered with an appreciative smile.

"Not to push, but the clock is ticking on this one," Rogers butted in again.

Sister Shareef nodded before exiting the room. Rogers turned to Lady Tech with a look he deemed as disapproving.

"What?"

"You could have gone with her for moral support," she shrugged. "That's the boyfriend thing to do."

"Boyfriend takes a backseat to trying to save the world from a hostile alien invasion. Now that the children have left the room, how bad is it? What shot do we have to win this without Dennison?"

"If I had some Intel and twenty maybe thirty years to prepare, we might have a sliver of a shot. Right now, to quote Vince, we have no chance in hell."

"Elaborate for me."

Lady tech rubbed the bridge of her nose before going into more detail.

"Let's see, their ship shut down communication all over the planet, and considering that they came with just one, I'm pretty sure it was equipped with tech and armament capable of global devastation. They also sent down one warrior capable of fighting on par with Freedom, who then had a massive controlled power boost that completely outclassed her. Then there was the second one. His base energy readings were so monstrous it nearly crashed my entire system.

I'm going on a hunch that those two were the head honchos, and those underneath them might be a tier or two down on the power level chart."

"Still, two that powerful is too much," Rogers said while shaking his head.

"We're in the realm of mortal gods," Lady Tech concluded. "We've somehow got their attention, and not in a good way. Things are not going to fair too well for us if we don't get some straight answers quickly."

"The second the Eye of Ra shows up on your radar, you let me know," Rogers instructed.

"Sergeant Rogers, I have the White House and the Joint Chiefs of Staff ready to conference with you," Maxine announced. "Will you be taking it in your office?"

Rogers glanced at Lady Tech before answering.

"Negative, Maxine, patch them through here. They're going to want to hear what we both have to say."

~ ~

Less than an hour later, Sister Shareef touched down onto the Sanctuary runway within a Tornado piloted by Maxine.

The entire flight, she sat in silence in her head, while Vincent sat uploaded into a Replicator body with the appearance of a bald Middle Eastern man in his mid-twenties with golden irises. He was dressed in a standard black and grey IMPACT suit the team wore, with black boots minus the Regulator emblems on the shoulders.

Now and then, Shareef swiped away tears. She fought not to break down as her mind tortured her with unanswered questions about where Sophia and Kimberly could be, and what was happening to them.

As the back-cargo bay door opened, Shareef took a breath pulling herself together before standing. She turned to Vincent, already up waiting for her to exit.

As expected, she walked down the bay door ramp to a waiting crowd of Sanctuary Council members and villagers who cautiously walked up to her with a mixture of fear and concern in their eyes.

"Is everyone alright?" She asked.

Hector Lopez, Sanctuary's Head of Construction, and one of the senior Counsel members stepped forward to speak.

"We're all fine, but Sophia's house has been blown off the map! And Earl …"

"What's happened to Earl?" Shareef asked with a lump in her throat.

"He's in really bad shape. What the hell is going on, Sister Shareef? Have we been invaded?"

His question ignited the natives of Sanctuary to ask their own questions, many in different languages. All aimed directly at her to answer.

She began to quell the crowd by first raising both her open hands into the air.

"Everyone, please! Calm down! I will explain everything!"

Vincent stepped in, repeating Shareef's request with an authoritative tone in languages she could not speak.

"Thank you."

"You are welcome."

"This is what I do know, and can tell you," Sister Shareef said. "The initial attack which took place here was from an Extraterrestrial force. We currently do not know the provocation behind this attack. What we do know is that both Sophia and Kimberly are off-planet."

Her explanation ignited the vocal rumbling again with more confusion.

"Define off-planet," Indrajit Singh, Sanctuary's Chief of Finance and Junior Counsel Member nervously asked, stepping in.

Shareef swallowed the lump in her throat before carefully elaborating.

"I mean…Sophia and Kimberly are currently not on planet Earth."

Panic erupted amongst the crowd, which set off her irritation.

"Everyone, please, calm down!" Shareef yelled with a forceful motherly tone.

It worked as the villagers fell silent once again, waiting for her to speak.

"Now, unfortunately, that is all I can tell you about what happened. The one thing I need you all to understand is that this is currently the safest place on the planet right now. Also, you are not alone! Until Sophia and Kimberly return, I will be here for you! Now, if you are not a Council Member, I ask that you please leave and return to your homes! Please! Thank you!"

Hector nodded in agreement before joining in.

"You heard Sister Shareef, folks! If you are not a Council Member, please go home! We will update everyone as soon as possible!"

The rest of the Council members joined in with Hector to help send the villagers home. Reluctantly the crowd dispersed, leaving Shareef, Vincent, and the Council Members on the tarmac.

"So, who's your friend?" Indrajit motioned.

"Hello Indrajit Singh, I am Vincent, Ms. Dennison's personal A.I. system currently uploaded into an artificial body."

The introduction shocked and stunned everyone standing on the opposite side of Shareef and Vincent.

"I knew it!" Indrajit yelled while pointing. "I knew it!"

"You didn't know, jack!" Hector shot back.

"Vincent, is that really you?" An astounded Ms. Gertrude inquired.

"Yes, Ms. Gertrude," Vincent answered. "I am detecting an elevated heart rate from you; did you remember to take your pressure pills today?"

"Yes, I did," she nodded with a smile.

"Vincent is here to provide aid and support while I'm away," Shareef explained.

"You're not staying?" Hector asked.

"I can't," Sister Shareef shook her head. "Not until I bring our girls home. If you remember the android sisters, Vincent is just as capable as they are."

"No offense, Vincent is going to protect this entire island?" Indrajit skeptically gestured.

"Although I am capable of doing so with this body, we have brought additional resources," Vincent informed them.

Before the question could be asked, attention was turned to the commotion coming out of the back of the cargo bay door. Once again, everyone except for Shareef and Vincent stepped back as a ten-foot-tall slender matt black two-legged mech walked down the rampway.

Its visor glowed white along with the other white lights emitting from different parts of its armor. It was more humanoid than Sam, aside from its bipedal feet, the mech was built for speed and agility. In its hands, the mech carried a massive rifle the size and length of the main gun of a tank in a matching matte black finish with glowing blue lights on different parts of the firearm.

"That's a big gun," a wide-eyed Hector acknowledged.

"This is a Sentinel mech body, which I also control," Vincent introduced. "It will ensure that the shores of Sanctuary remain secure."

"Well, I feel more secure," Indrajit admitted.

"Can you please take me to see Earl?" Shareef requested.

~ ~

Minutes later, Shareef stood by Earl's bedside unprepared for what she looked down upon. She could no longer fight the tears that ran down her cheeks at the sight of a comatose Earl with his entire foot missing on his left leg, while his shin and foot were gone from his right leg.

Head Nurse Adetokunbo somberly brought her up to date on his condition.

"We were only able to save his leg up to his shin; the foot was too damaged to be repaired. His shin and foot on his left leg were completely gone when Kimberly brought him in. He also suffered three cracked ribs. He fought with us not to give him pain medication. He did not want to break his sobriety. There was also some infection, so he has a bit of a fever, which we are treating. He's been in and out since the surgery."

"Who performed it?"

Shareef inquired, knowing Sophia was the only formally licensed surgeon on the island.

"I did," Head Nurse Adetokunbo answered.

A surprised Shareef looked at her with amazement and gratitude.

"Where I come from, I've seen similar wounds like these caused by landmines and other weapons," She explained. "Dr. Dennison is also an excellent teacher."

Shareef leaned over a bit to hold Earl's hand, which was limp in her grip. Their romantic fling after her release from prison was brief, but the friendship remained and grew.

"Whatever you need, anything. Just let Vincent here know, and I will make it happen."

"Thank you, Sister Shareef," Head Nurse Adetokunbo smiled. "We will take good care of brother Earl."

~ ~

Before she returned to the Tornado, Shareef, Vincent, and Hector stopped by what was once

Sophia's home. The aerial view did not do justice to the devastation up close.

Although the smoke had clear, the raw burnt smell remained wafting in the air. What jarred Shareef was the blast pattern that went all the way to the beach.

"Nothing's left," she whispered with a headshake.

"We swept the area for anything that was still intact that would mean something to her," Hector huffed. "We didn't find much."

"Hector, can you do me a favor?"

"Name it."

A sternness built up in Shareef's voice as she spoke.

"I'm bringing our girls home, one way or the other. Can you make sure they have a home to come back to?"

Hector's face said it all as she spoke.

"Already ahead of you. Just go get them."

CHAPTER 5

Approximately six hours after the Thracian attack of Earth, the clones of Horus's creation reached the adult development growth stage.

The Ancient took his time inspecting each of the pods as Dr. Alexander followed behind him.

As Meskhenet's voice projected from each pod, giving a run-down diagnostic of their health and physiology, Horus nodded with approval.

After the first sweep of inspections, Horus spent his time strolling between the three female clones. A half-hour later, he moved between the third pod and the fifth pod.

An hour later, Horus found himself rooted in front of the fifth pod stroking his chin.

A nod followed as his lips parted.

"She is a perfect vessel. Meskhenet, awaken her."

"As you command, Lord Horus."

The pod began to make a soft humming sound as Meskhenet proceeded to drain the amniotic fluid from out of it. A hissing noise began to mix with the humming as fresh air was pumped into the chamber.

Just like infants, the clone awakened, letting out a brief cry of discomfort from the harshness of fresh air entering her lungs for the very first time. With a weak flailing hand, she cracked the heavily enforced glass of the pod.

"Opening pod door," Meskhenet announced.

On cue, Horus's enslaved staff that was submissively waiting in the background sprang into action. As the pod doors opened, they gently assisted the female clone in sitting up to examine her.

Horus folded his arms, wearing the face of a proud father as Dr. Alexander stood next to him, looking on with amazement.

Despite his predicament, this was still the first time the doctor had witnessed the successful birth of a superhuman clone.

"Magnificent, is she not, slave?"

"She is beyond magnificent my lord," Dr. Alexander said earnestly. "They are all the pinnacle of evolutionary perfection."

"Well, of course," Horus arrogantly scoffed. "They were created by me."

Dr. Alexander answered with a head nod coupled with a submissive bow.

"I must prepare for the transfer. Until that time, this child is in your care, slave. She is an extension of me, which means she is me. Move her to the room prepared for her. Warn the other slaves to reframe all personal interaction with her, aside from feeding, cleaning, and dressing. Those that disobey will suffer greatly before they die."

"Yes, my lord," Dr. Alexander obediently nodded for a second time.

~ ~

As commanded, the clone was transferred to the examination room, which was outfitted with a bed. While in the care of the staff, she slept extraordinarily little, ate a lot, and had to be repeatedly cleaned up after.

She also critically injured a female staff member after being startled from feeling a shower for the first time.

The staff switched to bathing her by hand after that.

They dressed the clone in a white two-piece sports bra and bottoms. Like her sisters still in slumber, she was an identical triplet in her early twenties with a curly long brown mane and brown eyes. Unlike them, she was a full six foot one inches with a cocoa brown complexion and a faint white glow to her eyes.

When not being tended to by the staff, the clone spent her time examining either her bed, clothes, or denting the dull grey metallic walls with curious hand slaps.

At the top of the double mirrored observation deck, a worn-out Graves stood next to Dr. Alexander at what would have been their experiment.

"Her strength is increasing," Graves whispered.

"And it will continue to grow," Dr. Alexander nodded. "Like her genetic parents, she will continue to draw energy toward her. At her current level, no EVO on the planet can match her."

Graves cleared his throat to Dr. Alexander's answer. Both men's attention was grabbed by the sight of Horus entering the examination room below them.

"Slaves, remove thy insignificant selves from this room immediately."

All non-powered beings quickly exited the room, leaving Horus alone with the female clone.

He strolled up, examining her. Like a toddler, she curiously touched different parts of his body and clothing. The clone began mimicking his movements as Horus ran his hands across various parts of her body.

Horus finally cupped her face examining her eyes with the faint white glow within them. As she copied the gesture, a savage grin grew on his face.

"This one will definitely do."

Horus's eyes blazed a blinding white as he palmed the face of the infant clone. Her second sound was a cry of pain as she dropped to one knee. The young woman quickly grasped his hand using her immense strength to force his painful grip from her face.

~ ~

Within the observation deck, Graves and Dr. Alexander both stepped closer to the window with genuine curiosity.

"What is he doing? Graves whispered his question.

The doctor answered with an even lower whisper.

"He called it the transfer. I believe he's downloading the memories of his Sekhmet into the clone."

"All of her memories?"

"Yes," Dr. Alexander nodded. "Something similar to 'Search for Spock'."

"I vaguely remember that movie," Graves whispered.

"Before their defeat at the hands of the Annunaki, they must have mentally transferred all of their memories to one another in case one survived, and the other did not. The clone has a clean slate with little memory," Alexander continued his explanation. "By imprinting Sekhmet's memories into her, she will believe that she is Sekhmet. Becoming Sekhmet."

~ ~

A stronger Horus kept his vice hold on the clone, forcing her onto her back, which arched as she struggled to escape.

"Horus! Horus!"

Her first actual words caused Horus to power down, releasing his grip from her. He quickly picked her up, holding her in his arms.

As he held her close, Horus's lips trembled while his eyes became glassy. There was hesitation in his voice before he asked his question in Ancient Egyptian dialogue.

"What is your name?"

The female clone had a dazed, painful visage on her face as she looked up at him, trying to focus. She slowly stretched out her left hand, touching the right side of his face with her fingers while responding in the same tongue.

"Sekhmet …I am …your Sekhmet."

"What is the last thing you remember?"

"Our kiss, after we finished copying each other's mind before our next scanning test. In case one of us fell. You altered the restructuring pods to increase our power so that we could slay the Annunaki scum and take rightful rule of Earth."

She ran her hand across his bodysuit with a smile noticing how regal he looked.

"Have we succeeded?"

Horus, no longer able to contain his emotions, pulled her close as he wept bitterly, both surprising and unnerving her.

"My love, what has happened? Why does thou weep?"

With a semi-dazed expression, she scanned the foreign room.

"Where are we? What transpires here? Horus?"

~ ~

Forty-five minutes later,

Sekhmet stood quietly in Horus's designated chambers, staring into a mirror at a face she did not recognize while he stood behind her looking on. Her hands trembled as she traumatically touched her new face, hair, hands, and different parts of her body while he debriefed her on what happened after her death, including his imprisonment and release.

"The deterioration of your original body was too great to repair," Horus sadly said. "I found the last viable egg within you and cloned it within a restructuring pod I had built, adding the blood of a female demi-god and my seed to return your strength and bring you to your proper age."

Sekhmet turned to him with thick tears that fell from her eyes.

"I …have failed you …my love."

A shocked Horus rushed over to Sekhmet, wrapping his arms around her as she wept bitterly.

"I was not strong enough to stand by thy side, to toe the line …my failure casted you into an unspeakable hell! I am not worthy to …"

Horus silenced her with a deep kiss as he held her tighter.

As he released his lip lock, she gazed at him with a dazed visage.

"Never speak again of failure to me, my love," Horus whispered. "The success of our enterprise back then was, at best, a sliver. Twas your memories that kept me sane all these centuries. Your memories that gave me hope that I would find my way back to you. Now task has been completed, this world will soon bend knee to us, our enemies will be dead at our feet, and our empire will spread throughout the stars. We have won my love. We have won."

A smile finally came to her face as he wiped her tears away with his thumbs.

"You have brought me back to your arms, I shall pay my debt to you by laying the heads of all those who would oppose us at your feet. Your name will be spoken with fear and reverence throughout the cosmos, my love. I shall make it so with blood, fire, and broken bones."

Horus waited no longer, savagely lip-locking with her while tearing her top and bottom from her body. She attempted to do the same with his bodysuit but found it more durable than it appeared.

"Pull downward from the collar, my love," he smiled.

Sekhmet pulled the collar realizing how pliable and elastic it was.

"Interesting."

With one motion, she yanked it down to his shin and grabbed his bare hardened member leading him onto the bed on top of her. The ancient quickly kicked off his boots, using his legs to free himself from the bodysuit. She then spread her legs apart, wrapping them around him to carnally unite the lovers once again.

CHAPTER 6

Planet Anu,

Sophia stood silently in the Hall of Healing, waiting. Her mind had yet to process that she had stepped through an interdimensional portal and was now standing on an alien planet several billion light-years away from Earth.

Her eyes remained fixed in the direction where a medical team of six took Kimberly on a floating gurney the second they arrived. She took a step to follow them when Bastet, her escort, stepped into her path, blocking her.

~ ~

"You can proceed no further, Sophia Dennison."

Sophia was prepared to fling her out of the way when a calm Bastet dropped to one knee with her head bowed.

"Please, Sophia Dennison, allow our healers to tend to your daughter. Her safety is secured on the honor of myself and my family."

Her gesture took the fight out of Sophia. Her answer was a slow nod, which rooted her in the spot she stood in, refusing to move until she heard the news about Kimberly.

~ ~

Now and then, as she waited, thick tears fell from her eyes staining her face, and her outfit as memories, both good and bad of Kimberly, played out before her. It began with the days she found out she was pregnant, and watching her belly grow amidst a capital murder trial. It skipped to the day she gave birth to her and held her in her arms, and the second time she saw her at the Mountain View facility after her third resurrection. After her fourth resurrection, she remembered hovering from afar watching her in the care of Mark and Michelle Armitage as she went to school, had a birthday in a park, played in her room or outside, or slept.

Sophia muzzled her mouth to fight from crying on a foreign planet as she remembered the night she finally brought her home. Their first uncomfortable conversation, and the first time she almost had a heart attack watching Kimberly go orbital with just her leg power. Sophia stooped down to her knees, bawling into her hands as her memories brought back their first heart to heart under Sanctuary's starry sky, and the night they watched Frozen and sang the theme song together.

She was forced to endure the time Kimberly powered up to save her from Peace, nearly ripping her head from her body, and then again with an additional massive power boost from the Eye of Ra, snatching Sophia seconds away from entering a portal that would send both her and Peace into a blackhole trapping them forever.

Sophia's memories beat her over the head with the day Kimberly asked to stay with her permanently and decided to take her late aunt Veronica's name as her middle name. Her broken heart weakened her to the point she was forced to endure every single memory of her little girl, both good and bad. Laughs, disagreements, days they got on each other's nerves, days they held each other tightly to mourn, all became a weight Sophia was incapable of holding up.

She collapsed to her hands and knees hysterically wailing, as the heaviest of them all crushed her.

It was the horrifying vision of Prince Merc swatting Kimberly out of mid-air as she tried to save her again. He then mercilessly stomped down on the back of her head and neck as if she was a little animal. Haunting Sophia was the agonizing scream her little girl made before she went dead silent.

"I should …have taken you… to Mars," Sophia got out in between her sobs. "I should …have taken you… to Mars."

"In the name of Geb, Seshaw, help me please!"

A powerless Sophia in a catatonic state felt two sets of hands upon her helping her up and lifting her into the air.

"I have her Seshaw, summon a cradle transport immediately, please."

The person holding her in his arms had an exotic flowery smell to him, clothes as soft as silk, and a strong heartbeat. Within minutes Sophia was laid down on the plushiest cushion she had felt in her entire life. If it were not for the movement of the walls and ceiling, she could not tell if she was being moved.

Her head slowly turned to the left to see a man walking next to her. His skin was an almond brown, while his blonde hair was worn long with half the side of his head shaven. He wore a bright green and gold themed single shoulder tunic. Her ears picked up the loud rhythmic clanging of the large silver chained pendant he wore around his neck.

She slowly turned her dazed eyes to the right. The second presence she felt walking next to her was a being made of pure gold. Its head was that of a stork with the body of a nude woman. Its eyes glowed with a yellowish hue.

The sight of the bird-woman was enough to slowly bring her out of her episode. Sophia forced herself to sit up.

"The patient is attempting to rise," the golden bird woman indicated.

The transport she was on, which appeared to be their version of a gurney, came to a halt as the man on her left gingerly helped her sit up.

"Dr. Sophia Dennison, do you know where you are?" he asked.

"I am currently on the Eye of Ra's homeworld, Anu." She answered.

"Very good," he smiled. "How many fingers do I have up?"

"Two."

"Excellent, please follow them if you can."

Sophia did as he requested, following his fingers. As her head moved to track his hand, he switched them up.

"How many?'

"One."

How many?

"Three."

"How many?"

"Two…again."

"Very good," He nodded. "Now, if you sit still for a minute, Seshaw will give you a thorough examination."

"With all due respect, 'doctor' …"

"Forgive me," the Annunaki introduced himself. "My name is Thoth, the Chief Administrator for Anu's Healing and Science. The term on my planet is healer, but you can address me as 'doctor' if that makes you comfortable."

"With all due respect, Healer Thoth," Sophia said with a shaky voice. "I would prefer to know what is going on with my daughter."

"Respectfully, Dr. Dennison," Thoth pressed. "Aside from the psychotic mental break you just had from the trauma you endured, you overrode your cells' governor system to properly regulate the energies within you doing extensive near irreparable damage to your body.

Even with your regenerative healing, you will collapse if not looked after, which will not benefit your daughter if that happens. Please allow me to look after you, and then we will promptly discuss your daughter."

A reluctant Sophia nodded in agreement.

"Seshaw, if you may."

On command, Thoth's golden familiar stretched both her hands out.

"Please extend your palms out face up."

Sophia raised an eyebrow at the nude golden stork headed woman before doing as requested.

Seshaw took hold of both her hands. Her eyes began to radiate brighter as Seshaw began Sophia's examination.

"Blood pressure is 140 over 90; pulse rate is 140-60. Detecting sixty percent cellular deterioration. Cellular regeneration to repair internal damage is steady."

Seshaw's diagnosis left Sophia stunned and bug-eyed.

"All of that just by touching my hands," she gasped.

"Touching your hands allows Seshaw to get an accurate reading of your blood pressure and pulse rate, while she bio scans your body," Thoth smiled. "Patients also find it calming and soothing while they are being examined. Seshaw, please dispense a double dosage of Jerra's Milk and Starflower."

Seshaw released her so that its right palm could crack open, producing five capsules, four orange the size of an Earth zero capsule. The fifth one was larger, clear, the size of a triple zero pill, and glowed a yellowish-white hue.

"I take it; you will be explaining your prescription to me," Sophia said, pointing with widened eyes. "Particularly, the pill that is glowing."

"Of course, Dr. Dennison, the orange capsules are called Jerra's Milk, it has a bittersweet taste going down," explained Thoth. "It is a genetic bonding agent that will increase the rate of repair to your cells. The 'glowing pill' is called Starflower, its energy output is half that of a blue dwarf star. It was created to replenish the energy of individuals such as yourself."

Freedom's eyes narrowed at Thoth's thorough description of Starflower.

"You've treated individuals like me?"

"Come now, Dr. Dennison," Thoth answered with a simple smile. "With all that you have been through and experienced, is that so difficult to hear?"

"You wouldn't happen to have water?" She inquired. "I still have a gag reflex when it comes to pills."

"Of course, Seshaw."

Seshaw quickly removed its right hollow breast casing with its left hand. Sophia's eyes widened again, witnessing the faucet underneath dispensing clear blue water into the metal breast. It brought a bright, chuckling smile to Thoth that Sophia caught.

"Apologies," he said while waving his hand. "A fond memory manifested into my mind."

Sophia nodded, choosing not to delve further, taking the breast casing and pills.

She popped the five capsules and downed the water. Sophia made a slight yucky sound while handing back the breast casing, which Seshaw reattached back to its chest.

"You were right about the bittersweet taste…"

Sophia winced and shivered as her eyes began to glow brighter than usual.

"Holy …!"

"Starflower gives the patient an immediate boost of energy. The rush will subside soon enough."

"Tell me this is not prescribed as addictive," Sophia groaned. "Because it feels really, really good."

"Although there have been cases, it's infrequent for Cosmivorses such as yourself to develop an addiction to Starflower; once a Cosmivorse's cells are fully replenished, your body becomes self-sustaining, regulating its energy intake. A Cosmivorse would have to ingest over one hundred capsules to feel the same euphoria causing an energy overload to the body; the body would then bleed off what it does not require."

"The addict would then have to up the dosage," Sophia interjected.

"Correct," Thoth nodded. "The subject would seek out higher concentrations of energy such as stars, supernovas, dark matter pockets, or edges of sinkholes. This causes a permanent overload of the body. The cells eventually lose their regenerative trait and begin to deteriorate in time, causing death."

She somberly nodded to Thoth's explanation.

"Can we discuss the condition of my daughter now?"

Thoth nodded in agreement.

"She is currently being treated within one of our restructuring pods. She is stabilized, but her journey to recovery is long. She has, unfortunately, sustained a significant amount of psychological trauma due to her physical injuries."

"Please elaborate," Sophia requested.

Apprehensiveness formed on Thoth's face as he was unsure whether it was a good idea to go into the gory details. The pain and distress in the human's visage before him said there was a possibility she would snap whether he told her or not.

Thoth made sure to carefully choose his words.

"She sustained multiple head fractures. Also, all of the bones in her upper torso from front to back, including her spinal column was shattered."

A yelping sound came out of Sophia as she doubled over on the cradle transport. Thoth instinctively reached out, grabbing her to prevent her from falling off.

"Oh god," Sophia whimpered as molasses tears streamed from her face. "Oh, god!"

"As I have stated, she has passed the worse," Thoth pressed with a soothing tone. "With the aid of our restructuring pods, we have repaired the damage that was done. That and her body's superior regenerative capabilities have kept her clung securely to mortal coil."

"I want to see her," Sophia got out in between sobs. "Can I see her?"

"Yes, you may," Thoth nodded. "I must bid thee caution. She is currently in a comatose state."

Sophia wiped her eyes and slowly nodded before sliding off the cradle transport to stand on her feet.

"This way, please," Thoth gestured.

Sophia followed him down the hallway further into Atticala's main Hall of Science and Healing. She allowed herself to briefly relax and let her eyes wander around observing the alien world she was on and its residents.

Through the large transparent glass floor to ceiling windows, she saw structures like Ancient Egypt, Mayan, and Incan empires back on Earth. Anu's 'pyramids' and 'temples' were hi-tech alien buildings constructed from either gold, silver, or clear-cut diamond-like crystal materials. They all gleamed due to Anu's blue star.

Her eyes then wandered to the people that either stood or passed them in the hall. Full-grown Annunaki males ranged from six foot four to almost seven feet, while the females stood between six foot two and six foot eight. Like Thoth, they had standard human proportions. Their skins had a weird shiny smoothness and varied in shades like pale white, light grey, dark grey, fox reddish-brown, caramel bronze, cocoa brown, or midnight. Men and women both wore onyx black or platinum blonde hair either bone-straight stopping at their shoulders, fully braided or braided with one side shaved off, or bald. A few, mostly the younger generation, added streaks of colors to their hair. What set them apart from humans were their eyes; they were one size larger with a bit of a slant.

Sophia blushed from the fashion of the planet. The styles they wore were straight out of the history books and movies she watched about ancient civilizations from Earth, except the materials were higher quality, sheer and revealing. The Annunaki were not a modest species.

"Here we are," Thoth gestured. "The Hall of Healing."

The enormous hall was filled with a sea of metallic golden pods. The majority of them were open while a few were closed.

As they made their way through the sea pods, Sophia noticed the condition of some of the inhabitants.

Some slept comfortably on top of soft white cushions, while others floated in a state of sleep within a green liquid.

Her body rattled as she timidly approached the pod that housed her daughter.

Large uncontrollable golf ball tears fell from her eyes as a whimper squeaked out of Sophia looking down at Kimberly minus clothing floating in a state of sleep within a translucent green liquid.

"What do you have her in?" Sophia got out with a cracked voice.

"It's a type of nutrient bath," Thoth began to explain. "Many of its properties are close to amniotic fluid. We find that reintroducing patients back into this simulated state of birth helps with cellular repair and growth. They also prevent the issues of bedsores, infection, and allow us to administer heliclorian cells for operations."

"Heliclorian cells?"

"Like your world's work with nanotechnology. Heliclorians enter through the orifices of a patient's body and locate the damage or afflicted area for treatment or repairs."

"Her cells do not see the heliclorian cells as a threat?" She asked.

"Excellent question," Thoth smirked. "The answer is no. Heliclorian cells can communicate with cells identifying themselves as non-threatening. They will then work together to heal the body from damage or affliction. Once they have completed their tasks, they become inert and are consumed by the regular cells for additional nutrient."

A fleeting smile came to Sophia's lips, both impressed and appreciative of the treatment Kimberly was receiving. The next question she asked with a lump in her throat.

"Is she in any pain?"

"Seshaw, please display a scan of Kimberly Dennison, set all her vitals to Earth medical parameters."

Upon command, Thoth's familiar projected a 3D image of Kimberly's muscular and nervous systems, brain scans, bone structure, heartbeat, and breathing per second.

"As you can see, all of her vitals are currently normal. She's in no pain despite the massive amount of physical trauma she endured," Thoth pointed out.

"Then, the cause of her coma is psychological?" Sophia asked.

"I am afraid so," He nodded. "Normally, we would have a resident telepath enter her mind and communicate with her on the astral plane. However, her mind being in a constant state of flux would make communication dangerous for both the telepath and her."

"Telepaths… why am I not surprised," Sophia whispered.

With a shiver, Sophia placed her right hand on the glass of the pod, where Kimberly's head resided.

"I can't protect her…she keeps getting hurt…because of me."

Thoth walked over, standing by her side, looking down at Kimberly with her.

"I have two daughters of my own," He said with a soft smile. "Seshat, my youngest follows in my footsteps pursuing the field of science and healing in these very halls. My first-born, Tefnut, became a warrior like her mother.

True to her mantle, she travels from galaxy to galaxy, leaving for human days, weeks, sometimes months, depending on the mission, whether it be apprehending pirates, smugglers, diplomatic negotiations, or giving militaristic aide or support to fellow species under the Dominion Council.

When she returned here to the homeworld, I would purposely avoid her for no more than a half of your human hour. I would be somewhere weeping with joy and giving thanks to the departed for watching over her and returning her to me."

Sophia smiled while wiping her eyes, remaining silent listening to Thoth's story that she knew had a point to it.

"One day, I fell asleep underneath a tree in our garden in the middle of reading research notes. Tefnut, at the time, had been away with a joint unit hunting down a pirate syndicate that was targeting supply transport ships. When I finally awoke, there she sat, right on the ground next to me with the brightest smile on her face and tears in her eyes.

Fear instantly overtook me; I asked her what was wrong if something had happened. She calmed me down and reassured me nothing was wrong, the mission was a success, and that she was simply happy to be home and see me.

My child, a full-grown woman, and a highly decorated warrior then laid her head down in my lap like she did when she was a youngling and went to sleep."

Thoth paused as he swatted mist from his own eyes.

"On that day, realization struck me. Indeed, a parent should not bury a child. However, we as parents sometimes forget that our children still need us, even when they can stand on their own. They will always crave our love, our counsel, and, most importantly, the fleeting time they have with us before we return to the Awakening.

Death is inevitable for all of us, but my daughter dawns armor and takes up arms to help preserve peace in the universe and lengthen the time we spend together, even at the risk of her own life. Your daughter seems to be no different from mine."

"It's hard to see it from that point of view," Sophia whispered. "When you're looking from this side of the glass."

"We agree on that," Thoth nodded.

"May I ask you a question?"

"Of course."

"You said that I was a Cosmivore. You said there were others like me in the universe."

"Correct," Thoth confirmed. "Cosmivorses are the only beings currently in the universe capable of drawing from energies within the celestial spectrum for sustenance. This can only be achieved when a subject's cells develop a high form of intelligence to handle the complexity of containing and regulating massive amounts of energy through the collective body.

Just like humans, the majority of species across the universe rely on some type of star for life. Our bodies retain heat and send electrical charges throughout our nervous system for us to function. Cosmivorism is classified as the next level of evolution for sentient species."

"My daughter changed my cellular structure while I was pregnant with her," Sophia said.

A surprised Thoth nodded while rubbing his chin.

"Although it is plausible, symbiotic transmission from child to mother is very rare. It usually happens when the mother is under a severe amount of physical or emotional distress."

His answer brought a sardonic smirk to Sophia's lips, not directed toward him.

"Being on trial for the murder of your husband that carries a death sentence can bring on a lot of stress."

"What's surprising is the difference in power levels between the two of you," Thoth pointed out. "Without the aid of Awakening energy, both you and your daughter should be at a Planet Eater level, with her levels being much higher than yours."

"Her powers of energy absorption activated much later than mine," Sophia pointed out. "I have been absorbing energy for nearly a decade in Earth time."

"Time frame is not a factor," Thoth shook his head. "Through symbiotic transmission, your daughter's cells shared their genetic coding with your cells to safely unlock your dormant coding."

Thoth's revelation stunned her.

"You're saying …" Sophia swallowed while gesturing to herself, "That this …is…all…me?"

"Yes," Thoth nodded. "However, due to the age of your cells, the rate of energy absorption should be much slower than that of your daughter's. The readings Seshaw took from you estimated your absorption rate to be that of a Star Eater."

"Which is …higher, then that of a Planet Eater, correct?" Sophia asked with narrowed eyes.

Exponentially higher," Thoth informed her. "Seshaw, if you would."

Through her eyes, Seshaw fired a holographic projection on the energy levels of Cosmivorses.

"As you can see, Cosmivorses are measured by the following levels: Planet Eaters, which is determined by the size of a life-sustaining planet's core. Next is Star Eater, measured by the size and energy output of a star…your output falls in the line of a bright giant blue star, which is extremely impressive."

"Do you happen to know the levels of the two who I fought on my planet?"

Thoth glanced at her and cleared his throat before answering.

"The Thracian High General Princess Attea …"

"She's a princess?" A miffed Sophia asked.

"Why yes," Thoth nodded. "She is on the level of a Supergiant blue star, while her brother, the crown Prince Merc is a Hypergiant blue star."

"The way the Princess tapped and controlled her energies against me," Sophia slipped in. "Is that a technique I could learn?"

Her question forced Thoth's mouth to part as a jolt of shock hit him, making her nervous.

"Princess Attea was forced to use the Flow technique against you?"

"That's what you call tapping into the additional energy from your cells?"

"No," Thoth said while shaking his head with his hands up. "What you did was called Governor Releasing. As you probably know, your cells control and regulate the massive amount of energy stored within them. Governor Releasing is commanding your cells to stop monitoring the energies within you. This grants you an immense power boost but at the cost of cell deterioration destroying your body.

The Flow technique allows external energy to flow rapidly through a Cosmivorse's body, multiplying their physical attributes without directly storing energy."

"Similar to wind or water turning a windmill," Sophia deduced.

"Exactly," Thoth feverishly nodded. "Some of the most powerful Cosmivorse's in a Flow state have been known to destroy whole planets with a single strike or energy release."

"Well, she sure as hell rung my bell when she clocked me in that state." Sophia scoffed.

Her flippant response caused Thoth to narrow his eyes and lean into her personal space, unnerving her.

"Princess Attea struck you while in a Flow state?"

Sophia stood her ground, shifting her eyes left to right, wishing he would move and unsure how to answer.

"Um, …yes."

He leaned back, remaining locked on her eyes, which told him she was not lying. It made him both uneasy and extremely curious.

"Then, by all rights, you and I should not be having this conversation Dr. Dennison," Thoth said bluntly. "Any opponent on her power level or higher like her brother could survive such an attack, but anyone your level on down would have died instantly the second she connected, and that is the best-case scenario."

"What's the worst case?"

"Total regenerative system failure in the traumatized area she struck. It is diagnosed to be one of the most excruciatingly painful ways to die, and there is no treatment because system failure begins in the first five seconds if the blow connects with either the head or any area with vital organs."

It was then that Sophia realized why Thoth was giving her such an astounding look of disbelief.

"There are three other categories," Sophia pointed, wishing to draw some attention from herself. "White Star Eater …"

"The third most powerful level a Cosmivorse can grow to," Thoth turned unwillingly, getting back into the discussion. "Only a handful of beings in the universe hold that title…one being the Queen Mother of Thrace, Furia."

"Merc's and Attea's …mother."

"Why, yes."

Sophia slowly nodded before asking about the final levels."

"The last two are Galaxy Eater and Universe Eater."

"Universe Eater is based on a hypothesis," Thoth gestured while explaining. "One has never been recorded to exist. However, experts have theorized that if Galaxy Eaters exist, then it is plausible for a Universe one to eventually come to be."

A sharp chill ran down Sophia's spine from his explanation.

"There are beings…out there…that contain energies within them equivalent to a galaxy?"

"Why yes, three have been recorded," Thoth answered. "One is deceased, one has not been seen for eons, and one currently sits as the High Region of Thrace, Lord Nelron."

A lump filled her throat as Sophia nearly choked on her question.

"This Lord Nelron…is also Merc's and Attea's…father?"

"Why yes," he nodded.

"That's…one hell of a family," Sophia said while clearing her throat.

"They are quite impressive," Thoth agreed. "For mortals."

"So, this Flow technique," Sophia once again inquired. "Does it have any side effects?"

"Extreme fatigue after the technique is released," Thoth answered with curious eyes. "Especially for those who use it for the first time. It becomes tolerable the more one uses it. However, the most experienced practitioners can succumb to it, the longer they remain in the Flow."

"You wouldn't know how or who could teach me this technique?"

Thoth gazed upon her with a simple smile and head tilt as Sophia formed a stern glare not directed toward him in hostility. She folded her arms, waiting for answers.

"There are texts and visuals on the technique," Thoth calmly answered. "But the best way to learn is from another Cosmivorse who has mastered the technique. You do know you will soon be taken to the Dominion Council Inquiry to answer the charges of terrorism and mass murder?"

Sophia glanced at the four fully armored Annunaki warriors who shadowed her since they were assigned to be her guards. They stood away off, casually observing her and Thoth.

She nonchalantly turned to Thoth as if they were not even there.

"Oh yes, I am fully aware and can't wait to stand trial so that I can clear my name. But the second, my name is cleared …I'm going to be looking for some payback. It would be nice to even the playing field when I meet the siblings again."

A knowledgeable Thoth who believed he had seen and witnessed everything during almost two thousand years alive shook his head in disbelief.

"You do understand that there are very few beings in the known universe who would seek

Princess Attea, much less the Crown Prince for a confrontation?"

Sophia looked down at her daughter, floating silently within the pod. Her eyes returned to Thoth with an ominous, sinister glare that he knew was not directed towards him.

"Well, there's a first time for everything."

CHAPTER 7

Planet Thrace, Prince Merc's flagship Morgorn sailed out of warp speed drifting into his home planet's orbit.

"My prince, we have reached the homeworld; your royal transport is also prepared for departure."

"Connect me to Embaro," Merc commanded.

Before his communications officer could execute his instruction, the officer's ears twitched as a high-pitched chirping sound came from his earpiece.

"What is it?" Merc demanded to know.

The officer quickly spun his seat around to him.

"My prince, I am receiving a message from the royal court communications. They wish to address you personally."

Merc subtly shifted his jaw from left to right as he sat uncomfortably in his seat.

With a head nod command, the communications officer turned back around, bringing up the ship's main screen. An older Thracian woman with a dreaded sky-blue hair styled into a Mohawk, emerald scaly skin, and ice-blue eyes appeared wearing a silver and dark blue kimono-style outfit. Around her waist was a thick corset maroon-colored belt with a golden circular main plate. A creature standing on its hind legs with the semblance of a bear's body with a hawk's head was etched into the plate encircled with Thracian markings.

She gave him the traditional Thracian bow respecting his title before speaking.

"Prince Merc, praise be to the elder gods for you and your crew's safe return home."

"High chancellor Nuwata, thank you for your kind words. Do you bring a message from my father to me?"

"Your father wishes for you to make an appearance at court today. He would like to converse with you on a small matter."

"Inform him that I shall make an appearance after I return home, remove the filth of travel and adorn proper attire ..."

"He has requested that you come directly from your ship to court just as you are dressed once you have entered Thrace's atmosphere."

Her polite tone had hidden sternness that matched her visage, which grew a lump in Merc's throat, knowing that she was an extension of his father's authority not to be disobeyed even with his royal station.

"It shall be fulfilled," Merc answered with a nod.

Her face softened with a smile from his answer.

"We look forward to seeing you at court once again."

As the transmission ended, Merc fell back into his seat, sulking with an unnerved countenance while his left leg twitched violently.

His mind began to race with thoughts and strategy while using the sharp tip of his thumb as a chew toy.

"Uh, my prince."

Merc's eyes slowly fell upon his second in command, Ashtor, who made an uneasy gesture to what he was doing.

"You …you instructed me to bring attention to whenever you did that …detestable habit."

Merc snarled as he gently pulled his thumb from his mouth. He shot to his feet, standing tall and authoritative.

"I head to my royal transport, Ashtor, you control the helm upon my return."

"Yes, my prince."

Merc exited his command deck, heading toward the lift that would take him to the ship's docking bay and royal transport. He balled his fists, cracking his knuckles as his mind swirled with thoughts of the conversation his father wished to speak with him about.

~ ~

The crown prince sat in silence, drowning in his thoughts as his royal transport, the shape of a sleek golden boomerang, entered Thrace's atmosphere.

His eyes were disengaged until his long ears twitched as he sensed his ship nearing the capital of Senical.

The capital was a gleaming white high-tech amalgamation of buildings similar to the Roman, Grecian, and Chinese empire. He stood up and made his way to the door during his ship's descent, landing on an airship pad.

As expected, the second the craft touched down, and the door slid open, waiting for him was the capital's elite guard known as the Crimson Fang.

A small unit of Thracian soldiers totaling fifty tasked with guarding the entire city.

Each warrior had matching thick, gleaming blood red metallic bracers and greaves on their arms and legs etched with deep Thracian markings. All of their hair, regardless of the style, was colored maroon.

Attached to the thick belt on their hips that had the texture of leather was a black scabbard housing a sizeable two-handed sword with a pointy curved dull red metallic cross guard and grip sphere-shaped pommel with intricate Thracian etchings carved into it.

Males in the unit wore black leather kilts that matched their shin-high Grecian sandals and thick black combat harness that formed an 'X' shape across their chest with the straps.

The females' outfits were comprised of a black single-shoulder dress with a kilt style to the skirt that also matched their shin-high Grecian sandals and thick black combat harness that formed an 'X' shape across their chest with the straps.

Attached to the harness were blood-red metal epaulets fashioned in the head of an animal that looked like a sinister serpent with two thick massive upper fangs. Yellow glowing gems were set into each of its four eye sockets within the skull.

Also attached to the harnesses and epaulets was a long flowing blood-red cape that had the look of dull, heavy leather that moved and swayed like silk.

All fifty had eyes that glowed a bright orange-red hue revealing their unbridled power.

All fell to one knee in unison while smacking their left breast, greeting their prince while bellowing a thunderous chant.

"Thrace! Thrace! Thrace!"

The Crimson Fang remained on their knees with their head bowed as Merc descended the hovering pearl white steps. The second both his feet touched Thracian soil; they rose to stand at attention, gripping the hilt of their swords while placing their free hand behind their backs.

Making her way to him was the Lieutenant-Commander of the Red Fang. Her scaly skin tone was similar to his own, with specks of red and pink in it. Her single shoulder dress and the battle harness was a matching blood red, while her serpent themed metallic epaulets were a bright golden color, with gleaming red gems in each of the four eyes sockets of the skulls.

Like her unit, her dreaded full hair which hung over her shoulders was dyed red, while her glowing orange eyes teetering closer to red emitted brighter than everyone under her command.

"My prince, welcome home."

"Thank you, Lieutenant-Commander Elzra."

"I am to inform you that the Queen-Mother is in the throne room, waiting to lay eyes upon you before you meet with your father."

A low growl rumbled from Merc's throat as he kneaded the irritation from the bridge of his nose.

"Is my father in the throne room as well?"

"Nay," she shook her head. "He is in the royal garden entertaining his great-children."

"I shall make my way to the throne room then."

"Two of my soldiers will gladly accompany you for a proper…"

"Nay," Merc waved off her gesture. "Your unit has far more important duties than to coddle the likes of me."

"As you wish, my prince," Elzra answered with a Thracian curtsy. "Although it is no bother at all."

Merc walked off by himself to the main palace, a human ten-block walk from the airship pad. Along the way, soldiers and civilians cleared a path and either saluted or curtsied.

The main palace was the size and shape of a Roman Coliseum with a dome top covering it. It was constructed from a gleaming milk-white stone that faintly beamed in the sunlight of Thrace. Part of the dome was built with the precious white glass-like stone that glimmered with spectral colors.

The glass panels, which were located over three of the vast gardens of the palace, slid away from time to time, allowing in actual air and sunlight.

As he approached, the large round main door of the palace rolled away, granting him entrance.

Merc with blinders ignored the nobles that were either sprinkled or gathered here or there, all giving him a respectful greeting as he made a beeline to the throne room. Now and then, his eyes glanced at statues, paintings, ancient weapons, and armor from past warriors and nobles from his bloodline along with other dedicated patriots of Thrace over the eons.

As he neared the entrance of the throne room, a green scaly skinned Thracian male, with ice-blue eyes, dreaded yellow hair styled into a Mohawk dawning a pearl white toga snapped to attention at the sight of him. Around his waist was a thick brown belt that had a silver circular main plate with the same creature that was on High chancellor Nuwata's corset with different Thracian markings.

As Merc stepped through the entrance, the young Thracian male made a throaty announcement of his arrival.

"Introducing the Crown Prince Merc, the second born of High Region Nelron and Queen-Mother Furia, returning the court!"

Inside the entire throne room was the same gleaming milk-white stone with dashes of gold and purple.

Decorative wise, the throne room was bare and airy save for the twelve colorfully rich cloth tapestries revealing crucial historical times in the Thracian empire, and the six massive onyx and gold-colored stone statues of former High Regions lining the throne room three to a wall.

The stone created the six thick steps leading up to the two immense thrones sculpted from the floor and flowed several feet up to the ceiling.

High ranking nobles and servants paid their proper respects to him, while family members depending on their distance to him, greeted him with a hand wave or head nod.

One particular male Thracian, with orange and black scaly skin and a full head of dreaded jet-black hair, jumped in his path with a toothy grin, and his arms stretched out for an embrace. He wore a blue single shoulder toga and an oversized metallic silver and gold belt similar to what Roman gladiators wore on Earth. It possessed Thracian markings and a sculpture in the middle of a creature that had the appearance of a big cat and a hawk with its massive mouth open. Thick golden bracers adorned his forearms with Thracian etchings that glowed blue.

The power within his eyes burned bright orange.

"Brother, welcome home!"

Merc smirked as he embraced his youngest brother.

"Nordaru, you make me feel as if I have been gone for eons."

"One never knows when it's their last day in this universe," Nordaru gruffed. "One must treat their loved ones as if tis the final time, they shall see them. How was your campaign on that backwater planet? Is Attea home?"

"She's still off-world attending to other matters," Merc answered while clearing his throat. "I shall …"

"You shall delay no further and approach the throne. Nordaru, you've given your brother proper greeting, now stand aside."

The dominant female authoritative voice made Nordaru's long elfin ears twitch as he bore a scolded visage. He mouthed the words that they would converse later while sliding out of Merc's path, allowing him to continue to his first destination.

Sitting lazily on a plush sky-blue cushion upon one of the two thrones was the Thracian Queen-Mother herself, Furia.

Her skin was a deep scaly ash grey, fitting tightly on a curvy, muscular, athletic physique. Ancient battle scars marred different parts of her body, including a massive slash across her hardened face belonging to a woman in her late fifties that started from her left brow across the bridge of her nose down to her right jawbone. Her sharp white finger and toenails matched the rows of flesh tearing feline teeth within her mouth.

Her long-dreaded green mane was pulled back into a ponytail that hung over her right shoulder, putting her deep red glowing cauldron eyes on display. Adorned in a scantily white long Grecian styled dress, the Queen-Mother idly held in her right hand a hefty gunmetal gray double-bladed war ax that had Thracian etchings and cracks throughout the blade and handles emitting a pulsating hot green supernatural glow as if it was alive.

In her left palm, she held a naked dark blue scaly skinned humanoid male infant with tiny rows of spiky dorsal fins that ran up his spine to the top of his skull. The baby, with his eyes closed, greedily suckled on her exposed left breast.

Merc respectfully fell to one knee, downing his head, staring at the floor, waiting to be acknowledged.

"Mother."

The Queen Mother's long elven ears twitched as she looked down at her son with narrowed eyes.

"Rise, boy."

Merc obeyed his mother's deep throaty, sensual command. He fell into a casual stance staring up at her from her throne.

"Mother," Merc asked with a wagging finger. "Isn't that one of my bastards suckling on your tit?"

"Aye, it is." His mother grunted.

Merc asked his next question very carefully.

"May I ask why you are nursing the child, and not his mother?"

"His mother is a worthless, spineless, Zerakian sow." His mother answered bluntly.

Merc's ears picked up teary sniveling, while his eyes moved, glancing at a light blue-skinned female Zerakian adorned in a sky green Thracian noble woman's dress and fine jewelry. She stood off to the side amongst the rest of the court. Her bald head was lowered to the floor as her large spikey grey stone dorsal fins protruded from the top of her skull down her back.

"Oh." Merc coughed.

"I sat here watching her fumbling around to feed the pup," his mother scoffed. "Complaining that her nipples ached from him suckling too hard. You and your eldest brother almost tore mine off till I gave you proper flicking to the nose. I told her to do the same, and then she whined about hurting the child.

So, I ordered the wench to bring him hither. The child did not even require a flick. Her leaf-thin skin is no match from my half-blooded bastard great son's gums," she cackled. "Zerakian milk tastes like Dorac piss anyway, Thracian milk from his dear old great-mother will ensure he grows and stands powerful amongst the proud ranks of the Thracian empire."

Merc's eyes became narrowed with curiosity as he used two fingers to beckon the child's mother to come forward. As she timidly obeyed standing before him, Merc loosened the top of her dress, taking hold of her engorged right breast. The Zerakian female trembled while covering her mouth as Merc suckled her nipple, tasting the milk for himself.

He released her wearing a disappointed visage.

"Find your way to Embaro," Merc ordered. "He will construct a proper diet for you, which you will follow while nursing my son. Until then, you will reframe from feeding him. A wet nurse will be assigned to your duties until you are fit. Do we have understanding?"

"Yes, my father's child," answered the Zerakian mother.

With a dismissive wave of his hand, she scurried out of the courtroom bitterly weeping.

Merc sighed as he turned back to his mother, still glaring at him from her throne.

"So, where have you come from?"

"From roaming throughout the universe, going back and forth." Merc nonchalantly answered.

"Bring not your coy tongue to me boy, less you wish to taste the back of my ax, your father would have words with you."

"So, I have been informed. I take it he's in the main garden."

"Entertaining his legion of great-whelps," Furia nodded. "He waits for you there."

Merc's eyes mirrored the narrow slant windows in his royal transport as he caught his mother's underline hostility toward him.

"Have I done something to upset you, mother?" Merc flatly inquired. "You appear to be more perturbed than usual."

"Inquire once again after you have had words with your father," Furia coldly answered her second born. "If you dare."

Out of nowhere, the half breed child within her palm ended his suckling of her nipple. He slightly opened his eyes, emitting a choking sound. Merc watched as his mother skillfully laid the infant belly down across her knee while still wielding her ax. She then raised her hand, delivering one powerful slap across his back.

The baby's dorsal fins lit up as he let out a throaty belch and fired a thick circular energy beam from his mouth, cutting through the steps leading up to the throne.

Those present rejoiced with sounds of adulation. The Queen Mother cackled, lifting her great-son to a sitting position on her thigh. The child let out a smaller burp that puffed out smoke, followed by joyful infant squealing noises.

"That's my boy," Queen-Mother Furia grunted. "The only good thing about seeding Zerakians."

She placed a kiss on the forehead of her great-son, who went back to greedily suckling on her exposed breast before turning her attention back to her son.

"I have no further need of you other than to see that you still breathe air, remove thyself from my sight, and attend to business with your father."

Merc's jaw shifted as his nose flared, and ears twitched, hiding his displeasure for his mother's words and tone while showing her utter respect by taking the knee once again and bowing.

He rose to take his leave from the throne room, heading down a hallway leading to the central royal garden, all the while feeling his mother's burning eyes on the back of his neck.

Merc entered the central garden with his mind racing at light speed. He took his time walking down the mirror gleaming green stone pathway surrounded by vibrantly colorful trees and vegetation from his homeworld. Along with the foliage were small undomesticated animals such as pink and red creatures similar to sparrows with red and white feathers, three eyes, one being on the forehead, and two fluttering wings.

At his feet, scurrying past him were creatures similar to squirrels save for them being the size of domestic cats. They had jet black thin, matted fur with a thick black and white bushy tail, and deep burning red caldron eyes. Their long ears, similar to foxes from Earth, twitched as they curiously stopped and looked at the Crown Prince.

His thoughts were on the fact that he knew he was walking into an ambush. The question that befuddled him was how unpleasant it was going to be for him.

Merc's pace became slower as his ears picked up the sound of a very gruff and enthusiastic old voice.

"So, there we stood on the planet of Valmon, myself, Amun-Ra from Anu, and Sol-Thulo from Sar in thick of battle commanding a combined total of six-hundred of our finest warriors against six triage-Legions of Razcargian scum, which was three to one odds per warrior in their favor. Each side took heavy losses, neither side giving quarter."

Merc, finally reaching his destination, stood quietly listening on.

For a brief moment, a smirk fell on Merc's face as he remembered being a young child sitting attentively in that very garden with his siblings and cousins as either his great-father or father spun tales of glory.

His father, dressed in a royal purple pleated leathery skirt held up by a thick silver metallic belt with jewels and Thracian markings, sat on a curved white stone bench surrounded by a sizable crowd of his great-children whose ages spanned from toddler to teen. They sat or stood listening to another one of his epic tales.

Lord Nelron was a foot shorter than his son and appeared to have been forged from the core of Thrace itself. The top of his head was mostly bald save two golden blonde rope thick braids that started on each side of his temple. They ran down the side of his skull to his tailbone, where they hung. His long full beard of the same color hung with the shape of a blade stopping in the middle of his chest.

Nelron's bluish-grey scaly skin had the appearance of hard raw metal, while golden-white light emitted through his eyes from the power coursing through his cells. His world-shattering physique contradicted the face of a man by Earth standards in his late seventies. Battle scars and cracks within his skin faintly pulsated the unbridled energies within him that secured his continuous reign as the High Region of Thrace, among other titles bestowed upon him throughout his staggering lifespan.

In the middle of his tale, a massive beast came from out of the foliage and approached Merc emitting a screeching growl that would vibrate the bones of a lesser being. It was the actual creature etched in the main plate of High chancellor Nuwata's corset belt.

The animal was twice the size of a polar bear with fiery red fur. Its head and face resembled that of an eagle or hawk down to the razor-sharp grey beak that had the piercing strength of a rhino tusk. It also came armed with a set of five thick black claws on each of its four paws.

What made it more terrifying to behold was its bright yellow piercing eyes, devoid of all emotion similar to that of a Great White Shark.

Merc smiled as the beast did the exact opposite of its appearance, nuzzling the side of its face against his thigh seeking affection from him, as a deep chirpy purring sound came from its gullet.

He complied by rubbing the top of its head with one hand while giving its chin a good scratch with the other.

"Durongo," he whispered. "How is my favorite Corursid today?"

Durongo grunted, plopping down on its hind legs while raising one of its paws, placing it on his forearm as Merc continued to pet it.

"That day on Valmon would be remembered as one of the bloodiest and destructive battles in the Razcargian Conflict." Lord Nelron said, nearing the end of his tale. "We lost nearly three-quarters of our initial forces that day but succeeded in wiping every single Razcargian scum off the face of the planet and liberating the people of Valmon, who would later bravely fight alongside us to end the conflict.

In that battle, we lost Sol-Thulo, who single-handily slew more Razcargian scum than I ever could with his mighty sword, Black Nova. I had the honor of carrying his body off the field of battle and delivering him back to his family, where I knelt before them and told them of how he fought and died the perfect death."

"Whatever happened to Black Nova?" A young onyx and purple scaly skin Thracian boy with red dreaded hair styled in a Mohawk inquired.

"It was retrieved from the battlefield," Nelron answered with a smile. "Given to Sol-Thulo's eldest daughter, I believe, where it will be passed down her bloodline.

The moral of this story my children are the failings of pride. My pride before the battle nearly cost me from discovering one of the greatest warriors I would have the pleasure of meeting, someone I have the honor of calling my friend to this day, all because he was not Thracian.

Be proud to be Thracian, my children, revel in it but do not allow it to blind you to the self-worth of others around you who are not. And so, ends my tale, and my lesson."

As the children clapped and rejoiced at the heroic story told to them by their great-father, Nelron's long elven ears twitched as he looked down at one of his youngest great-daughters. Her head was down, and she had a sad look in her eyes.

"Why do I see sorrow in your eyes, child?" Nelron asked.

The little girl with her orange braided hair styled into a Mohawk, dark blue scaly skin, ice grey eyes, and a mousey nose gazed up at her great-father with a face close to tears.

"Great-father …I am part Razcargian by my mother …does that make me scum?"

"Stand and come forth, child." Nelron motioned with a hand gesture.

As the child slowly got up from where she sat and approached him, Nelron lifted her, setting her down on his lap.

"Here, my words, little one, and all who are of my bloodline before me. You may have come from Razcargian womb, but you were seeded by a Thracian. And once you have one drop of Thracian blood within you …"

"You are Thracian through and through!" The children around him howled, finishing his sentence.

"When your mother conceived you, she no longer became scum in my eyes. She became my daughter. And you are the great-daughter of the High Region Nelron, a mighty Thracian princess who will fight, kill, and die for the glory of Thrace."

Nelron's words caused the young girl's face to light up with joy. She giggled as one of the most powerful beings in the universe tickled her belly while placing a kiss on her forehead.

Finally acknowledging his son with a glance, he proceeded to break up the congregation of off-springs before him.

"Now, off with all of you, I must have words with your father and uncle. Go, eat, play, and fight. We shall have tales of glory for another day."

"Yes, Great-father!" all the children screamed in unison.

As they departed, each child halted before Merc, giving him a proper Thracian curtsy acknowledging him as either their uncle or father.

With his hand, Merc halted the little girl that sat on Nelron's lap.

"Father," she acknowledged with a curtsy.

Merc, with a narrowed stern gaze, stooped down, getting eye level with his daughter.

"Now Chana, after all of my teachings, did you believe you were Razcargian scum?"

A devious little smile grew on the child's face, bringing a smirk to Merc's visage.

"Very cunning to get more of your Great-father's attention."

"Tis, as you said, father, the smallest skill can be sharpened to deliver the deadliest blow."

"Give thee proper kiss for my teachings and be off with you. Take Durongo, while your great-father and I have words."

Chana wrapped her small arms around her father's neck, pecking him on the cheek before running off to play with her cousins and siblings.

"Come, Durongo! Let us go play!"

Durongo unleashed a booming screeching roar as it stood up and trotted off following Chana.

Now alone with his father, Merc switched from squatting to falling to one knee with his head down, displaying his unwavering respect and loyalty.

The High Region rose to his feet and beckoned his son with a hand gesture.

"Rise and come closer, boy, let me get a look at you."

Merc did as commanded rising again. He strolled over to his father, who looked him up and down as if he were sizing him up. Nelron grasped both his son's arms, examining what he created with fatherly pride.

"I remembered the day I pulled you from your mother's slit," Nelron savagely grinned. "At the time, you were smaller than your other siblings, a bit feeble. But as I cleaned the blood from you, and gave you proper strike, a powerful war cry came from your gullet. On that day, I knew you would grow to become a force of nature throughout the universe, second only to me."

"I live to meet your expectations and serve your will, father."

Lord Nelron moved closer to his son, staring into his very soul.

"And what is my will?"

Merc answered without hesitation.

"The growth and prosperity of all citizens of Thrace, my lord."

His father's ears twitched as he released his son and clasped his hands behind his back while giving him a semi-nod of approval. Nelron's simple 'innocent' gesture drew a look of concern on Merc's face.

"Does something trouble you, father?"

"Should I be troubled?" Nelron asked with a shrug.

Merc straightened up, more careful to stay within the line of sternness and respect as he addressed his father.

"I was taught to never answer a question I do not understand, father."

"Then let me be plain with my inquiry."

Merc stood his ground as his father leaned in, whispering in his ear.

"Do I appear to be so weak and feeble that you can freely plot and conspire to your hearts content hiding secrets from me?"

Merc skillfully kept his poker face from chipping while his insides turned. Another lump plagued his throat as he tactfully answered.

"Father … I …"

A booming animalistic roar capable of crippling the king of beasts itself came from the High Region. His eyes blazed bright, matching the intensity of his canine daggers protruding from his upper and lower jaws. He hovered inches away from his son's throat displaying intention to bite it out. Merc standing his ground, roared back with lesser intensity, while submissively lowering his head.

Nelron emitted a low growl as he calmed himself.

"Please allow me to complete train of thought before you attempt to refute me with a lie, my son."

Merc slowly nodded in agreement.

"Did you really think that I would be unable to read the chain of events and link them back to you?" Nelron shook his head in disbelief. "A human who happens to be a star eater on my planet, strategic attacks on diplomatic ships within different sectors of the human territory. What confounds me is how you coaxed your sister into this asinine scheme."

"Attea …is blameless in this father."

"I shall give you one final opportunity to reframe from lying to me, boy before I tear your head from your body."

Merc lowered his head to his father's calmed whispered threat.

"Quietly from the shadows, I have watched your past ventures and allowed them," Nelron said with a huff. "Knowing that they neither threatened the security of Thrace, aided in the flourishing of our great empire and furthered your position as the next Region to the throne. All the while, believing that you were learning. That you understood there were certain risks afforded to take, and other ventures never to be attempted."

Nelron leaned closer, getting mouth to left ear with his son.

"Your lustful ambitions now threaten the empire and our people, and I am to partially blame. The aged rust on my mind and my love for you have blinded me to the truth that you are still too stupid to know when to pull out."

A chilling growl came from his father's gullet again as Nelron reared his fangs inches away from his son's throat. Merc this time uttered, not a sound as he kept his eyes closed and his head down, taking every inch of the verbal berating being administered onto him. Nelron snorted as he retracted his fangs strolling away to think.

"Your plan was dead before it was even conceived because you are part of me. What you thought, I had already considered when I aided in fashioning the laws of Genetic Selection under the Dominion Council as ironclad protection against the likes of even myself. Do you know why?"

Nelron waited for Merc to respond. His son answered with a slow and earnest headshake, which brought a smirk to the High Region's face.

"To prevent myself and future generations from making the costliest of mistakes. Doing something selfish that might destroy the Dominion Council. The Council which has given our species the greatest of gifts. Infinite power and security through the forged bonds of our allies."

Nelron strolled back to his son, standing two inches in front of him.

"By itself, Thrace is a mighty, powerful, and prosperous empire. Being a part of the Dominion Council means that our might is near infinite because to challenge Thrace means to challenge all members of the Dominion Council. Our resources are unbounded, allowing us to beckon onto any of our fellow allies for assistance in all matters because if Thrace thrives, they too thrive, and the same can be said in reverse.

That bond forged is worth more than a hundred planets on any given day, and you have now jeopardized it for six measly planets."

Merc slowly swallowed the spit building in his throat as his father gazed upon him with a dull glare.

"Did you not appropriately scale the weight of your selfish actions to the consequences should you be discovered? Thrace's embarrassing expulsion from the Council, probable war with our former allies, and imminent vulnerability to our enemies who would wish nothing more than to see us fall. Did thought not seep into that thick skull of yours as you cast your die threatening the stability of your people?

Dare tell me what you did was for them, and then watch lying tongue be removed from your mouth with mine own hands."

Merc lowered his head, finding no refute to his father's ironclad argument. On the young ancient's face was a look never seen since he was a child, fear, and shame.

The Crown Prince softly whispered to his father the only logical answer to repair the immense damage he had created with his ambitions.

"You must deliver me to Council, father. I must abdicate my claim to the throne, and you must …"

"Silence thy tongue and fetch my pipe and herbs, boy."

Merc slowly raised his head, meeting the eyes of his father nonchalantly waiting for him to comply. He obediently walked over to the stone bench his father sat on, retrieving a deep metallic blue smoking pipe with ancient Thracian runes etched on the bowl. Similar markings were found on the top lip of the brown and tan wooden disc-shaped container sitting next to the pipe.

He carefully screwed the lid off, revealing glittering red dried up plant leaves inside of it. Using his thumb and middle finger, Merc plucked the herbs, carefully packing it into the chamber of the pipe. He then tightly screwed and sealed the lid back onto the container putting it back down on the bench before walking over to his father handing him his pipe.

The High Region strolled away from his son, taking a seat on the bench crossing his legs.

Nelron effortlessly focused raw sheering energy into his hand, which heated the metal pipe and set the herbs within it ablaze. He calmly placed it into his mouth, taking a healthy draw, and bellowed out white smoke from his mouth and nostrils thick enough to temporarily cover the lower half of his face.

He gave his beard a stroke before he answered his son.

"Thracians surrender to no one boy, not even to our own allies."

He took another small hit from the pipe, this time firing smoke from his nostrils before he continued.

"Time cannot be reversed, and the dead cannot be raised. Revealing your misbegotten treachery will inflict far more damage than just to our grand empire. We must instead divert your surging river into the ocean and never speak of it again. Any reparations you shall pay will be to me before you ascend to my throne."

Glowing blue mists of tears filled Merc's eyes, which he quickly wiped away.

"I am still worthy of your throne after all my failings, father?"

"Aside from Attea, who has no want of the throne," Nelron said bluntly. "There is no one worthier of becoming the next High Region than you. To be High Region, one must have an infinite and selfish love for his people. Something you have displayed time and time again, my son.

Your failing is in your ambition. You have yet to learn how to temper it. Learn from this all that you can and move forward to become the ruler you must be for your people."

"Yes, father."

"Also, know that your actions will greatly delay the day you will take rule," Nelron informed his son with a stern tone. "And you will pay dearly for your transgressions, boy."

"Yes, father," Merc acknowledged with a bowed head.

Lord Nelron used the long sharp fingernail on his index finger to mix around the remaining herbs within his pipe to get a few final puffs before getting down to business.

"You shall divulge to me thy full plan. Leave no detail absent from it. I shall take what is broken and forge a new one to ensure that you and Thrace remains blameless in this affair. You will then go and fetch your human and bring her to me so that I may deal with her. She now has one more role to play in this act."

CHAPTER 8

The Grand Canyon National Park, Colorado, the Project EVOlution base, upon Horus's mental command, Graves and Dr. Alexander stood with the apprehensive subservient staff waiting for their current lord and master alongside his resurrected queen.

During the time the reunited couple was away, Graves attempted to communicate with the doctor. Alexander, however, quickly reminded him with rapid eye movement of Meskhenet, the super Artificial Intelligence that oversaw the entire base, along with a returning Seker, Horus's cybernetic hawk familiar.

As the doors opened, everyone fell to their hands and knees, bowing down, making sure their minds were clear of any offense that could get them killed on the spot.

Breaths were held as a full in the buff Horus, and Sekhmet wrapped in bedsheets entered having a full-on conversation.

"So, humans spend most of their time looking at screens?" Sekhmet inquired in fluent English that she mentally learned from Horus. "For entertainment, information, and work?"

"Tis no different from the holographic images we learned from under the tutelage of Osiris and Amun-Ra," Horus pointed out.

"Still, at least they pushed our physical and mental potential before their betrayal," Sekhmet said while shaking her head. "Some of the things I saw on that screen were straight foolishness. What care I of the affairs of housewives? It is no wonder humankind's growth has been severely stunted. Once we take proper rule, I shall ban majority of these worthless 'programs.'"

"Not the show about the pale woman and the dragons?" Horus nervously asked.

"No, that was entertaining," Sekhmet nodded. "I will also keep sports such as the UFC and WWE but expand the rules to fights to the death."

"I, too, would love to see such matches!" Horus nodded with a savage grin.

The two ended their conversation to dully gaze upon their submissive subjects.

"Slaves! Raise thy heads and look upon in reverence the fruit of my labor!" Horus ordered. "Behold the Queen of all Goddesses! The Eye of Horus! Your mother, Sekhmet, has finally returned to rule by my side!"

Fear and terror were written all over the faces of everyone that lifted their heads looking upon her, which Sekhmet wholly enjoyed. She left Horus's side to stroll around the rows of mortals, many quaking, some whimpering, while a few more did both as she passed by them.

"Feeble children, you all shall find that I like your father can be a just and kind god," she informed them. "So long as my patience is not tested, and you give us what is deserving of gods, which is unconditional love and obedience. Any less is punishable by death. Do we have understanding?"

"Yes, goddess Sekhmet!"

The unified acknowledgment from all the mortals on their knees brought a bright smile to her face, which pleased Horus watching from where he stood. Sekhmet's smile remained upon her face until she stopped in her tracks and slowly gazed down at the human violently trembling at her feet.

Below her knelt, Dr. Henderson, the female lab technician who for many months had become the unwilling courtesan of Horus. Sekhmet's eyes emitted a brighter white glow as she slowly turned to another female lab technician two rows up, who replaced the chemist that suffered Horus's unhuman wrath for disobeying him.

Sekhmet slowly turned, walking back to her husband with a sinister smirk on her visage.

"I wish to be properly cleancd and clothed."

"As you command my love, I shall have …"

"I shall pick my own bathers," Sekhmet silenced him with a steel tone.

She slowly turned, pointing while giving a mental command to two male staff members in their mid-twenties.

Both men timidly got to their feet, glancing at one another. Their faces read they were about to be led to the gallows.

"You two shall give me a proper and thorough bathe."

Sekhmet, with the face of a cat who innocently had a mouse in its mouth, turned to see pure vexation plastered on Horus's visage at her selection. She sashayed her way through the wall he built, pressing up against his chest and whispered into his ear.

"I know what you have been up to before my resurrection …my love. Your wife now demands balance."

Horus lowered his head, becoming submissive, which dumbfounded both Graves and Dr. Alexander.

"Come now, children, less I remind you of my patience being tested."

The two terrified staff members both leaped forward, coming front and center with the ancient.

"This …this way …Goddess Sekhmet." Motioned the taller of the two men sporting curly brown hair and glasses.

The self-proclaimed Egyptian King of the gods stood still as Sekhmet walked away following the two men to the showers, while the rest of the mortals silently feared for their lives believing Horus would flip-out the second they left, taking his jealousy out on them.

Sure enough, the room violently vibrated while the ground underneath him slowly cracked.

Sekhmet waited as both men quickly removed all their clothing. The technician with the curly hair and olive skin scattered to the showers turning them on and began testing the waters to ensure they were an acceptable temperature, while the shorter man, another chemist with a bald head and pale white skin, got together clean rags, two luffas, and Dove Body Wash soap. Luckily for him, someone had scented Mandarin and flare flower scent stashed in their open locker.

This did not stop his heart from falling into his gut as he turned to a displeased Sekhmet, glaring back at him.

"What is this? Where is my bath?"

The chemist instinctually fell to his knees on the hard tile flower cowering.

"Forgive me…my goddess…but we have no baths in this facility…only showers to cleanse you."

The Egyptian Goddess of War scoffed as she read his mind to see that he spoke the truth.

"We shall change that very soon. What is that bottle in your hand?"

The chemist quickly crawled over to her, holding it up.

"It's called Body Wash soap, goddess Sekhmet. This one has a delightful scent to it!"

Sekhmet leaned forward to take a whiff as the chemist popped open the top and held the bottle higher.

"Not bad," she nodded with approval. "This will do, for now."

The chemist's heart, which returned to his chest, began to make rabbit beats as she unfastened the bed sheets covering her nude body underneath, allowing it to fall to the floor.

He forced himself to rise and follow her into the showers, where the equally frightened technician stood with his head bowed in servitude waiting for them. The goddess strolled up to the running water placing her hand underneath it.

The feeling of the wet liquid bouncing off her hand returned a smile to her lips.

"Warm water pushed through pipes. Impressive. Our backwatered species is not a complete loss after all."

With closed eyes, she stepped underneath the shower, thoroughly soaking herself, while her two servants quickly divided the rags and luffas between themselves and began pouring the body wash soap onto the luffas while saving the cloths for the rinse phase. With eye contact, they came up with a plan to clean the Goddess of War to ensure they were not getting murdered on the spot.

The second Sekhmet stepped from underneath the showers, both men went to work. However, the shorter bald male deviated from the plan going for the back parts of her body, forcing the taller man with curly black hair to address her front.

The lab technician suppressed his desire to shoot the chemist a dirty glare as both men began scrubbing Sekhmet, starting at her neck, working their way down.

"Put strong effort into task slaves," she hissed with sinister sensuality. "I will be greatly displeased if I do not feel properly cleansed."

Both men's eyes became glassy as they glanced at one another, knowing that the predicament they were in spelled certain death for them both no matter what they did. It did not help that either of them had to battle to suppress their involuntary natural urges as they were forced to stand nude and clean a beautifully naked woman capable of killing them with either her bare hands or a thought.

The man behind her had a more straightforward job as he soaped up and scrubbed her rear and the back of her legs. Her designated servant tending to her front had the grueling task of cleansing her intimate parts while feeling her eyes on him.

"You fear me, don't you, boy?" Sekhmet bluntly asked.

The Lab technician timidly nodded.

"Yes, goddess Sekhmet."

Brazenly she reached down, grabbing him by the shaft of his penis, causing him to squeal as he stood on the tips of his toes. The grip she had on him felt as if she wanted to rip it off.

Her actions also startled the chemist who knelt where he stood watching in fright, believing his associate was about to meet a gruesome end.

"You also desire me," She said with a sensual smile. "Pumping blood doesn't deceive."

"I beg your mercy, goddess …"

Sekhmet silenced him to a whimper by using a finger to lift his chin so that she could look into his terrified eyes.

"You will not be punished for being a man, slave. You are mine to do as I please. And it pleases me that you desire me. The both of you."

At that moment, the Chemist behind her bowed his head, concentrating on the wet tile floor.

"Now, suspend all fear, conduct thyself like a proper man with cock, and clean your goddess properly."

"Yes, goddess Sekhmet!" Both men acknowledged.

Tossing away all inhibition, they both scrubbed her down thoroughly as commanded, remembering their lives depended on it. The chemist took an even bigger initiative placing his body inches within her personal space to help soap up parts of her front; he felt the technician was still too timid to clean correctly.

With a head motion, the chemist signaled to the tech that it was time to move onto the rinse cycle.

"May we rinse you now, goddess Sekhmet?" Asked the lab technician.

"You may," Sekhmet nodded. "But tend to my back. The sight of you bores me now."

The lab technician nodded with a weakened neck while fighting back the tears. The eager Chemist, not wishing to share his fate, quickly took a rag soaking it with fresh running water and stood before her vigorously wiping off the suds, while the lab tech moved to her back doing the same.

To save his life, he left not a crevice untouched on her body. He did not even flinch when Sekhmet placed a gentle hand on his skull. He just prayed that her touch confirmed that she was pleased, and he would live another day.

"Very good, slave," she smiled. "Now, finish my cleansing with thy tongue."

The chemist had no time to decipher her words as Sekhmet widened her stance and guided his head in between her legs.

With her other hand, she grabbed a handful of the lab technician's curls and pulled him to her rear to do the same.

A devious Sekhmet then mentally projected the pleasures she felt onto Horus, causing his emotional output of rage to rattle a big part of the facility and sink him further into the crater he stood in.

At that moment, every mortal that remained knelt within the room glanced at who was either on their left and right, knowing that they would soon be slaughtered in a jealous bloodlust.

What everyone in the room did not know was that Sekhmet was in Horus's head, giving him strict orders.

"Remain where you stand, bare what you see, and lay wrathful hand to no one."

"Yes, my queen." He reluctantly answered back.

A visibly aroused Horus stood with gripped fists and endured the sight of his resurrected bride brought to ecstasy by two mere mortals.

Sekhmet, with a satisfied gaze of euphoria, released the lab technician concentrating solely on the chemist bringing him to his feet by his chin with a gentle hand.

"You are a master of your craft, slave." She panted. "I am pleased with your work."

"Thank you, goddess Sekhmet." He smiled back. "I am here to please you."

At that moment, the chemist groaned in horror as Sekhmet increased her grip on his lower jaw, cracking it to force his mouth open. She lifted him higher onto the tips of his toes.

The lab technician, now on his rear, squealed and cried as he witnessed the Goddess of War take hold of the Chemist's tongue, slowly yanking it out with one pull, causing fresh new blood to spurt from his mouth onto her freshly cleansed skin.

Sekhmet dismissively released him, allowing the chemist to fall, smacking the floor with a painful thud. He was, however, more focused on his broken jaw minus a tongue as he curled up into a sobbing ball.

"But …you said …he pleased you." The lab technician blubbered.

"That he did," Sekhmet nodded in agreement while looking over the ripped-out tongue in her hand. "And for that, he shall keep his life, he just cannot keep the tongue that now knows a god intimately."

A sinister Sekhmet then turned with a sadistic grin to the lab technician on the floor.

"Unfortunately for you, I was not pleased."

Her words of judgment brought the lab tech to hysterical tears as he attempted to scurry away on his rear.

"No! Please! No!"

"Dear child, your death shall not be by my hands," Sekhmet innocently shook her head.

His heart dropped at the sound of destruction as Horus effortlessly tore through walls to get to the showers. The last thing the tech would see after uncovering his arms from the flying projectiles of debris was a naked animalistic Horus towering over him.

His attempt to flee was futile as the Egyptian King of Gods pounced on top of him. The lab technician's horrendous end was met as Horus pinned him down, brutally sodomizing him in front of a cackling Sekhmet, shattering his neck and spine in the process. Horus then rose to his feet, lifting the broken man into the air by his limp neck.

The chemist closed his tear-stained eyes, as his ears were forever haunted by the blood-curdling screams of the lab technician being torn in half by an unforgiving ancient.

His eyes slowly opened to Horus drenched in fresh blood, staring down an enamored Sekhmet gazing back at him.

In one fail swoop, he rushed the Goddess of War, taking her up in his arms, carrying her over to the still running showers.

Their lovemaking was savage and animalistic, breaking up the walls and floor all around them. It blotted out the world along with the chemist that laid a couple of feet from them, still bleeding out not too far from the dismembered corpse of the lab technician.

~ ~

After their sinister sordid affair in the showers, the lovers chose four more servants to clean and attend to them, while a mortified Dr. Alexander had to pick people from his staff to see to the dismembered body of the lab technician and the seriously injured chemist.

Although he learned to keep his mind clear, frustration filled the weary doctor's face, unable to comprehend how two alleged beings of superior intelligence could inflict so much unnecessary death.

It was a question he had the answer to buried deep in his gut. He and his people were nothing more than playthings for the immortals.

As things quieted down a bit, Dr. Alexander had the painful displeasure of constructing a new attire for the resurrected Goddess of War. She stood barking orders at him on the design while wearing just a white towel around her waist and some purple flip flops.

It was more amusement for Horus as he stood off to the side, casually leaning against a wall as a silent spectator to the berating and abuse.

Meskhenet, the base's new super AI system, could have easily constructed Sekhmet's suit on command. Horus chose to use this as a lesson for Dr. Alexander. He, like the rest of his staff, was nothing more than a servant.

After its completion, servants were brought forth to dress her. Sekhmet stood admiring herself in a full-length mirror at her new attire.

Her new outfit consisted of a form-fitting dark grey mesh bodysuit, black half thigh-high boots with red piping, and a black and grey tactical bodice with the symbol of a red lioness head etched into the center of the chest. Her attire was accessorized with re-creations of an Egyptian queen headdress, thick bicep bands for each arm, and a three-piece loop necklace all forged from

Horus's synthetic Alder metal with the look of gold.

The softness of love fell upon Horus's face as he watched her girlishly stand on the tips of her toes admiring her new look. She turned to him, dawning an innocent smile.

"Do you approve, husband?"

"Your ensemble fits your station, my love."

"Goddess of War," She whispered to herself. "I love the sound of that …but why am I also called the Goddess of Healing?"

"Mortals' tall tales, my love."

"A lioness is such a fitting symbol for me," she said before her smile switched to a snarl. "But which son of a whore linked my bloodline to that of the filthy House of Ra? I am no daughter of his, and never will be."

"Technically, our rebirth is owed to those we once saw as our gods and fathers," Horus reminded her. "Though I loathe them equally for their betrayal, I am reminded that without them, we would not have the power that courses through our veins, nor the ability to cheat death."

Sekhmet gave him a playful leer.

"As sentimental as ever you are, my love."

In the middle of admiring herself in the mirror, Sekhmet glanced at the female servants she picked to see to her needs.

Once again, Dr. Henderson and the replacement female lab technician picked when the second was punished for disobeying Horus stood off to the side with their heads down, waiting to be commanded.

"You slave," she motioned to Dr. Henderson. "Come forward."

Henderson swallowing the spit stuck in her throat, did as commanded. She prayed that the distance she stopped was both reasonable and safe.

"Raise your head, girl."

Dr. Henderson slowly did as she was ordered while struggling to keep the terror she felt from her eyes.

"What say you of my look?" Sekhmet asked.

"May I ask how to properly address you before I answer, my goddess?" The doctor asked while clearing her throat.

A tiny smile grew on Sekhmet's face at the doctor's subservient question.

"I am your one true goddess, slave, Goddess Sekhmet will suffice, but you may also address me as mistress."

"You look …fearsomely beautiful, my mistress Sekhmet," she quickly answered. "There is no goddess or female mortal in all of the universes that can rival your beauty."

Her compliment drew a broad smile on Sekhmet's face causing the resurrected immortal to move closer and tower over her. Henderson, having survived her ordeal with Horus, kept her composure while her fellow female lab technician, a foot behind her, became even more distressed.

Sekhmet moved into Henderson's personal space, looking her over.

"Such eloquent words, I see that you are well educated, especially in the history and customs of ancient times. In my days, women were not fit to be scholars. Wives, mothers, and whores were the titles we were permitted to hold. Whether you were poor, rich, or noble was determined by the house you were born into, or the man that picked you.

Through your eyes, I see much has changed. So, answer me plainly, how does it feel with all your education to be reduced to the whore of the King of the gods?"

A smile came over Henderson's face as she looked Sekhmet in the eyes, knowing that she was both taunting and purposely bating her.

"Like anything, there was an adjustment phase," Henderson said with no hesitation. "But I soon learned my place and duty to my one true god. It has been an honor and pleasure being a servant and whore of Lord Horus. I pray that I may be of some service to you as well."

Henderson's answer drew a brighter smile on Sekhmet's face.

"I do like this one, my love. She knows her place. You choose your concubine well."

"Although she takes cock well, she pales in comparison to you, my queen," Horus reaffirmed.

"I care not that she sampled your cock," Sekhmet snarled. "I care about the seed germinating in her belly."

The ominous revelation made the room ice cold. Tears fell from Henderson's eyes, which weighted her head. In her mind, she now stood before her executioner.

Tears also fell from the female tech next to her, who also believed Henderson's fate was sealed.

A silent and devastated Dr. Alexander watching from the sidelines slowly turned to Horus, whose reaction to the revelation that he impregnated Dr. Henderson was cruel and dismissive.

"You feared that I would find out," Sekhmet continued. "Feared of what I would do to you. Did you not, slave?"

"Yes, goddess Sekhmet," Dr. Henderson answered with a whimper while clutching her belly.

"Though I blame you not for how it happened, order must be restored to my house on this day. That child can never see the light of day."

It began with a painful groan followed by an agonizing scream from the female lab technician who stood behind a shocked and horrified Dr. Henderson.

Dr. Henderson covering her mouth, wailed hysterically as the young woman fell to her knees while thick blood seeped through and poured down her pants legs.

"Lose that child in your belly, and your fate will be more horrible than hers," Sekhmet warned. "Calm thyself and witness order restored to house."

Every mortal in the room ears would forever be scarred by the woman's death cries and the chilling sound of something being rip out of her with telekinesis.

Finally, the room became silent.

Shivering, Dr. Henderson slowly turned and looked down at the young woman staring back up at her with the torturous expression of her death still on her face.

As the blood that began to flow underneath her and Sekhmet's shoes, the Goddess of War used her finger to raise Henderson's chin to make eye contact.

"Order has been restored," She said with satisfaction. "First concubine keeps one bastard of Horus. He will be of use to us when the time comes."

A mentally broken Dr. Henderson fell to her knees into the warm pool of blood with her head bowed and somehow found the words.

"Thank…you…goddess Sekhmet…for your mercy."

Sekhmet looked down upon her and placed two fingers on the top of her head.

"Your gratitude has been received today, slave."

The Egyptian immortal turned to saunter over to Horus, who watched her come to him with a Cheshire grin on his face.

It was immediately removed as Sekhmet grabbed Horus's jaw, slamming him violently into the wall behind him.

The act caused everyone else still alive to leap out of their skins as the stunned god's body cratered the wall.

An angered Horus did not say a word as he glared at his wife while she licked and bit at his lower lip before sinisterly whispering her warning.

"I am your queen and goddess returned. Whores may sample the mighty cock of Horus from time to time, but only the Eye of Horus shall carry his seed. Impregnate another mortal sow, and the next blood I spill will be that of a god. Do we have understanding, my husband?"

A savage grin formed on the face of the Ancient as he felt Sekhmet massaging his member, while she playfully lifted him off his feet by his jaw with her inhuman strength.

"Yes, wife, we have understanding."

As Sekhmet lowered him back down to the ground. An aroused Horus violently scooped her up by her rear while grabbing a fist full of her locks. Sekhmet allowed him to ram his tongue down her throat as she returned the passionate kiss sucking him in. A disturbed and traumatized Dr. Alexander lowered his head at the lustful scene.

~ ~

Per Sekhmet's command, Dr. Henderson was relieved of her duties, cleaned up, cared for, and confined to her room to concentrate on bringing Horus's child to term.

Horus then took his wife with a mentally worn Dr. Alexander on a tour of the EVOlution facility.

She was introduced to the enhanced soldiers Horus used his mental abilities to re-write and control. Her husband then took her down to the lower levels, where she came face to face with the machine that contained and monitored her former body.

Finally, they returned to the upper levels and the main observation deck, where an equally beaten Graves waited for them. Horus revealed to her their new children fully developed, lying dormant in cryostasis.

Sekhmet took her time going to each pod, examining the superhuman inside before solemnly standing over the fifth chamber that created her new body.

"I wish you had saved my old body," she whispered. "So that I may have looked upon it one final time."

Horus walked up behind her, placing a comforting hand around her waist.

"It would have brought you nothing but pain and grief, dear wife. Joy and happiness are all you deserve, for you have returned from the afterlife into my arms. Nothing, not even death, can ever separate us."

With a sad smile on her face, she clasped his hand, giving it a gentle rub.

The sadness quickly burnt away as her eyes emitted a white glow of bubbling anger that came through in her tone.

"Explain to me again, husband, why are we here hidden away instead of taking our rightful rule of this world?"

Horus's hand released her as she turned to him, waiting for an answer. It was clear to Dr. Alexander and Graves that the honeymoon was officially over.

"As I explained to you, wife, the world has vastly changed …"

"I understand that demi-gods are walking the Earth created from my own genetic material," Sekhmet snapped, cutting him off. "And only two by your words are formidable."

"There is also the descendant of Amun-Ra."

"And what fear should you have of him? Are you not the god of the sky and kingship? Did you not slay Osiris and Set to avenge me? What fear should you have of a mortal with diluted Annunaki blood?" Sekhmet furiously spat at Horus, "We are gods! Why do we resort to cowardly scheming to take rule, when we have power coursing through our veins to bring this world to heel?!"

Horus took a breath drawing in patience before he reasoned with her.

"I fear no half-breed mortal, wife. It is the backing of Anu and the Dominion Council that pauses our introduction to this new world."

Sekhmet opened her mouth to fire off a nasty retort but was silenced by Horus, who held up a finger.

"Allow me to finish before you debate me!"

Placing her hands at her hips backed by a narrowed glare, she allowed him to continue.

"As I said to thee before, my love, this world has vastly changed since our removal from it. Aside from the rise of demi-gods, mankind has significantly evolved their way of thinking. The majority of man worships a nameless absentee God, while others believe not in gods at all. This facility, which I have commandeered for us, is just a fraction of the technological advancements our mortal species has achieved over the centuries. They have split the atom, and from it built weapons of destruction capable of razing continents, possibly worlds.

The rise of technology has also strengthened their will and defiance. They have become a species that will not be quickly ruled, even by gods.

I have studied the history of human rule over the centuries until this current time. Every dynasty, every monarch, every king, queen, dictator, government who has dared to subjugate its people, who have ruled through fear and tyranny, who has not operated in the best interest of the people eventually falls never to rise again; it is not a foundation that can support our empire."

"But, we are gods!" Sekhmet seethed through her teeth.

"Which means nothing to them!" Horus fired back. "Like hundreds of gods who have come before and after us, our names and legacy are known to teachers of history, and fairy tales read and watched in books and television. They barely show allegiance to the popular God and his Son."

"He has a Son?"

"Born to a virgin," Horus nodded. "I have yet to comprehend how the ignorant masses could accept the plausibility of such an absurd event."

Sekhmet then silently gestured to the four restructuring pods, each housing a full-grown inert superhuman created by Sekhmet's eggs, Horus's sperm, and genetic material from Sophia Dennison.

The Sky god cleared his throat of irritation and continued.

"Majority of humans today would rather die than live on their hands and knees. Attempting to bring them to heel by bloodshed would bring us into a confrontation with the descendant of Amun-Ra, which would eventually bring us into an encounter with Anu, who has the full support of the Dominion Council. We would be undone before we even sat in our seats of power.

To acquire rule, we must appear not as their enemy but their ally. We must gain their love and respect, not their fear and hatred. We must shed our godhood and become what they will need, what they want."

"And what would that be?" Sekhmet demanded to know with a cocked head.

A sinister smirk grew on Horus's face before he answered his wife.

"Heroes. We must become heroes to the people of Earth."

A frustrated Sekhmet folded her arms while pouting. She wanted to desperately refute what her husband said to her, but knew he was the more tactical between the two of them. She also could not deny what he had shown her so far from the new world of man that brought weight to his argument.

Sekhmet giving Horus a side-eye, muttered her question.

"How do we accomplish this task?"

"The first act has already been completed when I revealed to them an enemy greater than they could ever imagine," Horus grinned. "The Thracian Prince's appearance has instilled fear in all of the nations of Earth. Their champion and her daughter have been removed from the planet as well, so their hope is now dwindling.

With our puppets in play, we shall appear as benevolent immortals risen from ancient times and reveal the truth about the Annunaki, the Thracians, the Dominion Council, and their intentions for this world, **our truth**. And with every man, woman, and child gripped with the fear of extinction, we shall bestow onto them the power to stand with us and crush the invaders at our doorstep."

"What power?"

"Bring them forward, slave."

Upon Horus's command, Doctor Alexander motioned to his staff to bring forward a metallic case on top of a trolley cart. As the case was opened by one of the male staff members,

Sekhmet's arms unfolded, falling to her sides as her mouth parted open.

She slowly strolled up to the case filled with forty vials, each with crimson red liquid within them.

"Is that what I think it is?" Sekhmet asked with a gasp.

"It is," Horus beamed while picking up one of the vials of red liquid holding it up. "Tis a modified version of the Aten serum used to evolve us into our godly state. I simplified it to target the dormant gene of the demi-god Sophia Dennison which resides now within all humans forcing it to activate and grow until it remains awaken, granting a regular mortal the powers of a demi-god.

With each injection administered of Aten, it eliminates and alters the host's cells as the demi-god cells multiply before going dormant. With each dose, the demi-god cells spread and remain more active, until finally, it no longer goes into dormancy."

"How many injections are needed before the transformation is permanent?" Sekhmet asked.

"Sixty vials," Horus answered.

"Three months." Sekhmet deduced.

"Correct."

A sneer of disbelief grew upon her face.

"So, thy answer to an already defiant species per your words is to grant them more power? Do tell me that your near eternal captivity has not robbed you of all your senses."

Horus gave Sekhmet a semi-calm glare warning her never to speak that way to him again before he answered.

"Has thy ever known a dog to bite the master's hand that feeds it?"

"Depends on the dog," Sekhmet answered with a snort.

Horus ignored her sharp tongue continuing.

"My version of Aten not only grants abilities, but it will also instill the undying faith, worship, and loyalty towards the champions that have been risen to fight by their side to save humankind."

A sinister grin grew on Sekhmet's face as she now understood her husband's devious plan.

"Mind control?"

"Mind persuasion to be more precise," Horus smirked. "The serum not only targets the dormant gene, but it also attaches itself to the central nervous system and the pituitary gland unleashing endorphins synonymous with love, admiration, and pleasure. Endorphins triggered by sight, sound, and even smell pertaining to us."

"They will love us without even knowing it," Sekhmet savagely grinned.

"They will willingly die for us, without even knowing it," Horus chuckled.

"What of those who are already demi-gods?" Sekhmet asked.

"I am quite confident the majority will stand with their fellow brethren and us against the coming threat. And like them, they will eventually bend the knee.

Those that do not shall be swiftly swept from mortal coil along with the rest of the opposition during the chaos of the war to come. When it is all said and done, the road to salvation shall lead through us."

Sekhmet stood there for a minute, attempting to make sense of Horus's plan.

"So, we create an estimated five to six billion soldiers, the Dominion Council is a united front of over thirty thousand species, maybe more since the centuries past. How do we overcome those numbers?"

"By forging our own alliances," Horus answered. "Meskhenet, reveal our network."

The massive screen in the center of the room came to life, revealing the planets and species Horus was currently in contact with. Sekhmet's eyes widened with amazement as she moved closer to get a look at the busy work her husband had been up to.

"The Volorion Empire, Tinra Oa Order, the Nation of Altar," she named a few.

Horus walked up to stand by her side while pointing to the screen.

"Nations of species that hate and despise the Dominion Council as equally as we do. Some I have bent to my will to secure their alliance, others I am in current negotiations with. All wish for the destruction of the Council so that they may return to the times before it was formed.

We will not foolishly recreate the failings of the Razcargian campaign, my love. To bring the universe to heel, we shall forge our army, unite these worlds under us, and eradicate the Dominion Council from existence. By the time they realize what is upon them, they will be taking their last breath of life. All of them."

Sekhmet turned, falling into Horus's loving embrace burying her face into his chest. As she raised her head, staring into his eyes, Horus leaned in to plant a kiss.

"So, what of the demi-god you murdered? The main reason you remain in hiding?"

Her stern question froze Horus's advance while wiping the confidence he had from his face.

He slowly turned with a scowl to the one mortal in the room who Sekhmet could pluck the information from.

Dr. Alexander kept his head down as a wide-eyed Graves became drenched in sweat, taking a futile step backward.

The Goddess of War snapped her fingers, refocusing her husband's attention.

"If you did not want your secrets known to me, you should not have your manservant around for me to freely read his mind."

"Nay wife, I hide no secrets from you," Horus defended himself while clearing his throat. "I merely…"

"Why did you murder this 'Sir Knight Light'?"

Horus let out frustrated air before he spoke.

"I underestimated him. Unlike these enhanced guards who I have altered to obey me, most demi-gods, these 'EVOs' are resistant to mind control. I had no choice but to dispatch him, and then become him to further my endeavors, the main one which entailed finding your remains to return you to life."

"Why in the name of the underworld did you drain him?!"

An enraged Horus released her, stepping back.

"Have you any idea what I have endured?" Horus howled back, wounded. "Buried alive for centuries! The energies that kept me alive dwindling to nothing! My hunger was insatiable once I broke free! I was also alone in this world! Alone!"

Sekhmet closed the gap between them, placing a hand on Horus's chest to calm him as the Ancient huffed and puffed his frustration on what appeared to be the brink of tears.

"Calm thyself, husband," she whispered. "Calm thyself. I am here by your side, never to be removed again. Now relay to me everything. Leave nothing hidden, so that I may aid you in repairing the cracks in this mighty foundation you have built for us."

CHAPTER 9

The Hall of Elders, the main capital building of Atticala,

Laurence entered the hall side by side with Anubis and Bastet to report to the Council of Elders.

They ascended the grand spiral steps, which led to the Hall of Elders. A hall constructed from pure silver Alder with etchings of hieroglyphics. Humongous Ember statues of past Elders that stood in chronological order of rule. Each glowed brightly with infinite Awakening energy, making the hall shimmer.

As Laurence passed the last three statues belonging to Set, Osiris, and finally Amun-Ra for the umpteenth time, a slight smile formed. It was caused by the memory of the first time he entered the hall after arriving on Anu after defeating

Anubis in combat on the desolate planet of Corazal.

Decades later, compounded by missions and adventures that took him to the far corners of the universe, no half-human had ever traveled. Laurence searched for knowledge and wisdom that he had hoped to return to Earth to teach the people of his first home a new way.

However, as Laurence's newfound love for exploration bestowed upon him a vast understanding of the universe, it also delayed his return to Earth by decades. That, along with a sad conclusion, he had kept to himself.

As the massive circular chamber door before them rolled out of the way, allowing them to enter the Chamber of Elders, a smile came to the trios face as they were greeted by Tefnut, the daughter of Ma'at, the first Eye of Ra, and Atum's eldest son Shu, the Eye of Nu in their respective armors. They were leaving after giving their report from their mission.

"Cousins." The trio said in unison.

"Cousins." Tefnut and Shu returned.

They gave each other the proper forearm clasp greeting an Annunaki warrior gave to another.

"How was thy mission?" Anubis inquired.

"Successful," Shu answered. "We escorted the Zengarian delegates safely to their conference and back without incident."

"We heard it's because you trio took the suspected human into custody," Tefnut added.

"Alleged suspect human," Laurence sternly corrected her. "We had to intercede to prevent the Thracian Crown Prince and Princess from creating a diplomatic incident."

"Have a care cousin," Tefnut warned him. "Earth is not a part of the Dominion Council."

"Nor are the bloody Volorions we had the misfortune of fighting," Bastet said while defending Laurence. "Yet, we were told not to create an incident with them."

Tefnut ignored Bastet's words focusing on Laurence.

"You overstepped by venturing to Earth and interfering cousin. She is not pleased with you."

Tefnut's eyes then went from Anubis to Bastet.

"None of them are."

Tefnut and Shu departed, leaving Bastet, Laurence, and Anubis glancing at each other with the understanding that they were walking into a potential hornet's nest.

However, their stride did not lessen as they entered the chamber room and walked through rows of towering golden columns that stretched as far as the eye could see. Each of them had gleaming silver hieroglyphics that told the history of the Annunaki.

Eventually, they reached the sea of steps where the Council of Elders sat in thrones forged from pure shining gold and silver Alder, fashioned to represent each House. The House of Set, being the eldest house, sat in the middle. To its right was the House of Ra, and to its left was the House of Khnum. To the right of the House of Ra was the House of Osiris, while to the left of the House of Khnum was the House of Nu.

Beings who lived thousands of years, possessing knowledge and intelligence that surpassed many species across the universe and their names were well-known to humans who had a sliver of understanding about Egyptian mythology.

Before them sat Isis, wife of Osiris, the third from the house of Osiris, first son of Osiris the second, and Bastet's mother.

Like her mythos on Earth, her beauty appeared to have no equal. Her skin was a warm honey brown while her silky pearl black hair was bone straight and hung down to her shoulders. Certain things were inaccurate about the tales told of her. She had large, piercing silver eyes and a toned, shapely physique of someone who had seen battle and won. Isis's features of a woman in her late forties – a mixture of gentle softness and not to be trifled with.

Her attire was a sheer gold and blood-red double shoulder strapped sheath dress. Around her left bicep, she wore a silver serpent that wrapped around her arm several times.

Next was Atum from the House of Nu, the first son of Nu resplendent in gold and silver, yellow and green. With his gray skin and thick, midnight black braid off his right shoulder matching his braided beard, he had the appearance of a Pharaoh of old.

Khnum, the second, from the house of Khnum, first son of Khnum, was the oldest, largest, and most intimidating of the elders. His bare-chested, muscular onyx-colored physique was covered in battle scars that he did not even attempt to hide.

Nephthys, wife of Set the third, from the house of Set, first son of Set the second, Isis's sister and Anubis's mother, was also a chilling, golden-eyed beauty, adorned in a sheer sky-blue version of an ancient Kalasiris dress. Her thick silky raven and royal purple braided hair had a gold tiara perched on top of her head fashioned in the shape of a Seni.

Finally, Ma'at, Laurence's great, great, great many times great aunt, and the first daughter of Amun-Ra sat in the seat of the house of Ra, the first son of Amun. She was dressed similarly to Nephthys in a sheer white and gold version of her Kalasiris dress with a deep plunge line that went down to her navel. Her skin was a deep bronze color, while her eyes were a warm hazel hue. Her pearl black hair hung straight down to the middle of her back.

Behind each of the Elders stood their familiar armors: Isis's armor was designed in the theme of a hawk creature with massive multi-colored wings attached under the arms to the torso. Along with it was Atum's stately emerald-black beetle-themed armor with a sheathed long sword; Khnum's minotaur-inspired armor hefting two heavy battle-axes; Nephthys' golden, forest-green graceful stork-like armor armed with a bow; and Ma'at's eagle-themed armor with twin short swords.

Monstrously exquisite and powerful weapons capable of operating independently of their wearers, obeying their masters, and mistresses sole command. Each with the ability to destroy whole planets if need be.

Laurence, Anubis, and Bastet dropped to their knees, smacking their forearms against their chests as they bowed their heads to the Council. They rose once again and at semi-attention, waiting for the debriefing to take place.

Tefnut's words rang true about the demeanor of the Council. The heat of irritation and disappointment could be felt raining down on them from where the trio stood. Anubis and Bastet could tolerate the glares from their uncles, but their mothers' disapproving glowers made them shift a bit where they stood. The same could be said for Laurence, who was forced to weather through Ma'at's piercing frown locked solely on him.

"Let us begin this debriefing with the sequence of events," Atum sighed, speaking in Annunaki dialect.

He glanced at the other Council members waiting for approval.

They each agreed with a nod.

"Anubis, Eye of Set of the house of Set," Atum began the debriefing. "What was the outcome of your audience with High Prime Vbzarma?"

"The High Prime had no intention of negotiating," Anubis bluntly answered. "Instead, he planned to execute us, take possession of our armor, and per his words, attempt to reverse engineer them for mass production. High Prince Nofarrzo also informed us during the battle with his War Legion, that an old friend of our fathers sent his regards."

Each of the Council members glanced at one another, perplexed and deeply concerned over the High Prince's words.

"Let us put the Volorion matter to the side for now," Isis stepped in. "Why did you three venture to Earth and interfere with the apprehension of the human Sophia Dennison?"

"I ventured to Earth to investigate why it was under quarantine," Laurence spoke up. "My intervention ensured the detainment of Ms. Dennison and prevented the possible destruction of the planet, which the actions of the Crown Prince and Princess nearly caused."

"That was not a part of your mission," Ma'at spoke up with steel sternness.

Laurence calmly turned to her, remembering at that moment that she was not his aunt, but the Council of Elder for the House of Ra.

"Forgive me, Elder Ma'at," Laurence responded. "But I am a child of Earth as well as Anu. If I regret anything, it is getting my cousins entangled in this affair."

"Once again, our cousin does not speak for us," Bastet said, stepping forward. "We happily accompanied the Eye of Ra to Earth to prevent the High Region's pups from botching a simple apprehension."

"Curtail your tongue, Eye of Osiris," Isis warned her daughter. "You are overstepping."

Bastet embarrassingly lowered her head while clearing her throat.

"Apologies, Elder Isis."

"It is understood that you are still a child of Earth, Laurence Danjuma," Khnum spoke with his signature rumbling tone. "But as a citizen of Anu, and an Eye, you are also bound to the laws here as well as that of the Dominion Council. The Council by vote delegates responsibilities to fellow nations that they entrust to carry out how they see fit so long as they are within the parameters of the laws created by the Council. Your interference in Crown Prince Merc's and the Thracian High General Attea's mission both disrespected and undermined the authority of the Thracian empire, who are our allies."

A stone-faced Anubis stepped forward.

"I was the elder in charge of this mission. I bear the responsibility for approving the venture to Earth; the burden of fault is my yoke to bear."

Anubis's words reeled both Laurence and Bastet causing them both to break rank.

"How dare you steal responsibility for this venture?!" Bastet spat.

"This yoke is not yours to solely carry, Anubis!" Laurence chimed in.

"Remember your places and where you both stand!" Anubis roared his authority.

Laurence slowly shook his head in disbelief, while Bastet scoffed and snorted at Anubis for admonishing them in front of the elders.

"You are all to blame for this infraction," Nephthys said with soaring vocals echoing through the room. "And you will be judged and punished accordingly for your actions."

Laurence, Anubis, and Bastet all solemnly yet proudly stood accepting the ruling and judgment of the Council of Elders.

"Princess Attea is currently en-route to collect the human," Atum informed the trio. "You will hand the human over to her, and you will give her proper apologies for your interference and undermining of their operation. Do we have understanding?"

"Yes, Elder Atum," the trio answered in unison.

"We must now address the third and final matter of this debriefing," Ma'at said, switching the subject with a steel tone. "An accusation brought to our attention by the Thracian Crown Prince. An accusation that this Council finds extremely disturbing pertaining to the child of Sophia Dennison currently being treated in our Halls of Healing."

Bastet slightly lowered her head, closing her eyes. Laurence could hear additional air blow through Anubis's nostrils, as he remained stone-faced while Ma'at's stern and confused eyes fell on him.

"Laurence Danjuma, Eye of Ra, step forward," Ma'at commanded.

The Eye of Ra briskly took one full advance forward, keeping his eyes locked on her. He could tell that she prayed the question she was about to ask him was false.

"You have been accused by Prince Merc of infusing a child with Awakening energy. Is this accusation true?"

"Yes, it is, Elder Ma'at."

Laurence's ears picked up Bastet whispering a foul word in Annunaki as his eyes stayed on Ma'at, the Head of his house whose face now bore a mixed emotion of disappointment with a douse of punching the soul out of her.

"You do understand that you are admitting to a practice that you know full well is condemned not just by the worlds under the Dominion Council, but by this very Council of Elders who was the first to bring a petition to outlaw this process?"

"Yes, I do, Elder Ma'at."

"Do you also admit that you not only performed this act, but hid it from this Council, and from me your House Elder?"

"Yes, Elder Ma'at," Laurence admitted with no hesitation.

"Do you realized what you have done, Laurence Danjuma," Ma'at frustratingly pressed. "What she could potentially become?"

"I do."

"Explain your actions to this Council immediately, Laurence Danjuma."

"Unfortunately, the explanation for my actions can only be relayed to your ears."

Laurence's answer drew concern from the remaining elders who turned to one another, while Anubis and a perturbed Bastet gave him perplexed expressions.

"With the permission of the remaining Elders, I would like to converse with the Eye of Ra privately on the astral plane."

As the other members nodded in agreement, Ma'at sat back in her seat, becoming motionless while her eyes turned white as milk. At the same time, Laurence's eyes mirrored hers, signaling that she had pulled him into the astral plane. As he lost consciousness, his body locked up, becoming as stiff as a statue where it stood.

~ ~

Laurence awoke in a cloudy pinkish-blue realm, which made him feel like he was standing in the middle of the Aurora Borealis. He briefly glanced at his astral form that was nude with the anatomical shape of a Barbie Ken doll. Standing before him was Ma'at also in her astral form, waiting for an explanation.

"Well, explain thyself, boy."

"I was given instruction to infuse the child with the energies of the Awakening by Amun-Ra, and I was further instructed to tell no one else of this but you, but only when you asked."

His answer removed the sternness from Ma'at's visage, replacing it with one of shock.

"You …communed with father? When?"

"After I almost died on Tyron-5 and was placed in an induced coma for several months. At first, I thought it was mere dreams until he began calling onto me at times when I was awake. He gave me much instruction over the years."

Ma'at's face mirrored the hurt she felt from him, keeping such a secret from her.

"Why would …?"

"I wanted to tell you so many times, but he sternly forbade me from doing so. He stressed knowledge of you knowing this would only bring you pain."

"But why now?"

Laurence moved closer before he answered.

"Almost eight human months before the attempted uprising on Earth orchestrated by evolved humans, Amun-Ra came to me and instructed me to infuse the power of the Awakening with a child that would ask for my help."

"But why would he instruct such a thing knowing it was forbidden?"

"He spoke of events that would threaten the known universe itself in the coming future. Vengeance from the shadows bent on extinguishing all life—a power held by one that could shake the universe. I asked for clarification on these events. He said these events could not be changed, only the outcome. He said the child would be one of the keys to changing the conclusions."

"One of the keys?"

Laurence answered with a nod.

"I struggled with the yoke he bore upon me, right up to when I infused the child with the power. The conflict of my actions changed when the child returned to me after the battle with the individual named Peace and the Zombie Nation. She asked for me to take the power of the Awakening away from her, that she no longer needed it after saving her mother."

Ma'at nodded, understanding his logic.

"Knowing that it was forever fused with her, I bled the power so that it gradually grew within her as she matured. We face dark times ahead of us and are headed toward a course that cannot be steered from. Defensive measures must be fortified to ensure that we are to survive what is to come. That also includes painful decisions, namely regarding me."

Ma'at's face read that she did not like where he was going with this conversation.

"Amun-Ra gave final instruction for you to deal with me after I made this offense, and you must carry it out when the time comes."

~ ~

Minutes later, Laurence's eyes reverted to normal as he awoke returning from the astral plane. He gazed up at Ma'at, who also returned wearing the same sad, painful expression she had after the conversation on the astral plane.

Her face communicated her feelings to him.

"Please don't make me do this ...please."

A hardened Laurence knowing what was at stake spoke back with just his gaze.

"You must."

The other Council members subtly glanced at one another, understanding what was going on, while Anubis and Bastet stood oblivious to what was taking place.

"Laurence Danjuma, our conversation behind the reason for your actions are deemed by my judgment to be inefficient, and you must be judged and sentenced for your actions."

Although they kept their composure, Laurence could feel the sinking of his cousins' hearts, especially Bastet, who grew a sisterly attachment to him over the decades.

"My only request from this Council is that we delay sentencing on the Eye of Ra for now," Ma'at humbly requested. "The one accord we acquired from our discussion is that someone has been plotting and scheming from the shadows, and it is imperative we uncover who that is. The Eye of Ra will remain reinstated until then."

"Agreed," Isis nodded.

"Agreed," Atum added.

"Agreed," Khnum grumbled in agreement.

"Agreed," Nephthys said, finalizing the consensus.

"Laurence Danjuma, you Anubis and Bastet are free to return to active duty, awaiting judgment at the predetermined time," Isis announced. "Carry out your onuses until then."

"Yes, my elders!" All three Eyes said in unison.

Laurence, Anubis, and Bastet fell to their knees, smacking their forearms against their chest, bowing respectfully to the Council. As they rose once again before departing the Council Chamber room, the Eye of Ra stayed with his elder telling her everything would be alright.

Ma'at's sad gaze said something differently.

"No ...it will not."

The silence between Laurence, Anubis, and Bastet stayed with the trio as they exited the Chamber room, through the hall, and finally out of the building where the sun of Anu shined down on them.

At that moment, Anubis spun Laurence around, grabbing him by the front of his armor and slammed him against one of the support columns of the capital.

Bastet stood shocked at what just happened, only because Anubis beat her to the punch.

"What did you do?" Anubis howled in his cousin's face. "What are you keeping from us?"

"Know me, cousin," Laurence said calmly. "When have I ever done anything that did not have purpose. That was not for the greater good?"

"I don't question your heart, cousin!" Anubis shot back. "I question your actions!"

"Actions that at this time, can never be known to you, either of you."

His eyes met with a frustrated Bastet, who looked like she wanted to step in and beat the truth out of him.

"How do you expect us to stand with you if you keep secrets from us?" Bastet shot back at him.

"This I can tell you," Laurence said with a steely tone. "There will come a time where you cannot stand with me."

"Getting a bit dramatic now, aren't we, cousin?" Bastet inquired with an irritated eye twitch.

Laurence took in some air and slowly exhaled. He then grasped Anubis' forearm. The Eye of Set reluctantly removed his grip from his chest plate.

"There are events taking place that will change everything," Laurence began to warn them. "Including us. But our charge remains the same, no matter the outcome."

The Eye of Ra turned to walk away when Anubis grasped his bicep, stopping him.

"And where are you off to?"

"To stand by Ms. Dennison when she is acquired by Attea before I return to Earth," he bluntly answered. "It is as Elder Ma'at stated, someone has been making moves in the shadows. We must flush them out. Earth may hold the clues to who we are looking for, and I intend to find them."

Anubis released Laurence, whose face became that of a predator on the hunt as he proceeded to walk away, heading to the Hall of Healing. Anubis and Bastet looked at one another and nodded before following him. They vowed to walk with their blood for as long as possible.

CHAPTER 10

Planet Thrace,

Peace walked silently down the halls of the main palace flanked by a male and female member of the Crimson Fang sent to fetch her from Merc's home.

Her attire for coming to court was a female Thracian garb similar to a Grecian style single shoulder lavender mini-dress. Six small ropes in the back of the dress around the waist were of the same color with metal weights similar to the color of gold poked out of ringlets. They were tied together, cinching in the abdomen as one would do a corset. On her feet, she wore open-toe sandals with straps tied around her shins that had the texture feel of black leather.

On her right arm, Peace was allowed to wear a single black forearm bracer that also had the texture of leather, making her feel like a gladiatrix.

She sported her blonde dreads out, hanging down her shoulders and back.

Peace wore her ice-cold assassin persona, while her stomach churned with fear and nervousness.

The fear and nervousness came from noticing that there was no soul around when she exited the carriage transport and was escorted into the palace.

Her eyes searched for a guard at their post or a servant making the rounds. No one was in sight, confirming her stomach's concern that she was walking into a dire situation.

Her eyes moved about her skull, combing for a possible opening to make her escape but could find none.

Judging by her escorts, they were on a more elite level than the other soldiers assigned to her. If they were on par with Merc or Attea, which she doubted, she would be dead before she threw her second punch.

If they were on her level, it would be a useless brawl expending unnecessary energy until reinforcements arrived, either subduing or possibly killing her.

She had to wait until the opportune time presented itself for her to escape.

~ ~

To settle her nerves, her mind briefly wandered to memories of the past few weeks spent at Merc's palace.

Aside from being his paid assassin, she shared his bed and other hospitalities.

The intimate time between them was primal and addictive as they fought to overpower the other with sexual euphoria.

From her count, the score was forty to forty-one in her favor, which was openly disputed by the two.

She always had a sinister smirk on her face when Embaro, Merc's Manor Lord, gave her a glare of disgust every time he entered the room. He despised her for defiling his prince the night before.

She remembered the time afterward when they laid around talking. She spoke mostly about her life before and after she became an EVO.

Merc surprisingly listened to her with a tentative ear, making his opinion known when he felt like it.

He informed Peace by Thracian law her father would have been put to death. Violation of a youngling and inbred contamination of one's bloodline was a capital offense on Thrace.

Merc also pointed out to her where she went wrong with her attempted takeover of Earth.

He answered light inquiries about Thrace and his life growing up as a prince. When she attempted to delve deeper, he gave her the same answer with a calm smile.

"Your beddings skills will have to become much sharper if you wish to know my secrets, little one."

She did not show it, but she enjoyed hearing him call her "little one."

She also knew Merc was tougher to crack than Rosen.

A smile accidentally slipped on her face, as she remembered one morning getting up and proceeding to put her clothes on.

"What are you doing?" He calmly asked.

"Getting up …need to stretch my legs."

"I am referring to your clothing." Merc gestured.

"What? You prefer me to stay au naturel?"

She struck a sensual nude pose as he sat up cross-legged on the bed.

"When they are together, males and females dress one another," Merc gestured her over to him. "It is a sign of respect."

With a scoff, she strolled over to him handing over her garments. He began wrapping her up in a sheer blue and gold flower pattern cloth the way the male Thracian did for her on his ship, making her underwear.

Her heart sped up as Merc's hands touched her thighs and in between her legs. As she looked down at him, she lightly ran her fingers, caressing his silk soft blue dreads.

Finished with her underwear, Merc stood up, taking the matching sheer sky-blue laced camisole summer dress in his hand. She raised her arms, allowing him to put it on her, then turned around to lace up the strings in the back to properly fit her.

She pretended to move her dreads from her face when she was wiping mist from her eyes.

At that moment, she wished she had been born on Thrace and not Earth, and how different her life would have been.

"All done," He sighed, releasing her.

Peace turned to Merc, looking up at him for the first time without her harden shell.

"So, I get to do you next?"

He responded with the same calm smile he wore when he called her "little one."

"If you'd like."

~ ~

Her senses returned to her nearing the massive throne room doors, which opened several feet before approaching them.

The sick feeling in her stomach returned with a vengeance. The majority of the room was empty; there was no one in sight save for Merc standing several steps down from the throne. Sitting in their respective seats was Furia seated with her legs crossed while her hands and forearms rested on the arms of her chair. She softly tapped her fingernails on her right hands against the stone armrest while her narrowed eyes locked on Peace, burning a hole through her.

The second eyes on her were Nelron's. He sat on his throne, casually, hunched over with his hands clasped together, wearing a dull smile. Unlike his wife, who appeared to want to tear her apart, he was less intimidating despite the enormous power coursing through him, dwarfing everyone within the room. For some reason, she both felt it along with its intensity the closer she approached.

"So, this is what being in a friggin anime feels like," she thought to herself.

It was one of the effects of her abilities. The first time she felt it was when Dennison showed up at the Amazon rain forest months after her first resurrection, and when Freedom unleashed her full power in Mexico, turning the tide to defeat her.

It only worked with beings either unleashing or possessing massive levels of energy higher than her own.

Nelron's power output caused the hairs on her skin to stand painfully on end, the feeling as if her blood were on fire, while her muscles violently cramped up.

What bothered her above everything else was the dismissive look Prince Merc finally gave her as she approached. She had seen that look concerning herself many times before.

It told her that she was no one in his eyes, and once again by herself.

As they stopped two feet from the first steps of the throne, the two Crimson Fang warriors fell to one knee while smacking their left breast with their heads bowed in servitude.

"Thank you, Nero, and Kuji, you may return to your unit." Nelron commanded, "We can take it from here."

"Yes, High Region!"

Peace hid the throat swallow she made as her two escorts rose to their feet and departed, leaving her with the royal family.

With her hardened shell back on, Peace turned to Merc.

"Kind of early to introduce me to the parents. Don't you think?"

"Remain silent until spoken to," Merc sternly ordered her.

"Hold thy tongue, boy," Nelron admonished his son. "You give no orders in this room."

A visibly embarrassed Merc lowered his head.

"Yes, father."

His rebuttal of Merc did not make anything less easy as she did not know how to read the room. She was not brought to them in shackles and chains, so she was not a prisoner. However, something was wrong from Merc's demeanor, and she had a clear idea of what it was.

Somehow, they had gotten wind of his side project to acquire Earth and were not too pleased most likely with the tactics in which he used to do it.

So, she decided to play her only card. Save her own skin.

"If I may speak your highness," Peace began using a respectful docile tone. "I was contracted by your son to do some jobs which he and his sister devised. All I did was carry them out with the promise of proper compensation and my …"

Peace was silenced by Nelron, who simply placed his finger to his lips for the universal request to stop talking.

Furia had stopped her tapping but kept her body part ripping visage on Peace, which became more uncomfortable by the second.

The High Region finally rose from his throne and proceeded to stroll down the steps toward her.

Her legs began to buckle as he neared by both the sheer intimidation he exuded and the output of his unbridled power pounding her senses into oblivion.

Peace used her only defense, standing at attention the way she was taught while training as a D.E.A.D.

As he stepped off the final step and neared her, Peace realized he was only two inches taller than her.

Nelron stood in Peace's personal space, looking into her eyes with disturbed fondness.

"The next tier of human evolution," He grunted. "Not a huge improvement, but I suppose your species had to start somewhere."

Peace clamped down on her tongue so as not to have it pulled out by the root from a smart retort.

It was maddening that she was incapable of reading the High Region based on reactions from his body or facial features.

"Where is the attire you found her in?" Nelron inquired to his son.

"Discarded, father," Merc answered.

"Can it be replicated?"

"Yes, father."

"Do so, make its appearance as authentic as how you found her in it. You are then to dress and return her to the sink vortex whence you found her."

"Yes, father."

Amid the conversation, a wide-eyed Peace savagely shook her head to process what her ears picked up.

"Excuse you, put who back where now?"

Nelron continued to speak to his son, ignoring her series of questions.

"Do not use a ship, a jump portal will suffice for transport."

"Yes, father."

Peace's eyes blazed her rage that could no longer be quelled. She did not know what pissed her off more, hearing with her ears that she was being sent back to a blackhole, or that she was being ignored.

Being who she was, snapping was only a matter of time.

"This is bullshit…this is fucking bullshit! We had a deal! Your son and I had a fucking deal! Now I carried out my end of this bargain, and I expect …"

The rest of her words were choked out of her.

However, it was not done by the High Region or Merc.

It was chilling that she never even saw the Queen Mother leave her throne or descend the stairs.

How she effortlessly wrapped her hand around her throat, hoisted her into the air, and held her there.

Her hand felt like a mechanized vice grip applying pressure if Peace was still a regular human. She attempted to fly off to break free, but the Queen Mother simply increased her clutch, employing more force and digging her sharp nails into her throat, which Peace felt as she gasped.

All Peace could do was to grasp her forearm to alleviate some of the pain.

Furia's deep red glowing cauldron eyes blazed her displeasure as she made her thoughts known.

"You do not echo under my roof, human."

Nelron took his time sauntering back to stand by his wife's side, looking up at Peace.

"Have a care, my love, we need her in whole for this venture to be fruitful."

He finally addressed Peace.

"Apologies, my dear, my son neglected to inform you that I have the will and authority to negate or alter any and all orders or dealings when it comes to him and the Empire of Thrace which you stand in. His ship that plucked you from that sinkhole belongs to me, the home in which you resided in, ate, and bedded my son belongs to me, which means you belong to me.

I hold no ill-will towards you child. If I were a lowly commoner from a backwater planet with meager skills such as yourself, given the opportunity presented to you by my son, I would have done the same to survive.

But as the High Region of the Thracian Empire, I must protect my people. And to do so, I must repair the damage my son has inflicted through his impulsiveness and greed, which is sadly unfortunate for you."

Nelron moved closer to Peace as Furia lowered her inches to the floor.

"You see, the human you and my son framed will go on trial before the Dominion Council. Her defense's counter for her innocent will be the claim that another is responsible for the assassinations. The Council will then send someone to fetch you from the sinkhole. If you perish before then, your body will be proof that the other human was solely responsible for the attacks.

However, if you still cling to mortal coil when retrieved, you will stand and testify that you were within the sinkhole during the attacks. Unless the other human and her defense can find another angle, she will be found guilty. You will be set free as human laws and conflicts do not fall within the jurisdiction of the Dominion Council.

And the Empire of Thrace will remain blameless during this entire affair.

Whatever my son promised you, I will honor it and compensate you a thousand times over. I will even grant you citizenship and domicile on one of our other homeworlds."

Peace did not wait for the threat to come, as she got out her question in the middle of being strangled.

"How…good…is your…word?"

An impressed Nelron requested his wife to ease her hold with a simple hand gesture, to which she complied.

"My word is bound to my honor. To go back on it, would be to dishonor my empire, my queen, and my family."

Peace's eyes briefly met with Merc's before returning to his father.

"My compensation is a half a million times …what your son promised me, a ship …I can pilot, and a map of the universe …so I can set up …wherever I damn well please."

Lord Nelron considered her request while stroking his Fu Manchu.

"Done."

"Where I come from…a deal is sealed by a handshake."

Peace raised her hand, spitting in it. Furia sneered in disgust while her husband grinned, and then mirrored her action. A simple grip and shake closed the new deal.

"And so, the pact has been sealed, child, along with your fate," Lord Nelron gave a serene sinister warning. "Should you go back on your side of the bargain."

"As if I'd be dumb enough to finger myself as the trigger woman," Peace snarled.

As the Queen Mother callously lowered Peace back to the ground, releasing her, Peace's eyes went back to Merc's own, who remained cold and unsympathetic toward her. He stood wallowing over the fact that his father pulled rank on him in front of a mere human and cleaned up his mess, making him feel infantile.

For a fraction of a second, she allowed him to see the hurt in her eyes that would never be seen again so long as she lived.

"Let's get this done, so I can get paid and the fuck out of here."

CHAPTER 11

Attea stood near her shuttle with two of her guards waiting for Freedom to be delivered to her.

Standing across from them in relaxed stances were six Annunaki warriors in full armor along with their familiars. They stood in a semi-circle locked onto Attea and company as they waited.

Her impenetrable shell as the feared Thracian High General allowed her mind to wander to events before arriving on the planet.

The one person out of two could instill bone-chilling fear into her made contact while en-route to Anu.

~ ~

Aboard her ship traveling at light speed to its destination, Attea found herself down on one knee with her head bowed and her forearm across her chest, paying respect to her father, the High Region.

"Father."

"Attea, my lovely child," Nelron softly smiled. "I missed your presence at court."

Slight embarrassment cracked all over her face from her father using a tone similar to when she was little.

"Apologies, father," Attea answered with a recovered tone. "I head to Anu to fulfill my charge given to Thrace by the Dominion Council to apprehend the human Sophia Dennison so that she may stand before the inquiry for …"

"I know of your charge, daughter. Do be so kind and excuse yourself to your quarters. I wish to converse with you privately there on a matter."

In an instant, the lump in Attea's throat rolled down into her stomach. It became a boulder as she rose to look at her father.

His calm, cheerful demeanor did not change, but she knew from his eyes. They told her what the conversation would be about in her quarters.

"Yes, father, I shall leave immediately."

Attea rose to her feet as her communications officer quickly transferred the High Region to her room.

Attea left the command deck, walking the hallways to her cabin with the boulder in her gut forming to the size of a mountain. It did not slow her stride as she made it to her ship's abode in a timely fashion.

The second she entered and stood before her father's holographic image, Attea fell to a knee for the second time keeping her gaze on the floor.

"Rise child," Lord Nelron commanded. "You've already paid me proper greeting."

Attea rose to her feet, standing at attention with her arms clasped firmly behind her back, waiting for her father to begin the discussion.

"Let's make this conversation minimal, my child," Lord Nelron softly exhaled. "I will speak, and you will answer with a nod, or yes. Do we have understanding?"

"Yes, father," Attea nodded while swallowing another boulder down her throat.

"You know why we are speaking?"

"Yes, father."

"You will continue with your charge and deliver the human to the Council for inquiry."

"Yes, father."

"And then you shall journey to Enuc's place of business and have a discussion with him. Do return with the information I require."

"Yes, father. It shall be done."

"Thank you, my precious child, I know you shall not falter in your duties. We shall speak further when you make your appearance at court again."

"Yes, father."

As the image of her father disappeared, the Thracian High General dropped her impenetrable shell trembling like a leaf. Attea covered her mouth, preventing the whimpers from escaping her lips even though her chambers were soundproof.

The soft kindness her father's words were dipped in did not mask the sour disappointment she saw in his eyes as he looked at her, which was the High General's one weakness.

Attea furiously wiped her eyes and took her time re-forging her indestructible mettle before she exited her cabin to retake command of her ship and carry out her orders.

~ ~

Attea's eyes flickered as she returned from her memories.

Memories that caused her to momentarily snarl as she cursed herself for not killing the female human on Earth as planned.

~ ~

Within the heart of the capital of Atticala,

Laurence strolled side by side with Anubis and Bastet into the Hall of Healing. There was little conversation between them and when they met up once again to retrieve Freedom.

Each of their familiars notified them of Attea's ship approaching Anu, which meant they had to prepare to hand Dennison over.

As they entered the room wading through the sea of golden restructuring pods, the Eye of Ra's visual was locked on Sophia standing with Thoth conversing next to her daughter's pod.

He watched as her eyes slowly lifted, finding his, while the expression on her face read that she knew why he was there.

Though she kept her composure, Sophia's right palm slowly rested on the pod, projecting that she was not ready to leave.

Thoth greeted the trio with a customary Annunaki curtsey.

"Eye of Ra, Set, and Osiris."

"Uncle."

Laurence returned the greeting with a bow of his own along with Anubis and Bastet. He then turned his attention to Sophia.

"Sophia Dennison of Earth, by order of the Council of Elders, we are here to collect you and turn you over to the Thracian Regime."

Sophia mustering up a sliver of peaceful resistance gestured to her daughter's pod.

"But my daughter has not recovered yet …the agreement …"

"The agreement was that we would treat and stabilize your daughter, Sophia Dennison," Bastet politely butted in with a sprinkle of sternness. "My uncle and his staff have complied with that portion of the bargain."

Thoth, in his reluctance, nodded, confirming what Bastet had said was true. Anger slowly crept on Sophia's face with the pressure of being backed into a corner.

"So, what is to become of my daughter?"

"The child will continue to be cared for," Anubis gently responded. "Once she is well enough, we will return her to Earth and her next of kin."

Sophia nodded, finally giving in. She turned to Thoth with a grateful smile on her face.

"Healer Thoth, I want to thank you for everything you have done for my daughter."

With a simple smile already on his face, Thoth replied with a promise.

"I shall watch over her as if she were my own."

His words brought a tremble to her lip as she responded with a nod. She then turned to bow down and kissed the part of the pod where her daughter's head rested and whispered something intimate for no one to hear.

As she rose, Sophia's demeanor changed to ice water as she slowly stood to face the trio.

"I'm ready."

~ ~

Setepenre, one of the central interstellar transport hubs of Anu, Sophia stepped out of the shuttle, walking down the steps flanked by Laurence and Bastet with Anubis bringing up the rear.

Her eyes immediately zeroed in on a waiting Attea standing by a Thracian transport shuttle with a male and female guard unit standing side by side to her right.

Surrounding them in a spacious semi-circle were the six Annunaki warriors from each House in a casual guard stance.

The walk to the waiting Thracian company that would take her into custody felt longer to Sophia than the actual shuttle ride to the hub.

As they approached, the six-person Annunaki guard parted, creating a dual three-person line facing each other coming to attention allowing the two parties to come together.

As they came to a halt a couple of feet from one another, Attea took a step forward to address the Eyes.

"Eye of Set, Eye of Osiris, and Eye of Ra, I am formally here to retrieve and detain the prisoner Sophia Dennison of Earth for delivery to Alvion Prime to stand before the Dominion Council."

"We are here to comply," Anubis acknowledged with a head bow. "As well as to apologize for our interference in your charge on Earth. Our actions brought disrespect to you, your brother, the Thracian Empire, as well as our respective Houses and nation."

All three Eyes humbly bowed before the Thracian princess.

"I accept thy apology on behalf of the Empire of Thrace," Attea accepted with a shifting jaw.

On those words, a male Thracian guard with a pink mohawk dread hairstyle stepped forward, removing a pair of claspers from his belt. Freedom exhaling unnecessary air from her nostrils, stepped forward with arms extended.

He took great care positioning the double loops over each of her wrists. As he placed his right thumb on an imprinting system in the center of the bar, the coils tightened, securing her wrists.

Sophia's forming knit brows revealed how impressed she was that the restraints with a fragile appearance were deceptively resilient under the slight force she gave it with the expectation that the claspers would break apart.

Freedom chose that moment to exert her last sliver of defiance, turning on her heels, giving the Thracian High General her back to have a face to face conversation with the Eye of Ra.

"You're human."

Her words did not break Laurence's expression as he watched Sophia's eyes switch between him and the other Annunaki present as she made a quick observation of the apparent differences between him and them.

"Or at least most of you are," she concluded.

"Yes, I am ... mostly human."

She took a full step getting into his personal space with a face that read she wanted to slug him.

"As soon as my daughter awakens and is well enough…she goes home...to my parents. Also, you do not tell her where I am or what has happened to me."

Laurence agreed with a head bow.

"You have my word."

Freedom cut him with her eyes as she turned and walked into Attea's custody. Sophia made sure her shoulders were kept squared, and her head held high as she fell in between the male and female Thracian guards. Her eyes purposely diverted from the Thracian High General as if she did not exist.

Attea maintained her professionalism even though her blood quietly simmered from the non-verbal insult.

She focused her attention on the Eyes, whose presence she was still in.

"The retrieval has been completed," Attea bluntly responded. "We shall now take our leave."

The Thracian High General performed a mandatory formal curtsey. The Eyes returned the stiff tension-filled farewell in kind with their own goodbye and good riddance.

As Attea turned departing, followed by her guards and new prisoner back onto her shuttle, Laurence's jaw shifted as he suppressed the urge to beckon onto Attea and converse with her earnestly about the events that took place on Earth.

Armed with the knowledge of the High General's unwavering allegiance to her Empire and family kept him from wasting words that would not be heard.

As their eyes lifted to the departing Thracian vessel ascending once more into the skies of Anu, Bastet was the first to break the silence by turning her head and firing a projectile spit onto the ground.

"Bloody Thracians."

"What be your next move, cousin?" Anubis coldly inquired. "Earth?"

"Yes," the Eye of Ra nodded. "My homeworld contains many answers to the turmoil that has been caused. Something far more nefarious is at hand, and I must root it out."

"When do you depart?"

"Not before I see Neith and the children."

"Agreed," Anubis nodded. "You have not been home since your arrival, neither Bastet nor I would hear the end of it if you abruptly left homeworld without seeing your mate."

Bastet turned to Laurence, snarled, and struck his midsection with a closed hammer fist that slightly doubled him over.

"What was that for?" He snapped at her.

"To remove that ridiculous look from your face along with the notion, you will never see us again. Go to your family, …be off with you."

The Eye of Ra rolled his eyes as his menos covered his body with a thought command. He lifted off, taking to the air to his home as Anubis turned to see the same look Bastet knocked off Laurence's face onto her own as her eyes stayed with her departing cousin.

~ ~

The shuttle ride back to Attea's main ship was in eerie silence. Sophia sat up straight with her shackled hands on her lap while her eyes focused on the thin slit window port that provided her a view to the outside world as the ship took off leaving the planet.

On the other side of the shuttle, Attea, for the first time in eons, was uncomfortable where she sat. With her arms folded and legs crossed, she mirrored Sophia's statue demeanor except for her eyes now and then shifting in her head to look at her human prisoner clearly and blatantly paying her no attention.

What confounded her with inner rage was that when she did it, her heartbeat sped up. She would then quickly turn away, pretending to look someplace else or stare off into space the second Sophia made the slightest movement.

Attea's screams of rage echoed in her skull at what was taking place in the confined space of her shuttle.

A mere backwater human brought out emotions she had not felt since her first time in actual mortal combat.

A large part of her wished to know why. The fear of the perception of weakness prevented her from speaking during the flight back.

The ordeal made her blood boil.

The second the shuttle docked with the main ship, Attea was pulled out of her brooding trance. It was the eyes of her subordinates, waiting for her to stand that woke her up. As she rose to her feet, Sophia did the same when Attea's soldiers got to theirs.

Eye contact remained nonexistent as her troops flanked Sophia while she brought up the rear.

As the door opened and the floors from the main ship became steps, Sophia followed the soldiers out into the shuttle bay, where her eyes beheld other shuttles, and personnel scattered about halting where they stood focused in her direction.

Instantaneously they all fell to one knee with their right forearm across their chest, and heads bowed. Sophia knew it was not for her.

As she descended the steps, they remained in that state until her ears heard the High General's boots touch the floor of the ship.

All rose in unison and waited as the procession left the hanger before they went about their business again. Sophia kept pace with the guards in front of her. Her eyes moved about the place, scanning her surroundings.

Even though she had never been on a starship before, it was pretty much what Sophia imagined. The walls, ceiling, and floor were the same metal grey color with a dull gleaming shine picked up by the thin strips of white light tracks that ran about the ceilings and walls.

Now and then, they would run into a crew member coming in the opposite direction who would either stopped or moved aside. They would snap to attention with their head bowed and an underhanded knife-edge hand across their chest.

The march halted at a waiting elevator. As the guards entered first and spun on their heels, turning around, Sophia followed suit. She made sure the visage currently on her face did not change as her eyes briefly met Attea's, who entered and turned standing in front of her.

She was close enough for Sophia to get a full whiff of her dreaded blood-red mane with a strong musky scent similar to peppermint.

As the elevator began a gentle descent into the lower levels of the ship, Freedom clenched her fists as a vile murderous thought filled her mind at the moment.

Even though she was sure to be brought down by the guards flanking her, it would have been the perfect opportune time to grab the High General from behind and either attempt to snap her neck or strangle her to death.

Sophia opted to release her sinister intentions through her nostrils, which a shorter Attea felt on her neck.

As the doors to the lift opened, the Thracian High General exited, leading the way as Sophia and guards followed.

Freedom counted in her head thirty paces from the elevator, followed by a turn that took another twenty steps.

In front of them was a reddish energy field separating the section they were entering from the rest of the hallway. As it dissipated, they went through, Sophia's eyes scanned the enormous spacious holding cells that lined both sides of the hall down to the wall at the end.

The cells on the left of her were bare save for a long metallic bench.

The cells, on the other side, had no benches. Instead, each of the three walls was a set of weird cocoon looking restraints for four appendages. A slightly nervous Sophia held her breath as they halted by the third row of cells.

Attea then turned and stood before the cell on her left. As a similar energy field from the hallway disappeared, opening up the unit, the Thracian High General, with a hand gesture, commanded Freedom to enter.

With cut eyes, she complied, walking in and taking a seat on the bench attached to the center wall.

Like on the shuttle, Sophia made herself comfortable crossing her legs as she zoned out, not even giving Attea a second look.

Wrestling to maintain her professional composure, Attea asked the disrespectful human customary questions one inquired of a prisoner under the Dominion Council.

"Do you require sustenance, something to eat or drink?"

"No."

"Do you need to relieve yourself?"

"No."

Attea slowly nodded to Sophia's blunt answers laced with the desire of her wanting the High General to just shut up and be out of her cell and sight.

As she turned to leave, also wanting to be out of the human's vicinity before she did something that would violate Dominion Council law, Attea stopped and faced Sophia.

"For the injuries my brother inflicted upon your daughter. You have my apologies. She was never meant to be a part of our conflict."

Attea's sincere and solemn apology meant more for repairing the dishonor her brother brought upon their family, caused Sophia's head to raise as her eyes locked onto the Thracian General for the first time since their encounter on Earth.

Sophia shook her head while fluttering her eyes in disgust as a sinister smirk formed across her face.

"All you had to do when you landed on my island, was walk up to me, and say, 'Sophia Dennison of Earth, I'm hereby placing you under arrest for the following trumped-up charges.'"

Attea placed her hands at her hips, slightly impressed and disturbed at Sophia's perfect imitation of her voice.

"I would have said you were full of shit. We would have argued; you probably would have threatened me with consequences of what would happen if I did not comply. I would have retaliated with a, 'I'd like to see you try.' Somewhere in our verbal disagreement, I would have slipped in that I knew about your Dominion Council, and that I also knew the Eye of Ra."

Attea's frown deepened as she switched to folding her arms, not liking how this conversation was going.

"And now knowing that you also knew him, you could have contacted him. He could have then walked out through one of his portals like he did, told you that you were full of crap, convinced me to surrender, and come to this ridiculous trial to clear my name.

And as irritating as I would have found it, I would have willingly surrendered myself to you. Peacefully."

The smile slowly disappeared from Sophia's lips, becoming a calm trembling rage.

"Instead …you blow up my house, and in the process maimed a man who I not only see as one of my good friends…but a literal second father to me. And for all I know could be dead from his injuries because I am not there to treat him. You then fight me across my planet, causing untold destruction and death to innocent people on my world, …like Steve-O.

And then…your brother comes down …and damn near murders, my child…"

Sophia fought to control her trembling as she wiped the forming tears at the corner of her eye.

"So, you can take your apology and choke on it."

Sophia leaned forward, delivering her steely summation.

"I am choosing to go before this Dominion Council, peacefully, where I will prove my innocence against these absurd charges and clear my name.

And then…then, I will be paying you and your brother a visit to finish what you started."

As Sophia fell back against the wall in her seat, Attea took a minute, processing everything she heard before she spoke.

"I did not mistake you for one who made hollow threats."

Sophia retorted with additional bass in her tone.

"I'm sitting here still breathing because neither you nor your brother could finish the job back on Earth, Super Giant Blue Star Eater. So, don't talk to me about **hollow threats**."

An eerie silence filled the room as official mortal enemies stared each other down.

"Now if you'll excuse me," Sophia said, breaking the silence. "I'm going to rest my eyes, so I don't have to look at you for the rest of the trip."

Sophia, with arms folded, lowered her head and closed her eyes, sliding into blackness, retreating into her thoughts while canceling out the world around her.

A miffed Attea snarled while her eyebrows went into a spasm of twitches.

The second time the same lowly human from a backwater planet made her feel both disrespected and powerless. This time it was under the roof of her own vessel.

An offense attempted by more superior beings who she either permanently injured or sent to the afterlife.

With gripped fists whose knuckles cracked with the urge to pummel someone, an enraged Attea spun on her heels, storming out of the cell, passing surprised subordinates to get as far away from Sophia as possible.

~ ~

Back on Anu, a descending Laurence landed in the front yard of his home.

The pyramid-shaped abode with a domed top built from a combination of white stone and mirror-like silver metal stood the height of a three-floor townhouse. It sat atop a land of neatly trimmed sea blue-green grass with a walkway created from the same stone akin to the house that connected it to a local road.

The second he retracted his armor and took two steps onto the pathway, Laurence turned to a savage high-pitched roar as something big came from around the rear of his home at high speed bolting toward him.

He braced himself with a big smile upon his face.

"Butch! Come here, boy! Come here!"

Hitting him with enthusiastic full speed in the midsection was the house Jacolla, a large animal with a head similar to a jackal atop of a muscular body rivaling a silverback ape. It vigorously wagged its long narrow whip for a tail while wrapping its tree trunk for arms around his waist to support it standing on its hind legs to nuzzle the top of its head against Laurence's bare chest, looking for affection as it welcomed him home.

Laurence reciprocated by vigorously rubbing its back of soft maroon matted fur while scratching Butch's chin with his other free hand. The act caused the house pet to rapidly stomp the ground with its right hind leg.

"Who's a good boy?! Who is a good boy?! You miss me? You miss papa? You keep the Babi kids off our good lawn?"

Butch's answer was to stand taller, placing its front paws each with five rows of thick black hook claws on Laurence's shoulders as Butch opened its mouth of pointy white teeth to slobber him with its long purple tongue.

"Down boy. Come on, let us go see mother together."

Butch obediently trotted next to Laurence, now and then brushing up against his leg. Laurence's eyes raised to the symbol of the House of Ra a couple of feet over the doorway, an eagle-like creature with a star disk behind it forged in metallic gold. The crystalline disk doors parted as they both entered the huge sunken foyer constructed from floor to ceiling with a gleaming wet, dark blue stone.

Laurence slightly sighed as he was received and greeted by the five-party detail, which included the Head Servant of the House and minor servants.

The female elder with a cue bald head adorned in a golden orange Kalasiris, thick golden bracelets, and giant shiny silver disk earrings the size of drinking coasters with hieroglyphic Annunaki etchings stepped forward with a traditional curtesy of Anu.

"Welcome home, Lord Laurence."

"Pakhet, I was under the impression that you and the staff had the day off today."

"Per tradition, attending servants are on call when either the Lord or Mistress of the House is off-planet," she reminded him. "Our service ends once you enter, are properly attended to, and then dismiss us. This is our way which you are privy to, young master."

"You are also aware that I hate when you call me 'master' and am quite self-sufficient."

"As the Head Servant of this House for over four of your human decades, I am well aware of your independence. But I must once again remind you that you mistake profession for servitude."

With a raised hand gesture, the four male and female servants followed her command flanking Laurence. With a defeated eye roll, he stood still as they took their time, removing his armor.

Laurence released Sol, allowing him to transform into his Seni mode, which caught the attention of Butch, who vigorously sniffed him all over.

"Your bath is drawn …"

"Thank you, Pakhet, but I shall bathe later," Laurence politely cut her off, "I would like right now to see my wife and children."

The servants nervously glanced at one another as they witnessed the stand-off between Laurence and Pakhet. The Eye of Ra stood his ground as the Head Servant of the House with narrowed eyes gave in to him.

"As you wish, my lord. The Lady is feeding the children in the solarium."

"Thank you, Pakhet," he nodded. "And thank you all for taking care of my household while I was away."

All five respectfully bowed before him as they answered in unison.

"We are here to serve, Eye of Ra."

Laurence passing Pakhet placed a gentle hand upon her shoulder, which she grasped with a motherly touch. She released him as he made his way down a long hallway, followed by Sol and Butch.

At the end of the hallway was a circular glass door with frosted Annunaki hieroglyphics. They slid splitting apart, allowing the trio to enter into the rear section of the pyramid that was pure glass. The slanted glass ceiling was partially parted open to allow fresh air to enter.

Inside was a mini jungle garden of exotic vegetation and small birds native to Anu that snuck in through the opening to find food.

Laurence's chest heaved heavy.

The thought of him coming home alive once again did not strike him until he saw his family before him.

Several feet before him sat his mate Neith adorned in a sheer green single shoulder Kalasiris dress. Silently sitting next to her was her feline shaped silver and gold accent colored familiar, Seret. Her long silky black hair hung down as Neith held a clear bowl partially full of orange thick mashed up food. She attempted to feed the contents using a spoon possessing a polished wooden texture to her infant son sitting in a floating youngling pod. A golden semi-circular egg-shaped transport for children with a magnetized propulsion system doubled as a highchair with a rudimentary AI system that followed simple tasks.

Next to him sat his older toddler sister in a similar pod leaning forward as she waited for her turn for both her mother's attention and to be fed.

"Stop! Come not a step further."

The stern command from his wife halted him in his tracks along with Sol, while a semi-whining Butch came to heel sitting on his rear.

Neith slowly turned to him, looking him up and down with her piercing green eyes.

"Give me this moment to look upon you, my love."

Laurence cleared the lump from this throat before he spoke.

"So long as the moment is fleeting and you within my embrace is lingering, my love."

"Aye, 'tis fleeting." She smiled.

Setting the bowl on the floating table next to her, Neith rose to her feet and took long strides as Laurence closed the gap between them with his arms open to ensnare her. His lips first touched her forehead, making its way down to her nose and finally her lips for a long kiss that halted the world.

Finally coming up for air, she cupped his face pulling him in for an intimate third eye kiss that brought mist to the Eye of Ra's eyes.

"Weep not my love," she said while wiping them away. "You are home, and we are well."

"Boba! Boba! Boba!"

Laurence turned to the sound of his daughter bouncing in her seat with arms extended out while calling for him. A broad smile filled his face as he held Neith while stretching a hand towards them.

"My little Amunet and Bennu come to me."

The pods obeyed his command, slowly bringing his children to him. Neith let him go so that he could stoop down and pick up both his children. He showered them, each with tender kisses.

Amunet had his skin color with a slight shine and her mother's eyes. She wore her grandfather's curly blonde hair as she reached out with her tiny plump hands to grab hold of his nose.

Bick bald Bennu with his mother's skin, had ice silver human eyes like his father. With curiosity, he grabbed at the thick chained amulet around Laurence's neck of the House of Ra bird, holding the Eye of Ra symbol in its claws. Blue ember stones fused with Awakening energy made up the glowing eye.

"You were on homeworld quite sometime before coming home," Neith inquired. "Were you at the capital?"

"I had to stand before the Elders," Laurence nodded. "And answer for my actions."

Neith's expression read that she understood what was in motion.

"They know …what you have done," Neith whispered.

"Yes."

"So, the events of your dreams are taking place."

Laurence answered with a slow nod.

Neith sighed as she rested her forehead against her husband's right arm.

"Have they judged you?"

"They have."

"And what is your sentence?"

"They have stayed sentence for now," Laurence answered while adjusting his squirming son in his hand. "The matter with Earth is more pressing than my infraction."

"I was informed of that as well, how dire is it?"

"Sophia Dennison was taken by the Thracian High General to be delivered to the Dominion Council for inquiry on the alleged charges. Her daughter, who was injured by the hands of Merc, is currently being treated in the Hall of Healing."

Neith's eyes fluttered in disgust at the sound of Attea and her brother's name. She calmed herself, getting back to business.

"We must make preparations for after your sentencing when it comes …"

"The sentencing will be mine and mine alone, Neith…you and the children..."

"Silence thy tongue!" Neith spoke in her native language with a sharp tone. "This day was long discussed, and decision was made by us both. There will be no deviation from plan."

Laurence reluctantly nodded in agreement.

"Unfortunately, my return home is brief. I must leave soon to return to Earth."

"Why?"

Laurence peered at his wife with fierce, narrowed eyes not directed toward her.

"For some reason, these current chains of events gravitate back to my original homeworld."

"Not the Thracians?" Neith asked with concern.

"No," Laurence slowly shook his head.

His mate could see the wheels in his mind slowly turning.

"I believe in their attempt to capitalize on this situation, the Thracians are both being manipulated and dragged into a more nefarious affair."

His statement brought a half-smirk to her lips.

"This would be almost humorous if it did not threaten universal security."

"Neith."

She ignored his playful scolding standing on the tips of her toes to silence him with a kiss.

"Come, let us get you cleaned and fed before you take up your charge again."

"I wish to do this with just you and the children," Laurence requested. "The staff can take their leave."

"I will ask Pakhet to stay and watch our young," Neith countered. "I want my time with you."

She lightly massaged his crotch before walking away back into the house, followed by Seret. Laurence kept his eye on her the whole time as he felt the weight of an unknown pressure upon his shoulders. His actions up until now were for a supposed great good based on dreams and visions that entailed conversations with a dead ancestor.

~ ~

Neith was the only one he confided in regarding what he was going through. His mind wandered back to the night they spoke after Amun-Ra instructed him on what he must do.

He could hear her words in his ears as she sat next to him in their bed, rubbing his back.

"You must do this."

"Say what?"

"You must do Amun-Ra's will."

"You're telling me to break one of possibly the highest laws implemented by the Dominion Council. A law enforced by our Elders."

"Visions and dreams are those communicating from the Awakening, you know this."

"Yes, I know this," Laurence answered with a face that did not believe it.

"Amun-Ra has foreseen a threat to the existence of all life throughout the universe. And he has tasked you to ensure this does not come to be. For the sake of our young …of all young everywhere, you must shatter the law."

"If I do this," he swallowed, "What of our family…you …the children?"

"Before that time comes, we shall make the necessary preparations," Neith calmly answered him. "No matter what, we shall be with you."

~ ~

The Eye of Ra was yanked from the past by his daughter. Amunet tugged on the other side of the chain his son pulled on. Both children ignored him as he pecked both of their little foreheads, as they were more fascinated with handling the amulet of his station.

"You two want to take a bath with Boba before Modufa gets me dirty again?"

They answered him with generic baby talk.

"Yes, let's go do that."

CHAPTER 12

Alvion Prime, Capital Planet of the Dominion Council,

Sophia walked down the steps of the shuttle with Attea following her. A shiver ran up her spine; the second her foot touched the smooth ice blue metal of the landing pad. It would be the second alien world she would set foot on since leaving Earth.

The entire planet of Alvion Prime, much like the Headquarters of the United Nations in New York and Geneva, was where the Dominion Council numbering over thirty plus thousand species, converged for the maintenance of universal peace and security.

Amongst the ice blue and fire red foliage of the planet were communities whose structures reflected various homeworlds under the Council.

Buildings and domiciles were created for world leaders, diplomats, and their families.

All roads led to the main building, which was a diamond white and ocean blue dome five times the size of the Sydney Opera house. Sophia's keen eyesight allowed her to see more detail to the structure despite the sea of windows that sparkled blindingly from the light of the white dwarf star above.

Her attention quickly turned to the transport and receiving party waiting for them before Attea's shuttle entered the planet's atmosphere.

The party consisted of six guards of different alien species. Their outfits entailed a shimmering deep blue bodysuit, dull silver and gold form-fitting chest plate armor, white gauntlets, and shin-high boots. The matching drab silver and gold helmets and black rifles they held reminded Sophia of more advanced versions of the Lazer Tag toys she once got for Christmas.

On the left side of each of the guard's breastplate was a symbol of the Dominion Council, a star with two galaxies circling it similar to an X.

Standing with them was a male Zerakian with a light bluish-green skin. His bald head had large sharp grey stone dorsal fins protruding from the top of his skull that got smaller as they ran down the spine of his back.

He wore black flaring pants that covered his feet, and a form-fitting long-sleeve silver shirt with the back held together tightly by strings between the dorsal fins.

Attached to the shoulders of the shirt was a thin platinum-colored chain. Hanging on it at the center of the Zerakian's chest was the symbol of the Dominion Council in silver alder metal and blue ember crystal. The blue ember, which created the star emitted a glow from the solar energy infused within it.

The transport parked behind the receiving party was a long, rounded slate metallic grey vehicle with a large tinted window wrapped around the majority of the alien car. It floated several inches off the ground by an anti-gravity propulsion system. The symbol of the Dominion Council was etched into what appeared to be the front hood of the transport.

Sophia turned to Attea, who moved into her peripheral view motioning for her to start walking. She did as commanded, advancing towards the waiting party with the Thracian High General flanking her left side following one step behind her.

As they got within a reasonable range, Attea issued another order.

"Prisoner, halt."

Sophia came to a stop as her eyes moved about her head examining everything and everyone around her. They became focused again as the Zerakian spoke.

"High General Attea, I see you finally brought the human."

"High Counsellor Mezcro."

"Has Sophia Dennison of Earth been instructed of the charges and her rights?"

"Upon acquiring her from Anu, I informed her of the charges and her rights."

"Curious as to why this was not done on her homeworld."

Sophia's eyes shifted between the two as a subtle smirk briefly formed on her face.

Diplomatic bureaucracy was alive and well even amongst the stars.

"There was some …complications …in the retrieval …"

"Complications?"

Sophia jumped into the conversation with a snapping tone.

"What you did to my homeworld…friend…my daughter was a complication?"

This time it was High Counsellor Mezcro whose eyes shifted between the newly created enemies. Sophia's demeanor read that she wanted to burst from her bonds and restart the battle that began between her an Attea on Earth.

Attea stood, welcoming her to try.

"Officers, take Sophia Dennison of Earth into custody for processing."

Upon the High Counsellor's command, two of the Dominion Council officers stepped forward and gestured to Sophia to come with them.

Slicing Attea with a dirty look, Freedom did as commanded. High Counsellor Mezcro stepped into the Thracian High General's line of sight locked on Sophia while the officers placed her in the transport.

"Know that there will be a formal inquiry into the methodology regarding the apprehension process of the prisoner."

Attea seeing the High Counsellor's words as a threat, took a step into his personal space.

"You expected me to hunt down an assassin and mass murderer, beckoning politely for her to come into custody?"

"Alleged assassin and mass murderer," Mezcro sternly corrected her, "There are laws and protocols that protect and separate us from baseless beasts. Your actions have exposed the Council..."

"Spare me with a lecture about politics, High Counsellor Mezcro," Attea stiffly cut him off. "The day the Council finally elects a Zerakian to fulfill the task of a Thracian warrior is the day you can lecture me on my methods."

Attea spun on her heels heading back to her ship, not waiting for the High Counsellor's possible retort.

"I have fulfilled my charge and delivered the human to you. I now have other matters to attend to, good day to you, High Counsellor Mezcro."

Mezcro waited until Attea was a fair distance away, ascending the steps of her shuttle before muttering something under his breath.

"Bloody Thracians."

Within the transport, Sophia sat quietly with her eyes slightly squinted. Employing her ultra-keen eyesight and talent for reading lips, she eavesdropped on the uncomfortable conversation between Attea and the High Counsellor.

Sophia relaxed, becoming a blank slate as Mezcro, with the sour taste of conversing with the Thracian High General still plastered on his face, marched over to the transport, entering it from the front passenger side cabin taking a seat.

As the vehicle began to move, Sophia played back the scene in her head while formulating how to use it to her advantage.

~ ~

Moments later, Sophia exited the vehicle looking up at half a golf ball building with large windows inside its dimples.

As she continued to observe her surroundings with fascination, the six-guard detail broke into two teams of three, each lining up in single file flanking her left and right.

The two in the middle stayed closest to her while the rest covered her front and rear.

The High Counsellor took his formal position in front of the procession. As he began to walk, the two in front followed. Sophia was on the move the second the two next to her gestured for her to start moving, while her ears picked up the boots of the final set of two bringing up the rear guard.

Once again, her head and eyes slowly rotated and began scanning and processing her environment.

Her heart began to slowly quicken as she beheld what only imagination transcribed to novels and the silver screen. Some resembled humanoid versions of mammals, birds, and reptiles from her homeworld, while others were beings, her mind could never comprehend until now.

What unnerved Sophia was the unnatural calmness in the atmosphere from everyone who paused and stared at her.

The expressions she saw were all mixed, ranging from fear, curiosity, disgust, and visible anger and hatred. However, despite the emotions coming at Sophia from left and right, her composure remained calm and reserved.

Though she kept her mettle, Sophia was quietly unnerved. She was familiar with walking through a hostile crowd calling her every name in the book. The faked politeness and civility threw her off as to what to expect from her current captors.

Being pulled from her observation, Sophia found herself approaching an elevator. The High Counsellor moved to the side, waiting as all six guards, including the prisoner, entered and about-faced to the entrance.

Mezcro entered last, retaking his position as primary lead. As the door slid close, he gave a verbal command.

"Prison Ward."

She barely felt the lift ascend, going several flights up at tremendous speed. The only giveaway that they were moving was the glass display panel with extraterrestrial numbers that quickly changed the higher they went.

Sophia felt the elevator slow down under her feet as the panel stopped at a final number. The second the doors open, Mezcro briskly stepped out, leading the procession again down a long white bare hallway.

Sophia's eyes locked onto someone waiting for them near the end of it.

Before the procession was a tall, slender androgynist shape within a bodysuit similar to the guards minus the body armor. On both shoulders of the bodysuit was the symbol of the Dominion Council molded in silver metal. Like Mezcro, a thin silver chain attached to the emblems connected to a funky looking triangular shaped magnifying glass created from silver alder and glowing red ember crystal.

What mystified her was the being's hairless skin that was as black as space itself. The only thing on their near blank face was slanted purple eyes with green irises and three long gill slits on each cheek. They slowly expanded and retracted, showing a blood-red texture underneath.

"Overseer Molctura, I turn the care of prisoner Sophia Dennison of Earth to you."

Molctura bowed and spoke with a soft female voice that sounded as if he was underwater.

"Under my supervision, she will be protected and cared for."

High Counsellor Mezcro turned to Sophia.

"Sophia Dennison of Earth, I take my leave of you. Overseer Molctura will process you. Please confirm if you understand."

"I understand," Sophia nodded.

Mezcro nodded and then bowed to Molctura before turning walking back down the hall whence they came from.

Overseer Molctura then turned to Sophia to address her.

"Sophia Dennison, of Earth, allow me to explain the processing phase to you. You will be scanned for our records, your clothing will then be removed and replaced with a standard issued prison attire. We shall then escort you to the Council room to meet with your Defender for the Inquiry."

"I get a defender?"

"All accused are innocent until final judgment and are provided a Defender knowledgeable and proficient in Universal Law and defense," recited Molctura. "Finally, you shall be taken to a designated holding cell until your inquiry. Please respond if you comprehend the processing phase."

"I do comprehend," Sophia cautiously nodded.

Although it sounded similar to the process on Earth, she was sure there were some added twists to it.

"Very good," Overseer Molctura returned the nod. "We shall now begin the processing phase."

Sophia turned to the sound of the wall to her left, sliding open. Within it was a bare white room with a circular platform in the center of it twice the size of a manhole cover surrounded by six vents and three rings of clear glass.

She turned to Molctura, who gestured for her to enter.

"Please enter and stand within the center of the platform, Sophia Dennison of Earth."

"Well, they haven't tried to kill me yet," she thought to herself.

Freedom complied, walking into the center of the three circles within the platform. Instantly it came to life, emitting a bluish-green light from each of the three glass rings. Although she was sure nothing nefarious was about to happen, Sophia swallowed the lump in her throat while her muscles began to tense up.

Each of the lights projected from the ground into the ceiling above her. They connected with the circular patterns similar to the ones on the floor.

The inner and outer lights began to rotate simultaneously in one direction, while the center light spun in the opposite direction.

Sophia's ears twitched as a female voice began to speak.

"Commencing scan of the prisoner, legal name Sophia Dennison, universal classification Cosmivorse, species classification Human, the planet of origin Earth, approximate age fifteen thousand three hundred and thirty solar cycles."

Her eyebrows raised upon hearing her age. After doing the math, Sophia realized the calculation was based on the daily rotation of the Earth around the sun.

"Prisoner's current attire scanned for reproduction records, proceeding with removal."

"Removal?"

Sophia's inquiring voice was elevated as the floor underneath her emitted a solid orange light that also shot to the roof. Sophia let out a surprised shriek, unprepared to be hit by an orange beam with no clue what it would do.

Much to her shock and disbelief, her outfit and boots broke apart, falling from her body.

An angered and embarrassed Sophia attempted to wrap her arms around her chest despite the Thracian manacles still restraining her while lifting a leg to cover her nether region.

"Seriously?!" She screamed. Seriously?!"

Powerful suction jets from vents pulled what was left of her demolished attire into the floor, as the alien A.I. gave Sophia instruction.

"Please keep both feet planted on the platform."

A livid Dennison reluctantly placed her left foot back on the platform, as told.

Her fit of embarrassment kept her from noticing the thick white milky liquid oozing out of the same vents that sucked up the remains of her destroyed outfit. She quickly looked down after feeling it touch her feet.

"What the ...?!"

"Please remain in place for the synthetic weaving process."

Her teeth began to grind uneasily as the white ooze began to quickly crawl up her legs, coating her body as more of the thick substance pushed from out of the vents. Sophia found herself involuntarily twitching as it began to touch places on her body that were either uncomfortable or sensitive.

Eventually, the white substance coated her entire body, stopping at each of her wrists and neck.

"Attaching membrane nodes."

All six vents on the platform that the white ooze came from expanded and angled upwards. Sophia defensively jumped as six oval-shaped green glowing gems in silver casings shot out of the vents and attached themselves to her back, forearms, thighs, and chest.

The light within each of the nodes began to flicker rhythmically as Sophia watched and felt in amazement as the slimy white liquid began to harden, becoming a form-fitting, intricately textured crisscross patterned material with the feel of soft leather against her skin.

The ooze also formed attached footwear similar to Japanese tabi with a type of sole at the bottom. Sophia could not help but run her fingertips across the sleeve of her outfit and the node on her left forearm with amazement.

With curious concern, Sophia slowly lowered her head, touching the node on her chest, which was the same size as the one on her back and bigger than the ones on her arms and thighs.

"Deactivating Thracian restraints," the alien A.I. announced.

The thin gold restraints disconnected from her wrists. Allowing them to fall to the ground, she watched as one of the vents angled back down and sucked it up.

Overseer Molctura's voice came over the audio system within the room, getting her attention.

"Sophia Dennison, your current attire is a standard issued conditioning suit. The nodes attached to the suit are capable of tracking, monitoring vitals, and administering both disciplinary and lethal force. We shall now demonstrate the disciplinary force of your suit."

A surprised screech was squeezed out of Sophia as she was violently brought to her knees and forearms, shaking the platform.

Her heart went into overdrive, beating out of her chest. Barely able to move, she felt a weighted pressure that, for some reason, not even her incalculable strength could overcome. With gripped fists, she painfully turned her forearms to see the nodes which were now apart her outfit emitting a red light that violently blinked.

"What you are experiencing is a powerful gravitational field subjecting your body to the appropriate amount of pressure to keep you subdued," Molctura calmly explained. "The reason why you are unable to overcome it is because the nodes implanted onto your attire are similar to the manacles you previously wore, which prevent your adrenal levels from elevating; the key component for accessing your reserve strength and energy-based capabilities. If you choose not to comply with instructions or resist for any given reason, this method will be implemented to subdue you, please comply with a simple 'yes' if you understand."

"Yes!"

Sophia's frustrated scream of acknowledgment ended the galaxy crushing pressure that kept her pinned. She remained where she knelt for a minute to stop the trembling of her body. Freedom took long inhales of alien air that she did not need, but mentally aided in slowing down the pounding her heart was making before getting her way back to her feet.

Although she kept her calm, Sophia could not hide the scowl plastered on her face from what occurred. It was gently removed as a holographic image of a generic female character the size of a one-sixth scale action figure wearing an outfit similar to hers floated before her.

"Should you somehow overcome the disciplinary method used to restrain you, a lethal protocol will be initiated," Overseer Molctura went on. "Each of the nodes implanted in your suit will inject you with an agent capable of destroying your body on a cellular level. Allow me to inform you that due to your heightened ability to repair and regenerate, the process of death is long and excruciatingly painful."

The nodes on the holographic image lit up, turning purple as there was a recreation of what Molctura explained to Sophia.

"Please acknowledge if you understand what I have just said to you."

"Yes, I do!"

Freedom, though rattled to her core, kept her exterior mettle titanium strong in front of her captors. On Earth, she was the most powerful being on the planet. Light years away from her home, her strength and powers counted for little to nothing and were effortlessly subdued by alien tech. She had to rely on other tools in her arsenal if she hoped to clear her name and leave this planet alive.

This was Texas all over again, and like before, she could not fall apart, even more so.

"Prisoner Sophia Dennison, please step off the platform and exit through the entrance."

Doing as instructed, Freedom left the platform exiting the room into the waiting detail of two guards instead of six.

"Guess I'm not a high threat level anymore," she thought to herself.

Overseer Molctura exited from the observation deck approaching Sophia, and the minimized guard detail with his hands clasped, taking a solemn stance.

"Prisoner Sophia Dennison of Earth, I shall now escort you to the Council Room, where you will meet with your assigned Defender."

Freedom nodded, impressed, not just that their laws were similar to many democratic countries on Earth, but in space, they believed and executed it on a sacred level. With a nod of her acknowledgment, the Overseer turned to lead the way as they followed with the two guards that originally flanked her taking up their original positions escorting her to the next location.

It was a shorter stroll around a curvy hallway to a seamless door that was a part of the wall that disengaged and slid open the second Molctura stood before it.

Sophia and the guards entered the bare white room with a metallic finish to the floors and walls. As the Overseer extended his hand out, a large part of the floor disengaged and rose to reasonable sitting height with the shape, length, and width of an old fashion surfboard.

With his other hand, he gestured for her to approach. As Sophia came closer standing where his hand guided her, another part of the floor separated, revealing a disk.

Taking a hint, she sat down. It firmly held her weight, barely dipping. She was impressed with how easily it glided, where she moved.

"Probably some magnetized propulsion tech, Erica would love to get ahold of this and compare it to her own."

Remembering where she was, Sophia clasped her hands, placing them upon the floating table, looking up to Molctura for further instructions.

"Prisoner Sophia Dennison, do you require sustenance or to relieve yourself?"

"No, thank you," Sophia shook her head, partially wondering what would happen if she said yes.

"If you require anything, simply vocalize your request, and someone will enter to attend to your needs. Your assigned defender will be in shortly to converse with you regarding your case."

"Thank you," Sophia nodded.

With nothing left to say, Molctura and the guards exited the room. Her eyes stayed on them until the sliding door closed before retreating into her thoughts.

"Super hearing or x-ray vision would be perfect in this situation, oh well."

Sophia sat silently, humming to herself while tapping her fingernails on the top of the metallic white table. She was slightly disturbed by how calm she was throughout the whole ordeal after leaving Anu.

Maybe it was because she knew Kimberly was alive, safe, and well cared for. Probably because she had been through a similar ordeal and experienced the worst-case scenario. It could also have been Sophia playfully moving about the floating seat to distract herself as she waited for someone to enter the room.

Sure enough, Sophia was not kept waiting as the door she was led through slid back open. An eyebrow raised as she narrowly missed who walked through the door. The being that entered was one foot tall. The best description Sophia could come up with in her head for the extraterrestrial that strolled up to the table dressed barefooted in a dull sea-green sheen two-piece alien version of a kung-fu outfit was that he was eighty percent Mogwai body wise with purple and tan fluffy fur and ears, and twenty percent Ewok in the face with a worn orange beak similar to a Furby.

A fascinated smirk formed on Sophia's face as she watched the being tap two times on the floor with his left foot. A section of the flooring he stood on disengaged and rose to come to the level of the table, giving her a clear view of him. She missed the stencil thin triangle-shaped spectacles attached to his beak and the small translucent yellow glass tablet in his right hand.

"Sophia Dennison of Earth," he introduced himself, "My name is Oozaru of the Sumaka tribe from the planet Edora. I will be your Defender for this inquiry."

"Pleasure to meet you, Oozaru of the Sumaka tribe from the planet Edora."

Oozaru adjusted his spectacles and raised his pad, tapping the screen, causing it to light up.

"The Accuser will be here shortly to present you with a deal of some sort. It is your right to take the offer or decline it."

"Okay." She nodded.

"I have to ask you this question, it will matter not your answer, I am still obligated to defend you."

Oozaru lifted his head from his tablet, looking her in the eyes before he asked.

"Did you commit these crimes?"

"No," Sophia firmly shook her head. "I did not commit these crimes."

His head tilted similar to an owl as his ears flicked before he answered her.

"I believe you."

It brought a calm smile upon her face.

"Good to know."

Oozaru's tablet began to emit a rhythmic blink.

"The Accuser is here. I will handle the negotiations. I advise you to speak when spoken to."

"Understood," Sophia nodded.

The door slid open again as Sophia's eyes once again widened, unprepared for who walked in.

Her shape was a dead giveaway that she was female. Her skin was fish scaly, red, and gold. Where her nose would be was a bump and small slits on both sides. Her eyes were as black as space itself, while rows of long tentacles on her head hung down to her shoulders like hair.

The outfit she wore was a form-fitting two-piece pink skintight business suit with a latex texture to it. The platform shoes she wore were a transparent, translucent material, while the nail polish on her fingers and toenails pulsated a soft mint blue color.

"Defender Oozaru," she smiled. "Pleasure to see you again."

"Head Accuser Novtia," Oozaru bowed. "Pleasure to see you again as well."

As she walked up to the opposite side of the table, Head Accuser Novtia tapped her foot on the floor. She stepped back, allowing a part of it to disengage and float around her. As the tile seat slid in behind her, Head Accuser Novtia sat down while setting the blue tablet similar to Oozaru's in her hand down onto the table.

"Before we begin, is your client comfortable with this language from her homeworld? Should we speak in another?"

Oozaru turned to Sophia, waiting for her confirmation.

"English is fine," Sophia answered.

"Do I have permission to converse with your client, Defender Oozaru?"

Oozaru looked to her once again for approval. With a nod, Sophia gave her consent for Novtia to speak to her.

"Apologies," she politely pressed. "I require verbal consent from you, Sophia Dennison of Earth."

"Yes, you may."

"Thank you," Head Accuser Novtia softly smiled. "Now before we begin these proceedings, Sophia Dennison of …"

"Ms. Dennison is fine," Sophia respectfully requested.

"Ms. Dennison," Novtia nodded, correcting herself. "I am well aware of how you were acquired from your homeworld from the Thracian Empire. There will be a full investigation and inquiry into their methodology and practice in your acquisition. If the Dominion Council finds that their actions were outside the guidelines of acquisition, there will be fines and judgments. You or your next of kin will be properly compensated for these offenses depending on the outcome of your Inquiry. Inquiry meaning trial should it come to that after our discussion here."

Although she kept her professional visage intact, a sharp knot formed in Sophia's stomach. The sound of "next of kin" told her there was a possibility of a very ominous outcome should she lose.

"Now I have to ask," Head Accuser Novtia continued. "After you were acquired, were you mistreated in any way? Physically or verbally assaulted, disrespected in any shape, form, or manner?"

A slightly impressed Sophia turned to Oozaru. He nodded, encouraging her to speak up if any such actions against her occurred.

She began with a slight head shake before answering.

"No, I was treated well while in custody."

"Very good," Novtia nodded. "Ms. Dennison, you are formally charged by the Dominion Council with acts of mass murder that claimed the lives of eight thousand four hundred and seventy-three people including three diplomats and the destruction of seven-star ships. These charges are also considered war crimes under the Council, which, if found guilty, brings along a sentence of death."

Sophia straightened up a bit more with her fingers clasped, sensing a "but."

"However, if you plead guilty to the crimes and provide us with detailed information on who instructed you on the execution of these attacks, the Council is prepared to hand you an immediate life sentence on each death to run consecutively."

Sophia slowly turned to Oozaru before looking back at Novtia with a response.

"Could you please clarify what you meant by someone 'instructing' me."

Head Accuser Novtia clasped her hands together, leaning forward with a soft smile.

"Ms. Dennison, the Council is convinced that you did not act on your own. Given the history of your species, we are confident that you were following the orders of one or more of your governments. We want them, not you. If you testify to this, you will be granted leniency."

"That's going to be very difficult to do considering that I answer to no government on my planet."

"So, you're confessing that these acts were implemented by your own hands?"

"I confess to nothing," Sophia bluntly said. "No one controls me, I did not attack any of these starships, and I murdered no one. The furthest I've been in space is halfway between my planet and Mars. That's it."

With a slow sigh, Novtia activated the tablet she brought with two taps. It glowed, projecting a clear image of what was supposed to be Sophia in her full gear with her hood covering her face hovering in space. The picture began to split, showing seven different images of her, each with a timeline stamp. With another tap, she allowed the footage to play.

Sophia's shell slightly cracked, revealing disturbing disbelief. Before her eyes was someone once again pretending to be her, sullying her good name and image, this time on a universal scale.

With a narrowed gaze, Sophia attempted to use her keen eyesight to zero in on the attacker to uncover her identity. Unfortunately, her ability did not work well on video images. Whoever the impersonator was moved like her, had a similar energy output, and purposely used it and the hood on the suit to cover her face and bare hands to prevent detection.

"The bitch knew she was being taped," she thought to herself. *"That's why she kept her hands charged."*

Head Accuser froze the final images of the assailant and pointed to them as sternness fell over her face and came out through her tone.

"These images were taken from the seven record capsules belonging to the ships that were destroyed. Will you still sit here and claim that this was not you who executed these attacks?"

"I will wholeheartedly sit here in front of you and say that I did not execute these attacks," Sophia said, returning the sternness. "With all due respect Head Accuser Novtia, this is not the first time I've been accused of a crime I did not commit."

"Yes, I am well aware of your criminal background, Ms. Dennison."

Novtia followed up her retort with three taps on her tablet. It projected Sophia's criminal record from Earth.

"You were charged and sentenced to death by the state of Texas for the murder of your husband …"

"And executed for that same crime," Sophia interrupted. "Which I did not commit."

"Technically, you were not executed," Novtia corrected her. "And records show you were never exonerated for that crime."

"The government of the United States also has not taken any further actions against my client, Head Accuser Novtia, "Oozaru stepped in defending Sophia.

"No, they have not," Novtia said with narrowed eyes locked with Sophia. "But Ms. Dennison is fully aware as to why. Aren't you, Ms. Dennison?"

"You do realize you are levying two completely opposite accusations against my client, Head Accuser Novtia." Oozaru countered. "She is either an assassin on behalf of her government or a tyrannical menace to her planet. She cannot be both."

"You are correct, Defender Oozaru," Novtia nodded. "And I answer thee by saying that I care not whether it is former or latter. All that concerns me, and the Council is the facts which are before us."

Head Accuser Novtia callously aimed a finger at the stilled image of the assassin dressed exactly like Sophia.

"And these tell me that you are indeed the guilty party Ms. Dennison. Spare yourself the humiliation of an inquiry and confess to your crimes. This will be your only chance to be shown some leniency from the Council."

"My client as already made her answer known to you," Defender Oozaru said, stepping in on Sophia's behalf. "She chooses to maintain her innocence. We shall see you at the formal inquiry regarding this matter."

Head Accuser Novtia's midnight void eyes remained on Sophia's own as the two remained locked in a visual standoff to see which one would blink first. Accepting defeat, for now, Novtia slowly turned to Oozaru and bowed with her eyes closed.

"I shall accept the final decision of the defense and relay it to the Council."

Without another word, the Head Accuser rose to her feet, picked up her tablet, and gave

Oozaru another formal bow. Sophia's Defender returned the act of respect.

"Defender Oozaru."

"Head Accuser Novtia."

Novtia finally turned to Sophia, giving her a customary bow.

"Ms. Dennison."

Sophia attempted to return the gesture from a seated position. Novtia turned to exit the room with a subtle switch to her step, leaving the defendant and lawyer alone.

"I take it you have a good idea of what happens next, Ms. Dennison," Oozaru asked.

"We're going to trial," Sophia answered with an exhale. "Which means you will be doing everything within your power to prove my innocence."

"You are correct."

Oozaru followed up by stepping off the floating section of the floor he stood on onto the table itself. He faced her, standing within arm's reach.

"To do that, you must divulge to me everything that took place during the time of the attacks. Your whereabouts, who you were with, what you were doing. This is how we shall create an ironclad defense within the next forty-eight hours before the official start of the inquiry."

Sophia instinctively coiled back a bit from Oozaru's words with a look of confusion plastered all over her face.

"Forty-eight hours?"

"Why yes," Oozaru answered with a slight nod. "Barring any official request for a delay to gather additional evidence missed, forty-eight hours is the allotted time for both accusers and defense to prepare before the official date of inquiry."

"Forgive me," Sophia swallowed. "It just feels like a very tiny bit of time considering my last trial took at least six months to prepare for."

Oozaru nodded and gave her what she believed was his version of a smile.

"I assure you, Ms. Dennison, our proficiency and technological advancements in trial preparation is to minimize the ordeal of an inquiry for both those on trial and possible victims. We will scourge the far reaches of the universe itself to uncover the truth. What I need to confirm is your whereabouts and activities during the time of the attacks so that my defense team can investigate and build counter-arguments to refute Head Accuser Novtia's case against you."

"Your team?" Sophia asked with a perplexed eyebrow.

Oozaru nodded while gesturing to his tablet.

"Yes, they have been listening in and taking notes via my Uni-Connect. Head Accuser Novtia's team was most likely doing the same via her device."

"Well, lucky for your team and me," Sophia smirked. "I have an excellent memory."

CHAPTER 13

Horus stood silent as his wife Sekhmet paced the floor. She was in the middle of processing everything he updated her with leading up to her resurrection. Off to the side, Dr. Alexander and Graves silently watched the disturbing change of role as the god of kingship became a docile puppy before the newly awakened goddess of war.

Sekhmet finally halted in her tracks, raising her head to the ceiling. Her brows knitted as her lips parted, preparing to speak.

"So, these are the chain of events as I understand them. You were freed by three thieves, one of them a lowly descendant of Amun-Ra himself. Upon dispatching them, you made your way to Aja Nabha Varsha ...now named this...India...and drained one of their nuclear plants, replenishing some of your depleted strength.

You then made your way North in search of me, where you murdered a high-ranking demi-god soldier within the government of this United Kingdom."

"Twas not my intention to dispatch him," muttered Horus.

"You then impersonated him, learning the ways of this new world and its ruling government while searching for me, which eventually lead you here, but not before you murdered another female demi-god in the same manner you murdered the soldier."

"She witnessed me in mid change, I had to eliminate her quickly," Horus grumbled his defense. "The child was also a troubled soul, draining her was more humane, and allowing her body to fall from that height was the perfect stage for her suicide."

A stern goddess of war finally lowered her head with rebuking eyes toward her husband.

"No husband, snapping her neck would have been more humane, or hurling her from the sky. Not murdering her the same bloody way, you killed the soldier. A way that has carved a clear path back to you, keeping you a prisoner here, and undermining your plan for universal domination."

"I have been laboring feverishly to remedy the matter."

Horus's left eye began to pulsate at the sight of Sekhmet's disapproving gaze.

"You did not toil hard enough to expunge …"

"Is there a time frame on how long you intend to berate me on my failings, wife?"

Sekhmet reared her fangs to say something. She took a breath and held a hand up to reign in peace to the room.

"You speak truth, husband. Languishing over the past will not repair the damage done…instead, we must forge thoughts together and create a new path. We must wipe the stain of these two deaths from your hands and place them upon another."

Sekhmet's visage went briefly blank, Horus's own followed as the two slowly turned in the direction of Graves and Dr. Alexander.

On the other side of the room, Graves's nerves began to burn similar to acid as the room became eerily silent. He found himself instinctively lifting his head to see both immortals staring at him. The lump in his throat began to choke him, while sweat formed, soaking the back of his shirt underneath his jacket.

"Repeat what you were thinking, slave," Sekhmet commanded him.

Grave's mind went blank with fear while Dr. Alexander's bones rattled where he stood as his eyes strained to remain locked onto the floor. Sekhmet's eyes fluttered in disgust while Horus kneaded the ridge of his nose in irritation.

"This one is worthless!" Sekhmet snidely gestured to Graves. "He's broken with fear, you should just put him out of his misery."

"No! No!" Graves yelled, jumping forward. "I remember …my thoughts, my goddess! I remember!"

Graves violently shook his head, followed by a neck crack forcing himself to get it together as his masters impatiently waited for his answer.

"We have … we have …to give …the world someone else…someone capable of executing both murders, …especially eliminating Sir Knight Light. But most importantly …if the assassin was somehow in league with this …this …Dominion Council…"

"We would ensure unwavering fealty from mankind," Horus answered with a savage grin.

"This may be what purchases our army, husband," Sekhmet smirked.

Graves's neck finally lost its strength as his chin fell into his chest. He wanted to collapse to the floor but forced his legs to keep their foundation from crumbling. He managed to appease his masters, knowing full well, they were only toying with him again. They already knew his thoughts; Horus and Sekhmet just wanted to watch him squirm for their amusement.

It was difficult for either Dr. Alexander or Graves to keep their constitutions as the gods began to stroll about the room formulating their plan.

"Now we must find a willing patsy to take my stain," Horus said while stroking his chin.

Sekhmet stopped mid-step and turned to her husband with confusion on her visage.

"Patsy?"

"A person who is easily taken advantage of, and can be used to place blame upon," Horus turned explaining to his wife. "A fool, my love."

Sekhmet paused, allowing the word to roll around in her mind.

"I like it. So where in the universe will we find a suitable …patsy?"

An eerie, sinister grin grew on Horus's face before he answered his wife.

"The who and from where has already been determined."

"Lord Horus and mistress Sekhmet, your heralds, have arrived," Meskhenet announced.

Graves's eyes quickly glanced at Dr. Alexander, who mustered the courage to look back at him. That brief eye contact told them that they shared the same thought. It was the first time they heard the mention of heralds.

Since her resurrection, Horus had already brought his wife up to date privately with his dealings. Graves speculated that Horus, though confined to the base due to his infamous actions, projected his influence across the planet. He was, however, not sure to what degree.

"Excellent, send them in Meskhenet," Horus commanded.

The two humans straightened up as Sekhmet strolled over to Horus taking her place by his side.

As the doors parted, Graves was sledgehammered with disbelief and doused with mixed emotions as the founding members of Vitruvian Absolute walked through the doors.

Ken Shiro, the CEO and founder of Northstar International strolled side-by-side with Saraswati Absolute.

Behind them, bringing up the rear in no particular order followed the Mercurian class EVO, Deacon Absolute, Ryu Absolute the Apollo Class EVO, and Diana and Maximus Absolute the Titan Class EVOs of the group.

As they got within a respectable distance of the two ancients, all six superhumans fell to their knees with heads bowed, prostrating themselves.

"Hail Lord Horus! Hail Goddess Sekhmet! Our one true gods, and rightful rulers of this Earth!"

Sekhmet turned to Horus with a smile of approval and nodded.

"Rise, my heralds," he commanded.

All six rose once again standing in a relaxed stance, Ken Shiro turned, giving Graves his attention with a calm ominous smile.

"Former Secretary Graves, it is so good to see you again."

Graves glanced at Horus before answering with a bit of bass within his throat.

"Ken Shiro …you're a member…of Vitruvian Absolute. You're an …infected EVO."

"The proper term is reborn," Shiro corrected him. "However, my rebirth did not occur during the first wave in 2008, like my brothers and sisters standing here with me. My evolution is owed to Lord Horus."

Graves's eyes found its way briefly back to a sinisterly snickering Horus, amused by him and Shiro squaring off with one another.

"He came to me one night, chose me to be his first herald, and unlocked my true potential. On that night, I dedicated myself and all that I have to him. Lord Horus brought Vitruvian Absolute into the fold as additional heralds, while my company's resources were put to task in aiding with my master's endeavors.

Through us, he and goddess Sekhmet will take their rightful place as lords and masters of this Earth, ruling over mankind, unifying us as one species."

"So, all of that talk about Dennison being the 'chosen one' to lead all superhumans was what?"

Graves looked in the eyes of each of the Heralds, expecting an answer.

Horus stepped in, speaking for his subjects.

"Necessary propaganda to both sow unification amongst the people as well as discredit the demi-goddess. The objective set to either crush or bend her to our will. The Dominion Council removing her from the playing field altogether works fine as well."

Graves lost strength in his neck again, causing his chin to hit his chest. He clutched his fist, purposely digging his fingernails into his palm.

"Careful Graves, your thoughts betray you," Shiro tauntingly warned him. "Your mind is filled with so many questions after this small revelation."

Shiro obediently stepped aside as Horus approached him, towering over Graves. Robert collected the mettle to raise his head and look him in the eyes with a face that demanded answers.

Horus, with a simple smile, chose to oblige him.

"A simple builder's lesson, slave. It takes many layers to create a solid foundation. Shiro's company brings legitimacy to the serum I created, while Vitruvian Absolute spreads a message of unification and evolution among the species. And with my queen resurrected, the final move on the board will be for you to legitimize us as mankind's last hope to survive possible extinction."

"How … how…do you possibly …expect us …humans to win such a war?" Graves asked while swallowing the lump in his throat.

His question brought a visage of disappointment on Horus's face. The ancient slowly shook his head while placing his hands on his hips.

"Poor deluded child…look at what you've become. All of these centuries, you focused solely upon these things to obtain power," Horus gestured to his surroundings. "When true absolute power was closer than you realized."

Horus, with a pointed finger, touched the center of Graves's chest. Robert's body began to vibrate as the ancient's eyes burnt bright, fueled by the savage grin on his lips.

"I have walked amongst beings that I once perceived to be gods, boy. And glimpsed true fear within their eyes. Fear placed there by us, by what we would become. I tell thee on this day, armed with this knowledge, I shall bring an entire universe to heel."

"You still haven't answered the question! How?! How will you do this?!"

An eerie, ominous silence filled the room as Grave's not only asked his question but projected it with a sliver of the authoritative bass he once had. Horus stood with a face slightly impressed that Robert conjured up what little mettle he had after the levels of abuse he put him through.

Everyone else, including his wife, wore a stunning visage that Graves's dared to speak to a living god that way. Dr. Alexander's face read that he was about to witness the grisly end of the former Secretary of Defense.

Horus, with a subtle hand gesture, stayed his wife and the rest of the wolves that wanted to tear Graves apart on his behalf.

Graves, with a face that said he knew he was already dead, let his words fly freely.

"There are an estimated seven-point seventy-seven billion people on this planet. Let's say you somehow manage to get three-quarters of them ready and able to fight for you after you changed them. How the hell do you expect them to defeat this Dominion Council that is as you said, over thirty thousand nations strong?"

"You doubt me?" Horus said with a smirk.

"Seeing as how I saw almost a day ago, one of theirs run serious roughshod over one of ours. A woman that was supposed to be the most powerful superhuman on the damn planet. Yeah, I'm feeling a bit doubtful that you can do what you claim you can do."

At that moment, Graves wrestled with his body to stay limp, knowing whatever Horus was going to do to him that very second would be more painful if he braced himself; instead, a living god began to cackle.

"Former Secretary of Defense," Horus recited, "You served your station well."

Horus quickly leaned in as if to whisper something into Graves's ear. Only what he said was both loud and clear and shook him to the bone.

"What gave you the impression that she was the most powerful being on the planet?"

Horus stood up, towering over Graves with his hands calmly folded behind his back, preparing to lecture.

"For those of you who chose to believe what your scientists say, it is said that the universe began with one massive explosion …the 'Big Bang,' as you call it. However, there was another argument posed millions of years ago that there was a series of these 'Big Bangs' that created different parts of what we call the universe. And as these 'Big Bangs' expanded, they brought forth life and many other wonders."

Horus began to take a stroll around Graves as he continued.

"One of the theories mulled around is what would happen to life forms born near the epicenter of one of these Big Bangs. Some of these would possess immediate superior traits, while others would have extraordinary latent potential spawned through evolution."

Horus found himself standing in front of Graves once again, looking down upon him.

"There are at least thirty thousand nations within the Dominion Council, possibly more. But compared to a fully evolved human with the power to raze an entire planet, thirty thousand will never be enough to defeat me. And as you just stated, we have seven-point seventy-seven billion potential soldiers with that hidden destructive power. Even with three-quarters of the population activated at that level puts this war in the palm of my hand."

Horus ears twitched to a violent cough from his wife.

"In the palm of **our** hands."

"That's …not possible," Graves managed to get out. "There are limits …"

A savage, maniacal laugh from Horus shook the room vibrating the two non-superhumans' bones.

"You who witnessed the Earth tremble from a mere human's movement still uses the word 'limits' in your vocabulary?"

Horus's insane laughter switched to an animalistic roar as he grabbed the front of Graves's shirt, ripping him off his feet into the air. The mortal in his grip hollered in shock as Dr. Alexander fell to his knees in a wail.

"You sniveling little piece of sheep dung! Do you know what stokes my rage?! My cruelty?! It is the realization that my wife and I's sacrifice all these centuries was for **nothing**! To finally be freed from my eternal suffering and find the likes of you holding the reigns of the world! And this is its results! Through your greed, shortsighted vision, and backwater thinking, you have poisoned our illustrious and divine gene pool and turned the human species into a universal **embarrassment** when we should be feared throughout every corner of it! Well, I say to thee on this day, **no more!**"

"Lord Horus, the rest of the members of your meeting are waiting on hold," Meskhenet announced.

Horus, with disgust, dismissively released Graves, allowing him to drop painfully to the floor.

"Away with you into a corner with the doctor," Horus ordered with a hand wave. "Until I have further use of you."

Graves got to his feet as quickly as his body would allow him. Both him and Dr. Alexander made their way to a nearby corner once again, standing side by side with each other. Both of them, with their heads to the ground, appeared to be even more worn and defeated.

A smiling Sekhmet strolled over to Horus, standing by his side as their heralds took their place behind them.

The theatre-sized visual screen came to life, creating images of five separate screens revealing alien rulers from different parts of the universe.

Meskhenet began her introductions.

"Presenting the High Prime Vbzarma of the planet Volori and his sons High Prince Volker and High Prince Nofarrzo."

Vbzarma sat sulking in his seat while his sons at semi-attention flanked his throne. Both bore a visage of miffed irritation, mirroring their father's emotions.

"Presenting the Grand Kan Fatra Kumzi of the planet Tinra Oa and his daughter Princess Kai Mefita Kumzi."

The massive Grand Kan sat cross-legged on a plush red and gold pillow that had the properties of a bean bag. The Tinra Oan was a humanoid amalgamation of an elephant and a rhino. His powerful husking powerlifter physique was adorned in an attire similar to sheiks from Earth. His rhino ears flicked now and then from the insects swarming around his head, while his stumpy elephant snout that stopped at the center of his chest swayed from side to side and expanded as he breathed.

His two thick white tusks were adorned with gold and silver rings.

His daughter sat next to him on her own pillow. Her broad hefty yet slightly curvy frame was draped in a sheer purple and silver two-piece top and bottom similar to a belly dancers outfit.

Her ears, arms, fingers, and trunk were covered in fine jewelry that teetered close to armor.

She sat with a lazily disinterested gaze while her father wore an ominously calm glare mirroring a bull ready to charge.

"Presenting Regent Maleen of the planet Pandor and her daughter Princess Syrtria."

The Regent sat calmly with her legs crossed, and her hands clasped upon a red crystal throne with glowing yellow Pandorian etchings on different parts of the seat.

The Regent's long toned slender form was clothed in a white and pink off the shoulder kimono styled dress. It amplified the demonic blood-red skin her species was known for along with her four-pearl black eyes, two where typical human eyes would be, while the other two were positioned at the side of her skull.

Atop her long thick white mane head was a crown constructed from the same crystal material that created the throne. It also glowed from the intricate etchings within it.

Her daughter Syrtia, a mini version of her mother, wore a blue and black off the shoulder kimono dress. She playfully tugged on a thick silver chain her mother lazily held on to.

It was attached to a sad and subservient male Pandorian with his head down, and his hands clasped behind his back, wearing nothing but a white loincloth. He winced in pain from the chain connected to his member underneath the cloth as the child mercilessly yanked on it for amusement.

She only stopped when her mother held up a finger, signaling to her that playtime was over. Syrtia obediently skipped over to stand at her mother's side. She folded her arms, adding a pouting face, and attempted to pay attention to what was going on.

"Presenting Grand Emperor Zoran of the planet Gregor and his son Prince Togar."

Grand Emperor Zoran, like his species, was closer to human than everyone else present on the screen save for his ice blue glimmering skin and piercing white eyes with black irises the size of dots. Like his species, Zoran's silver hair had a permanent slick back wet look.

His royal attire was an alien mesh between English aristocrats using rich white and blue material similar to leather and silk.

Attached to the shoulders of his long coat were five rows of golden-colored chains connected to a thick triangular pendant. A glowing crystal image of his face sat in the middle of it.

Togar, his eldest son, was a younger image of him with blood reddish hair. His attire was similar to his father's but with a white and black color scheme. Unlike his father, he did not have a chain or piece of jewelry representing his station.

As his father dismissively fluffed the frills of his shirt, Togar stood at the left side of the throne with a disinterested sneer upon his face.

"Presenting the Imperial Lord Hoovii Omni of the Planet Nowaru."

The Imperial Lord, unlike his other counterparts, sat at a conference table with four members of his council.

His appearance was that of a humanoid male squirrel monkey minus the tail with black and white fur covering everything save for his palms and face. His attire was an alien version of a Catholic priest's clerical garb with militaristic upgrades in a royal blue color.

His midnight blue eyes, devoid of irises, intensified the stern gaze he emitted, mirrored and backed by his loyal subjects flanking his left and right.

"I present to you all Lord Horus, God of Sky and Kingship and Mistress Sehkmet, the Eye of Horus and Goddess of War, the current rulers of the planet Earth and its territories."

Aside from the Volorions, everyone else looked at the couple with unimpressed gazes.

"Now that the introductions are completed," Grand Kan Fatra Kumzi dryly spoke first. "Why have you requested an audience with us human?"

With a calm smile, Horus took a step closer to the screen to begin the proceedings.

"Fellow World Leaders, I and my wife have brought you altogether because we share common interests. We all possess powerful empires, we all desire to expand that power, we all dream of the destruction of the Dominion Council, which continues to impede that power, mostly your own."

Horus's introductory statement brought various mixed reactions to the screen. Grand Emperor Zoran was the first to verbalize what he was thinking.

"Powerful empire? Isn't than an exaggerated statement coming from you, human, considering no one has ever heard of you until now? Also, isn't your backwater planet still in conflict due to multiple leadership?"

Zoran's questions meant more to insult than inquiring, did not chip Horus's diplomatic visage. Sekhmet's own began to crack as her eyes narrowed with murderous intention toward the Grand Emperor.

"I've never seen a human star eater before," Regent Maleen interjected. "Never knew it was a possibility."

"I and my mate's abilities extend far beyond that of star eaters, Regent Marleen," Horus calmly explained.

"Boast of your physical capabilities to your heart's content, a ruler you are not," Zoran scoffed while turning to Vbzarma's screen, "High Prime, what type of farce meeting have you dragged us into?"

"Why don't you curtail your tongue, Zoran, and allow Lord Horus to speak," Vbzarma shot back.

Zoran's eyes went cockeyed with disbelief that Vbzarma would both insult him while defending the likes of a lowly human. Lord Hoovii decided to inquire.

"So, what grievance would you have with the Dominion Council?" Lord Hoovii pressed.

Horus turned to him, and bluntly answered.

"They murdered my wife, who now stands before you and imprisoned me. Now that I have returned and resurrected her, we wish to see all of their heads on pikes after their disembowelment."

Horus's revelation brought an eerie skeptical silence to the meeting. The expression on each of the world ruler's visage was that they believed they were speaking to mad people.

"Echoing all of our wishful dreams will not impress us, human," Grand Kan Fatra Kumzi snorted, breaking the silence.

"No Grand Kan Fatra, we are the ones that will make those dreams a reality," Sekhmet said, interjecting herself into the conference.

"Human, if you wish for this 'meeting' to continue and remain productive, instruct your heffa there to stay silent," Grand Emperor Zoran ordered Horus. "Tis bad enough, you have a filthy Pandorian whore on here."

"You, Gregorian vuck!" Regent Maleen growled while slamming her fist on the arm of her throne. "For that insult, I should raze your entire vucking planet! I shall feast on your …!"

Sekhmet stepping forward, held up a silencing hand to Regent Maleen. She halted her rant, wondering what the human was up to. A sinister grin formed on Horus's wife's lips as her eyes trained on Zoran.

"You would dare disrespect a living goddess in front of her husband?"

"Religion of any kind is outlawed on my world with the penalty of practice being death, human," Grand Emperor Zoran shot back, "It was a distraction to the population's duty to the empire, my empire. So, your title means nothing compiled with the fact that you are a lowly muck raking human and a female."

A subtle smiling Sekhmet allowed the Grand Emperor to finish his insult before raising the intensity of the glow emitting from her eyes.

The act was chillingly instantaneous as an unknown force yanked Grand Emperor Zoran out of his throne, throwing him to his knees and proceeded to slowly strangle him.

His posture was that of a boa constrictor squeezing the life out of him before it swallowed him whole. His eyes bulged from their sockets while his skin pulsated a bright reddish color trait from his species when they were under distress.

The reaction to the attack from Sekhmet projected from several light-years away caused mixed reactions both in the room and on the screen.

Vbzarma and his sons were visibly uncomfortable that Horus's wife possessed the same abilities.

The Grand Kan sat unmoved with a face of granite, while a wide-eyed Princess Kai muttered something in her native tongue, suggesting powerful witchcraft.

As expected, Regent Maleen leaned forward with a sadistic grin looking closer along with her daughter, who also moved closer to the screen with great curiosity."

Imperial Lord Hoovii sat there watching with an unpleasant look upon his visage while his Council screeched in both sides of his ears in their native tongue that had the accent of howler monkeys. With a grunt and a hand raise, he silenced them.

Horus maintained his composure while mentally screaming in his wife's skull.

"What do you think you're doing, Sekhmet?!"

"Proving a point," she shot back, *"Watch closely."*

Prince Togar walked over, gazing down upon his father, suffering at his feet, …but not with concern.

"Prince Togar, your thoughts this whole time were the unbridled hatred you have for your father."

Togar slowly turned to Sekhmet, who effortlessly read his thoughts.

"A hatred stoked by your father's brutal execution of your mother, which he forced you to watch," she continued. "Executed for a false crime, so that he could replace her with his current wife. But the greatest wound is when he took your title as crown prince and gave it to your newborn brother."

Several guards ran into view, yelling in Gregorian, coming to the aide of their emperor, only to each suffer a telekinetic fatal brain aneurysm from the goddess of war.

An emotionless Togar watched as they collapsed lifeless in unison, smacking the throne room floor with sickening thuds. His attention returned to Sekhmet as she continued to converse with him.

"You dream night and day of vengeance. To spill your father's blood, claim your birthright, take his wife into your bed, and to rip your child brother limb from limb as he did your mother."

"Yes," Togar acknowledged with a nod.

"Because your brother has not reached the rightful age, he cannot firmly take the title crown prince, which means if your father dies here …the throne is yours."

As Togar's gaze slowly turned back to his father, Zoran gurgled his speech with horror imprinted on his face.

"On this day, I shall give you the throne. Your rule will be bloodless, unmarred from treachery. All you need do is kneel and swear fealty to my husband and me, recognizing us as your new gods. Do you swear to worship and give tribute to us until your end days, Grand Emperor Togar?"

In one swift motion, Prince Togar took the knee, reverently bowing his head.

"I do, goddess Sekhmet."

Zoran groaned his wails to his son, who refused to look at him.

"Grand Emperor Zoran."

His eyes, which were the only things he still controlled, slowly turned back to his executioner. Sekhmet gazed upon him with the same ominous smirk that became her trademark before something gruesome took place.

"Here on my world, the punishment for disrespecting a god …is death."

His high-pitched blood-curdling screams vibrated the audio systems as Sekhmet took pleasure in shattering his bones and popping several parts of his circulatory system.

His bottom jaw flopped down as thick blood poured from all of the orifices on his face. Sekhmet finally released him, allowing his body to drop face-first onto the throne room.

As the yellow blood began to pool around his body, the new Grand Emperor rose to his feet.

He turned to the sound of heavy boots and footsteps rushing into the throne room as additional guards and members of his father's council entered, huddled together with mixed reactions and emotions.

"You saw with your very eyes from the observation and council chambers," Togar spoke with authority while gesturing to his father's body. "My father's abolishment of our faith and religion has caused our gods to turn their backs on us. Now, he has offended gods from another world and paid the ultimate price. Because my younger brother is not of age to take the right, I am now your new Grand Emperor."

One of the Council members, an older Gregorian male wearing white and red robes and a gleaming silver chain with a round gold pendant with Gregorian etchings and a rectangular gem in the center of it, stepped forward seething.

"Lies and treason!" He hollered, pointing, "This traitorous welp and that human witch murdered your emperor! Seize him and …!"

His orders turned to screams as he fell to his knees. Clutching the sockets of his eyes as they were burnt out of his skull by a white flame. The act caused the guards and other council members to jump backward in fright.

Togar turned to the screen to witness Sekhmet once again come to his aide, further stoking his confidence.

"Chancellor of State Vrockmani, as of today, you are relieved of your duties," Togar declared, looking down at the newly blinded chancellor. "I give you my word that your daughter, the queen, will be well looked after once you and my younger brother are removed from this life."

He then turned to everyone else in the room with his hands slightly raised.

"As you all have now witnessed, the gods are with me, who else would challenge my rule?"

Everyone else still alive quickly assessed the situation strictly based on the pile of bodies in the room and promptly fell to their knees, prostrating themselves.

"Hail the eternal reign of Grand Emperor Togar the second! Hail Horus…"

"Do not hail," Sekhmet ordered. "Give proper praise."

Those on their knees quickly looked at one another and corrected themselves as they roared in unison once again.

"Praise be to Lord Horus and Goddess Sekhmet! Praise be to our new gods!"

Amid the commotion, High Prime Vbzarma glared at both his sons with a subtle warning to not even think about doing what Togar just did. Both men stepped back a bit with their hands up as the coup concluded.

Grand Emperor Togar turned, falling once again to his knees with head bowed.

"I swear this to my new gods. My soul is yours; my people are yours; my world is yours; my legion is yours."

Horus stepped forward once again, taking control of the meeting.

"Attend to your affairs, Grand Emperor Togar. We shall call upon you later to discuss matters privately."

Togar rose to his feet and acknowledged with a bow.

"One more thing, Emperor Togar," Sekhmet interjected. "Your father's corpse is not to be buried in the Grand Tomb, discard his body in the forest for the beasts to feast upon, so that he may never find his way to the next world."

"It shall be done, my goddess."

"Grand Emperor Togar, one quick question."

Everyone turned to the screen as the request came from Imperial Lord Hoovii.

"The deal that your father and I were conducting which you were privy too. Will you be upholding it?"

Togar quickly glanced at Horus and Sekhmet as if they were his parents. With a nod, they gave their approval.

"I shall honor the deal," Togar answered with a smirk. "As long as we sit down to discuss some slight alterations."

"Of course," Hoovii nodded.

Togar turned to bow to Horus and Sekhmet one final time before his screen closed out, leaving the remaining rulers with mixed expressions.

Grand Kan Fatra Kumzi once again was the first to speak.

His tone was laced with sarcasm.

"Impressive display of abilities, was your intention for the rest of us to submit to your will and pledge our undying fealty?"

"Although I found that very entertaining to watch, I agree with the Grand Kan," Regent Maleen chimed in.

Horus's eyes slowly scanned three of the screens before him, filled with disapproving looks, and got down to business.

"Lord Hoovii, your frost sales have been waning because the Dominion Council has deemed your narcotic illegal and banned it throughout the universe. Regent Maleen, you, much like Lord Hoovii, are forced to conduct your skin trading business, which has been a traditional part of your people's way of life for eons as if you were a lowly criminal."

Horus made sure to lock eyes with Fatra as he continued.

"And you Grand Kan…have never forgotten the day the Dominion Council took the Antecqua territory from your grandfather because several worlds that were under your rightful rule went to the Council beseeching their independence from you."

The princess gave her father a side-eye while the visibly irritated Grand Kan blew extra air from his trunk.

"So, you know our grievances with the Council," Lord Hoovii said, taking over. "And you, a self-proclaimed god, has come to remedy our ailment?"

"By joining us in a campaign to rot the Council from the inside out," Horus said bluntly. "And then burn its remains."

"Impressive play on words," Fatra Kumzi gruffed with a laced sarcastic tone. "How do you intend to do this?"

A soft smile formed on Horus's face before he answered.

"It has already been put into motion."

"The four leaders uneasily shifted where they sat as Horus calmly clasped his hands behind his back.

"There will be an event taking place rather shortly, I cannot tell you when nor shall I tell you where. But when it happens, you will know the authors of its creation. It will then spread like a disease-causing each function of the Council the fail and shut down one by one."

"If your plan is effective enough to put a permanent end to the Council, what need do you have of us?" Regent Maleen inquired with narrowed eyes. "Seeing as how you are gods."

"You speak truth, Regent Maleen," Horus nodded. "We have no need for any of you."

A disgusted sneer formed on the Regent's face; however, she kept her tongue steady, remembering Zoran's grizzly fate. Her daughter sheepishly stuck out her tongue before running to cower close to her mother.

"But when the Council falls, and it will …chaos will run rampant throughout the universe. The one truth that the Council did teach is the necessity of order. As four out of five of the largest most powerful empires in the universe not under the heel of the Dominion Council, I am extending the opportunity to be a part of the new order."

"Why?" Lord Hoovii bluntly asked.

"Because the universe is vast and endless," Sekhmet said, stepping in again. "And though my husband and I intend to rule it, we have no desire to become a Shepard to it. What time would we have for our marital duties if we took up such a yoke?

But with the universe divided six ways, order will be maintained, order that we will dictate."

"There's still a stipulation somewhere in all of this," Fatra Kumzi grumbled.

"The stipulation is a reasonable tribute to the ones who brought you to the table," Horus answered with a forceful tone. "And an understanding that although you will rule your territories the way you see fit, we stand above all of you and your future bloodlines."

Fatra remained rooted where he sat, unfazed by Horus's words. Regent Maleen leaned back in her seat with her lips moderately parted in disbelief. On Lord Hoovii's screen, his eyes widen to their limits while his Council screeched and howled in both his ears.

Fatra subtly shifted his eyes to High Prime Vbzarma and his sons' screen. He observed that they remained both quiet and passive, which was entirely out of character of the Volorion royal family.

His eyes shifted back to the sound of a fist pounding a table as Lord Hoovii shot to his feet with his canines reared.

"The Nowaru nation will never be subservient to …!"

"Sit down, mortal!"

Horus's voice was rolling thunder while his eyes blazed, similar to Sekhmet's earlier. A shaken Lord Hoovii felt a powerful force shove him violently back down into his seat while his advisors screeched and scattered away from him in fear.

Princess Kai's jewelry rattled as she leaned back, clutching her pearls while Princess Syrtria cowered again, burying her face in the skirt of her mother's dress for comfort.

The fleeting scowl on the god of kingship's face vanished as quickly as it appeared replaced with a calm sternness.

What he said next was delivered with an even authoritative tone.

"Allow me to make my intentions clearer. The purpose of this discussion was never meant as a request to any of you. It was intended for you to make a choice. Either choose to become a part of the new order I will be bringing to the universe or be crushed by it. And in case you doubt our capability, remember that you witnessed a regime change by my wife's hands before your very eyes."

Sekhmet's lips formed a savage smile as Regent Maleen made an uncomfortable shift in her seat.

"Make no mistake, the Dominion Council will be brought down, trampled and salted, something none of you were capable of accomplishing nor possessed the gumption to attempt in eons since their creation. Considering how much you will gain once it is done, what is being demanded of you is quite reasonable. You all should be gratefully groveling before us with gratuitous gratitude."

Horus paused, waiting to see if someone else would refute his words. He continued after half a minute of silence.

"There is a saying that 'Pride cometh before a fall,' each of you must decide if you will allow your pride to break your neck, or if you will take the knee and rise becoming wardens of a universe under my rule."

"Wardens of the universe …would be an additional title given to us?" Regent Maleen inquired with a lump in her throat.

"Of course," Horus answered with a nonchalant shrug. "You will require both of them if you are to properly rule assigned sectors of my universe on my behalf."

"High Prime Vbzarma, you have been both silent and passive throughout this discussion," Fatra Kumzi finally blurted out. "What say you to all of this?"

Horus stayed silent, clasping his hands behind his back for a second time and waited for Vbzarma to speak. The High Prime's eyes quickly shifted to him. He cleared his throat, sitting taller in his seat while interlocking his fingers together before putting thoughts to words.

"The Volorion empire has already chosen to become a part of Lord Horus's new order. I say this witnessing both his omnipotent power and intelligence firsthand, he is responsible for creating our global shield system."

Fatra Kumzi's left eyebrow raised while both Regent Marleen and Lord Hoovii dawned faces that were a mixture of impressed and disturbed.

"You have given us much to consider, Lord Horus," Fatra spoke for the trio. "Is there room for discussion amongst ourselves, or were you expecting an immediate answer?"

"By all means, go and discuss amongst yourselves," Horus chuckled with a playful gesture. "Understand that the intentions are for future meetings to be with more pleasantries …not …this."

Vbzarma's eyes lowered to the ground, while the other three stared at Horus with dull looks.

"End of day Earth time should be sufficient enough to discuss amongst yourselves and make your decision," Horus concluded. "Until then, good day to you all."

"This is the end of today's video conference, goodbye," Meskhenet announced over audio.

As the screens closed out, the heralds subtly exhaled with relief that the meeting was over.

"Well, that went very well if I do say so myself," Sekhmet said with a cheerful smile.

Horus slowly turned to his wife with a look she had never seen on him towards her. Written on his face was unbridled rage and disappointment.

"Heralds and slaves, please depart for a moment," Sekhmet requested. "Your father and master wishes to discuss something with me in private."

The heralds quickly glanced at one another, and with slight hesitation, they made their way quickly for the door.

Ken Shiro, leading the rest of the heralds out of the room, snapped his fingers at Graves and Dr. Alexander. Graves sneered with irritation as he forced himself to move along with Alexander following them.

Sekhmet folded her arms, standing her ground as Horus stepped into her personal space.

"What you did …," He began with a growl.

"Was a show of power," She snapped, cutting him off.

"Was both foolish and reckless!" Horus roared. "What if they had cut the feed?!"

"Meskhenet controlled the feed! Besides, Zoran had no intention of joining the alliance! Like me, you read his thoughts! He wanted to verbally debase you in front of the others, that could not stand! The others needed to see that we are truly gods not to be trifled with!"

"Yes, we are gods, our powers are vast, but we still have **some limitations**!" Horus yelled while holding up a finger cutting her off.

"As long as we and only we know of our limitations, we have none!"

Horus's nose wrinkled as his wife's words silenced him. She stepped closer to him with wounded frustration on her face.

"Why did you bring me back to life? To rule by your side or to serve underneath you?"

A pained look came upon his face as Sekhmet tilted her head, demanding an answer.

"You are my wife, my love! You were all of my thoughts while I was imprisoned! Of course, you are here to rule by my side!"

She placed her palm on his chest to calm him.

"I am also the **goddess of war**," Sekhmet pronounced with an empowered tone. "And I have just delivered to you the Gregorian Garrison, the **third-largest military force** outside of the Dominion Council. Also, we are now the official **gods of Gregor**."

Her words brought a deep smirk to Horus's lips as he found reason in them. He moved closer to Sekhmet, caressing her biceps.

"Our movement going forward must be in unity," Horus softly spoke. "That is all I request."

Sekhmet nodded in agreement. Horus lifted his eyes to the ceiling as he made his thoughts known.

"With the Volorion War Machine on a leash and the Gregor now faithful to us by **your** hands, we have acquired a formidable force."

"I have no trust in Vbzarma," Sekhmet scowled. "He fought to control his thoughts during the meeting, and his face revealed his disdain for you."

"Agreed," Horus nodded. "But his two sons are imbeciles, the only one with more sense than them is Vbzarma's queen. So, replacing him would be quite difficult."

"Would it?"

Horus tilted in, pecking his wife's coy smile.

"Whatever thought of defiance Vbzarma may have had was culled by your actions, my love," Horus said with assurance. "And if not, we will swiftly erase him and his entire bloodline from existence and reap the joys of their spoils."

"By nightfall, we shall have loyal allies willing and able to fight for us," Sekhmet said with a smirk. "What next?"

An ominous grin formed on Horus's lips before he answered his wife.

"We awaken our children, the generals of our future army, and prepare for war. Speaking of which, Meskhenet, how goes progress regarding our defenses?"

"Currently on schedule with ninety percent completed," she announced.

Horus gazed lovingly into the eyes of Sekhmet while holding her as he verbalized his approval.

"Perfect."

~ ~

Three thousand seven hundred and twenty-four point twenty-nine miles from the Grand Canyon, in the harsh, frigid land of the North Pole, a unit of twelve hulking four-armed bipedal jet black drones with gold accents and the Eye of Horus etched on their chest plate broke into two teams.

Six worked to move equipment and building material from an autonomous cargo ship. The other six toiled tirelessly to build a ginormous silver gleaming pyramid structure that almost disappeared into the environment.

Underneath the pyramid was a tunnel created by a gigantic boring machine controlled by Meskhenet.

Its destination was six thousand two hundred and twenty point thirty-five miles en-route to Antarctica. Following behind it were six tank-sized drones similar to the drones topside that moved about on tank treads.

Waiting for it to connect was a similar Pyramid being built by a replica unit of drones.

CHAPTER 14

Alvion Prime, Capital Planet of the Dominion Council,

Sophia sat silently on a table now filled with plates and containers of eaten food and drinks while her Universal Defender Oozaru paced on top of the very same table. He quietly went over all of the data she freely gave him, confirming her whereabouts during the attacks.

Most of the food was consumed by Oozaru, which shocked Sophia as she wondered how someone of his stature could pack so much away. She felt obligated to eat something, so he did not dine alone. She opted for their version of a burger, fries, and soft drink, comfort food for an uncomfortable situation.

Although the meat patty was a deep purple, and the fries were a bright shade of orange, they came frighteningly similar to the taste of home, which satisfied her.

Oozaru stopped mid-pace nodding to himself as he reviewed the information populating on his tablet from his external team.

"Yes, yes, this information will look favorable to the inquiry."

"I sense a 'but' or 'however' somewhere."

Oozaru looked up, adjusting his spectacles as Sophia sat with a face prepared for whatever he had to say after reading the uncertain tone in his voice.

"Unfortunately, the Accusation will cite that this is not a strong enough defense," Oozaru said bluntly.

"Care to elaborate?" Sophia asked, with a tone of frustration not directed toward him.

With a couple of taps to his tablet, Oozaru projected the holographic image of a spaceship.

"This is a Femadorian Star-Class vessel," he began to explain. "It's hull like the majority of vessels is forged from Velspar metal ore."

"Let me guess, virtually indestructible," Sophia smirked.

"Nothing is indestructible," Oozaru shook his head. "However, the metal is durable enough to endure light speed travel without energy shielding."

Sophia's brow furrowed from what he said.

"Light speed travel, your ships don't travel through portals?"

Her question made Oozaru furrow his brows until he realized what she was talking about.

"Oh, you're referring to the dimensional portals used by the Annunaki. Alas no, star vessels do not employ that technology."

"How come?"

"Far too dangerous, ships that size experienced various system failures once they entered the stream. Some have stalled and were trapped mid-jump, never to be seen again; others lost control and drifted into the stream, which tore them apart. Because we were never able to recover the vessels or the recorders so that we could assess the failure, it was agreed upon to never use dimensional portal technology regarding star class ships or larger again."

Sophia nodded as Oozaru added the alleged assailant to the holographic image.

"Based on the recorders taken from the wreckage of the ships, radar confirmed the whereabouts of the assassin an estimated ten human miles away before the assault. What do you know about your Cosmivorse physiology, Ms. Dennison?"

"Aside from the research done by me and Dr. Erica Champion on Earth," Sophia shrugged. "Healer Thoth was kind enough to give me a detailed lecture on Anu."

"Healer Thoth," Oozaru smirked. "A wonderful individual must visit with him once again soon. Good, I can surpass the boring details and go to the heart of the matter. Team, please project the ranking chart."

The screen image changed to a colorful chart of various columns, each with a number and multiple species. Sophia's stomach began to turn as she began to look it over.

"The Dominion Council has always made it it's business to monitor, rank, and track your subspecies, due to your destructive potential," Oozaru said while pointing to the chart. "As you already deduced, this is the current list of Cosmivorses from various species throughout the known universe."

Her eyes went to the Onomians at the bottom of the list that numbered in the hundreds. As her eyes went up, the numbers became smaller as the ranking became higher. Her palms became surprisingly clammy at the final three spots. The first spot, for some reason, was faded and held by a Zamekian named Uza, spot number two, was held Thrace culminating from the royal family and high-ranking soldiers.

"The chart was updated after you were processed," Oozaru explained while uncomfortably clearing his throat. "Originally, the nation of Zengara held the number three position …no more."

Sophia's eyes found the number three spot now occupied by an image of Earth and a portrait of herself from the chest up. Her eyes slowly turned to Oozaru, who, for the first time since meeting her, had a slight look of distress upon his face.

"And these …are the ones with the destructive capability to do what you are accused of."

Sophia found herself involuntarily fluttering her eyes in disgust as every other species underneath her was removed.

"Seriously? This is utter bullshit. No one else in the entire damn universe is capable of doing this, but me?"

"This revelation has sparked great concern with the Dominion Council, and before you inquire, only four members of the Thracian Royal family are capable of executing such attacks, two of them you have met."

"And everyone else has some kind of ironclad alibi," Sophia concluded while pointing to the top of the chart. "What about this, Uza…?"

"He is neither confirmed to be alive or dead," Oozaru quickly cut her off. "And it could not possibly be him."

"Why?" Sophia asked with a slightly nervous tone.

Oozaru kept a stern eye lock with her, as he explained.

"Because there would have been no wreckages to find had it been him, not even the recorders."

Sophia leaned back a bit, remembering there was no backing to her seat as she threw up her hands.

"Help me to understand this, Defender Oozaru."

Oozaru sighed as he walked across the table in arms reach of her.

"As I stated earlier, Velspar ore can withstand light speed travel without protective energy shielding. All ships were destroyed by a single concentrated blast, or by the assailant ramming through the vessels with one blow. Only energy with the destructive force of a blue star is capable of doing this. Only an assailant possessing this power can deal such a blow, especially from such a short distance."

He quickly held up a hand, signaling he was not done with his explanation.

"Let us say we could explain the energy attacks, there are…some, not many palm-held energy-based weapons capable of drawing that power through a portal stream and firing it. That still does not explain the physical power this individual employed to tear through the ships. Curiously, this method was used on at least one ship during every assault."

Sophia, understanding Oozaru's last sentence, leaned forward, clasping her hands on the table before she spoke.

"Which means someone wanted there to be no doubt that it was me."

He nodded in agreement.

"There's still one massive hole in all of this," Sophia said with a sneer. "How the hell would I know where these ships were traveling to in the first place to attack them, and what would be my motive to do so?"

"Motive is never needed to charge one with a crime," Oozaru answered her. "However, because each ship was traveling within Human territory, the Accusation will cite it as your species response to defending their borders. Regarding how you obtained the intel on the vessels, trajectories, …that is a bit more complicated."

Sophia ignored the first part of his explanation, which blew her mind, and focused on the second half that stunned her.

"Complicated my ass, you're accusing the Eye of Ra of giving me …!"

Oozaru held up a stern hand, stopping her from finishing her sentence.

"Let me be clear, Sophia Dennison of Earth. No one is accusing a Royal member of the House of Ra of such a nefarious action, especially with no solid evidence."

Sophia realized he was silently reminding her that they were being monitored and recorded.

"However," he continued. "A verbal confession implicating the Eye of Ra would have him brought before the Council and impeached."

"Well, that's not going to happen because there's no confession," Sophia scoffed. "Aside from not speaking to the Eye of Ra in over a year, he gave me no location of any ships, and I never asked for any."

"As I stated, the Accusation is not interested in motive," Oozaru said while adjusting his spectacles. "Our universal laws are dictated by unwavering facts and evidence. And these are the facts."

Oozaru raised a red pointy small claw finger at the holographic image of her face.

"All current evidence is directed towards you, Ms. Dennison. The Accusation cares not if they draw a confession from you on any alleged accomplices. Your conviction will be enough to spark further necessary action."

Sophia's head lowered as her hands balled up, becoming two trembling fists.

"You mean ... they burn me, and then ...they burn ...my people."

"The latter, I cannot confirm," Oozaru said with a solemn tone. "The former you are correct about."

Her first instinct was to hammer the table in frustration. She elected to take in some of the alien air within the room and get her mind running. It was processing everything she had seen and heard, and everything Oozaru told her.

A chill vibrated from the top of her head down to her tailbone. It was from a frightening thought that she kept dismissing since her arrest. With the facts and evidence laid at her feet, there was one conclusion she could not deny.

"I am not the only one ...from my species ...who could have done this," Sophia swallowed. "There is another."

Her revelation caused stunned Oozaru to take a step back from her.

"What? How? Why did you not relay this to me ...?"

"Because I believed there was no way she could be a factor in all of this," Sophia huffed.

"Please clarify."

"Her name is Peace, she also went by the name Number Three, an ex-Special Forces operative who specialized in assassinations. She and three others were responsible for murdering my husband and framing me for it and other atrocities."

Oozaru turned to his tablet to see news reports on Peace from Earth.

"This woman attempted to overthrow all of the governments on your planet."

"She almost succeeded until the Eye of Ra, and I defeated her. We did it by chucking her into a black hole."

His eyes widened by her answer. Oozaru's head shook like an actual owl getting back to focus.

"And you believe this individual is still alive?"

"Her base level strength was greater than mine," Sophia answered, looking him in the eyes. "I was only able to defeat her by tapping into my reserves. If there is a sliver of a chance that Peace survived and escaped, she is the only logical answer for these attacks."

Oozaru nodded as he stroked his beard shaped fur chin.

"My team will investigate this and share our findings with the Accusation. You wouldn't happen to know the location of this black hole?"

Sophia shrugged.

"You'd have to ask the Eye of Ra that; I didn't care to know."

"We shall confirm the location from him and investigate," Oozaru concluded.

"Will this delay the inquiry?" Sophia asked.

"No," Oozaru shook his head. "This will more likely take place during the inquiry. My team and I must convince the Accusation and the Council on the validity of these new findings. To begin a search for someone in a void is neither a safe nor easy matter. However, if the evidence presented is credible, they will proceed."

Sophia's eyes narrowed with concern as she picked up some distress coming from Oozaru as he lowered his head a bit.

"What is it?"

Oozaru raised his head to look her in the eyes.

"As a Council member, this is very distressful information."

"You're a member of the Dominion Council …defending me?" Sophia asked with a shocked tone.

"Of course," Oozaru nodded. "It is one of my many duties as a member of the Council."

"Huh."

Sophia reset her focus as Oozaru continued expressing his troubled thoughts.

"If this evidence is valid, this Peace individual did not orchestrate these attacks by herself."

"That did come to mind," Sophia nervously answered.

Oozaru walked across the table, standing in Sophia's personal space as he looked up at her.

"Let me be forthcoming, Ms. Dennison, I lost colleagues and good friends in those attacks. I willingly took this case to unveil the truth and bring those responsible to justice."

"Shouldn't you be on the other side for that?" Sophia asked.

"Justice is only acquired when both sides of the law play their part to seek it," Oozaru answered. "My part is to ensure that the wrong party is not falsely accused and sentenced. However, as a Dominion Council member, this case seems to be pointing to something far more nefarious."

Sophia calmly clasped her hands on the table.

"Like …an inside job?" She asked with an ominous laced voice.

Oozaru's face told her what he would not verbally say out loud. It was in total agreement with her.

"I suggest that we end this session here, Ms. Dennison. My team and I shall continue to work on your defense. Get some rest and prepare for the impending inquiry."

CHAPTER 15

The Grand Canyon National Park, Colorado, the Project EVOlution base,

Graves and Dr. Egan Alexander once again stood side by side, this time behind the heralds of Vitruvian Absolute.

All of them stood as witnesses to Horus and Sekhmet dawning visages of proud parents as they strolled by each of the remaining four reconstruction pods that housed the dormant and sleeping superhuman clones, generals for their future army and the coming great universal war.

"They are quite pretty," Sekhmet nodded with approval.

"Naturally, they come from us," Horus informed her.

"Not just us," she sneered. "Some of them come from that infernal woman."

"Genetics stolen from you, my love," Horus gently assured her. "Rightfully returned for our use."

A smile returned to her face as Sekhmet nodded in agreement. She pointed to the pod housing, a male clone with onyx skin and cue ball head with the look of his genetic father.

"Let us write this one's mind first, I know how you always desired a male son. Meskhenet initiate the cerebral probe for mind writing."

"As you command, goddess Sekhmet."

A slot opened up on each side of the pod. Each had a digital handprint that lit up. Within the pod itself to small ports opened up, allowing for two long silver metallic probes the shape of drummer sticks to extend. They each came to a stop touching the clone's temples.

As husband and wife placed their right hands on the digital print, the light on the panel turned from white to green.

"Ready to begin?" Sekhmet asked.

"I still do not see what was wrong with the regular process," Horus pouted.

"I will not have my children undergo the same harsh treatment you projected onto me for my awakening," Sekhmet snapped at him. "You're just miffed because you did not think to add this to the pod."

Horus threw her a quick sarcastic sneer before getting serious again. Both their eyes began to glow brightly as they worked together to write the clone's memories, which they created.

Within the pod, the clone's eyes began to rapidly flutter as his body gently twitched.

~ ~

Billions of light-years away on Alvion Prime, Capital Planet of the Dominion Council, Freedom sat quietly laying on her back within her detention cell.

Even on the softest, most comfortable cushion she ever laid upon in confinement, she could not rest as her mind rambled. It was busy playing back the events in 4D that lead up to her trapped within another prison cell.

Sophia mentally rewound, fast-forwarded, and paused memories looking for a clue, which she probably missed. She zoomed, searching for an agent spying on her from the shadows working to scheme and frame her.

She left out a defeated exhale, concluding that she would find nothing in her memories.

This plan had to be constructed amongst the stars.

Sophia did make a promise to herself.

"When I get out of here, this will be the last fucking time someone puts me in a box."

She switched her mind to more calming thoughts.

Kimberly was alive, stable, and safe. Despite it all, she trusted the Eye of Ra to take care of her. If she hoped to see her daughter or her homeworld again, losing the trial was not an option.

And if she did happen to lose, Sophia had to make sure alternate measures were taken.

Although the Dominion Council was made up of thousands of highly advanced and intelligent nations, they were not invincible.

Freedom nonchalantly examined her suit constructed to both restrain and suppress her power, searching for a chink.

The six orbs attached to the suit were vital to restraining her. Damaging or destroying them would be crucial to her release. She was considering it based on her conversation with Thoth.

Never once did he mention that a Cosmivorse possessed her defensive healing genetics. Which meant that ability was unique only to her. There was a possibility that she could overcome the poisonous toxins the orbs would inject her with should she attempt to destroy them.

Her thoughts of escape were interrupted by the sound of footsteps approaching her cell.

She took a breath and sat before as the oval door to her cell slid open. Standing in the doorway was Overseer Molctura and two guards.

"Prisoner Sophia Dennison of Earth, it is time for the inquiry."

Freedom nodded and rose to her feet. She glanced to see the cushion once again on her bed deflate flattening out as the frame slid back into the wall, becoming part of it.

"Okay."

Molctura and the guards stepped back a bit, allowing her to enter the hallway. As the door to her cell slid close, the guards took up their position, flanking her left and right.

"Let me say that you have been a model prisoner while in my care. I hope I have been the same to you as your Overseer."

"You have, thank you," Sophia nodded with a faint smile.

Molctura, with no more words, turned standing in front of Sophia. He took a step beginning the march.

Freedom took the cue following suit, with the guards heading to the inquiry chamber.

~ ~

Minutes later, Sophia's procession went through a sizeable oval hallway heading toward a circular door with a symbol of the Dominion Council laser etched onto it. As they neared it, the doors parted, sliding away from each other into the wall.

Freedom's eyes widened as her breath was taken away.

The inside of the Hall of Inquiry was gigantic, rivaling the size of a baseball stadium, but more formal than the US Senate. The color scheme was a milky white with accents of blue and silver about the room. As far as her eyes could see were rows of representatives from different planets and species seated behind long metallic silver desks that ran the length of one side of the room to the other.

Each of them sat in soft, marshmallow height chairs.

Her heart sped up a bit, realizing that all eyes were on her. Like her arrival, Freedom could feel the wave of mixed emotions that bombarded her as she made her way to the front of the chamber.

For a second, she felt smaller than an ant, until a familiar sensation washed over her.

It caused her to involuntarily snap her neck left and right, searching for him. The closer she got to the front, the more her blood began to boil, and her hairs became needles.

Being around EVO's with lower power levels never triggered the ability within her.

Peace's monstrous and continuous power surge made it impossible for her to be detected.

His power was both massive, controlled, and focused.

As her eyes finally fell upon him, Merc dawned in traditional dignitary garb returned the subtle murderous glare she gave him.

Sophia forced herself to pry her eyes away from the Thracian Prince, focusing back on the selected Tribunal officiating the inquiry.

The proceedings were similar to Earth trials with one side for the defense and one side for the prosecutor. A cylinder-shaped witness stand was placed in the center of the room.

It was the divider in the room for the Tribunal bench. It was tall, elevated, and made of a shimmering white stone material comprised of six seats for the judges chosen to preside over cases.

Sophia was escorted to the defense table. Oozaru sat in a miniature chair on top of the table, going through his notes on his tablet.

She glanced over to her right to see Head Accuser Novtia at her table with what appeared to be a member of her staff doing the same.

As she sat down, Sophia's mind briefly wandered back to the interrogation room, where Oozaru explained the trial process.

~ ~

"The inquiry is slightly similar to your trials on Earth," he began. "With the exception that instead of a judge, we have a Tribunal of six selected members of the Dominion Council. Your jurors will be the remaining members of the Dominion Council, not overseeing, defending, or prosecuting this inquiry."

"All of them?" Sophia asked with a raised eyebrow.

He slowly nodded.

"All of them."

Sophia sat back in her seat, attempting not to be stunned as Oozaru continued.

"The duration of the inquiry lasts as needed for both parties to present their evidence and witnesses. Deliberation takes a mandatory two of your Earth days. During that time, Council members can request evidence to review and debate amongst themselves to reach their verdict. The Majority vote determines the judgment, which is announced on day three. The Tribunal will then retire for a day to determine the sentence."

Sophia slowly nodded, processing all that Oozaru had said.

He answered her question after reading her facial features.

"If you are inquiring what our odds currently are, I will not lie to you, Dr. Dennison. It will be an uphill battle. A battle that is not unwinnable. In the end, all of the Council Members' desire is to bring the responsible parties to justice, which means placing doubt in their thoughts that you are the responsible party."

Words that were supposed to give Sophia a wave of reassurance painted her face with skepticism. History on her planet had taught her that if justice could not get the one responsible, it would be satisfied with a sacrificial lamb.

And she had no intention of taking Isaac's place in this scenario.

~ ~

"All rise!"

The request from the Chamber guard pulled her from her thoughts as she stood up along with everyone else as the Inquiry Tribunal entered the room through a side door.

"Introducing the Inquiry Tribunal, Council Members selected by their peers to give fair judgment of the inquiry of Sophia Dennison of the planet Earth on the charges of terrorism, mass murder, and the destruction of Dominion Council property.

All remain standing for Tribunal Sashal, Vice Prime Minister of Femado!"

As with both males and females of her race, Femadorians, both male and female, were hairless humanoid beings with a large round head, five fingers and toes, large dark jet-black slant eyes, and tiny ears wrapped in pinkish-grey skin.

She was adorned in a single shoulder white and sky-blue outfit similar to Shaolin monks with open-toe Grecian sandals on her feet.

"All remain standing for Tribunal Shogonite Faustra of the Sar Republic."

Like his species, Shogonite Faustra had the appearance of a purple furred humanoid fox with sprinkles of white covering his entire body. Like Earth foxes, Sarians also had long bushy tails. The color scheme of his attire was similar to Vice Prime Minister Sashal. His three long busy tails hung out of a hole in the back of his outfit, which was a combination of samurai kimono meets three-piece English business suit. Like his Earthly counterparts, he walked barefooted on digitigrade hind legs with three toes. His black-trimmed claw toenails matched the nails on his three fingers and an opposable thumb.

"All remain standing for Tribunal Nephthys, Head of the House of Set from the Nation of Anu!"

Sophia's eyes slightly widened; during her time on the planet overseeing her daughter's care, she never came in contact with a ruler of Anu.

The mother of Anubis was a golden-eyed ancient beauty coated in deep bronze ageless skin with pearl black hair that hung straight down to the middle of her back.

Nephthys entered adorned in a slightly modestly sheer white fitted skirt and bustier top made from several thick blue pearl beads.

"All remain standing for Tribunal Mulfus Siral, Interim Grand Sai of the planet Glissand!"

The Interim Grand Sai was of an aquatic humanoid species. Similar to Femadorians, his slate grey-blue body was hairless but scaly with tendrils similar to cephalopod limbs attached to the dome of his head. Two-gill slits made up the nose on his face. The artificial light in the chamber caused Mulfus's fire-red eyes to gleam.

His outfit consisted of a very airy two-piece shirt and pants with sandals that appeared to be made of a blue material similar to seaweed and algae sponge.

"All remain standing for Tribunal Fenian Dayra, High Lourdes of the Southern Territory of the Navar Empire!"

To Sophia, the female Navarian was a tall, slender, hairless pointy-eared elf with two fingers and a thumb on each hand and three toes on each foot. She had a boney ridge that ran up her nose, stopping at her slightly domed forehead below her eyebrow. Her skin was a minty sea green hue that, for some reason, matched her eyes and hair, which was long, heavy, thick, with a wiry dread texture.

Unbeknownst to her, Navarians was one of the oldest species in the universe who stopped showing physical signs of aging after reaching maturity. Instead, the High Lourdes's veins underneath her skin and hair revealed her actual age as they emitted a medium bright glow.

She wore a form-fitting blue and white gown of a wet look material with a flowing skirt and incredibly low U-shaped exposed back.

"All remain standing for Tribunal Marcus Salt, the Vice Maul of the Kergan State!"

At that moment, Sophia wished she had her iPhone.

The Vice Maul's humanoid reptilian physiology, which closely resembled dragons, was proof that lizard people from space were real. His hulking bright red muscular scaly body minus a tail was carried atop two digitigrade hind legs with three toes. His toes had nonretractable brown claws similar to the ones on his three fingers with a thumb. His sizeable thick skull had boney ridges running from the top of his head down to the base of his spine. Inside of it blazed yellow emotionless eyes.

His attire was a weird hi-tech amalgamation of Roman Gladiator meets Scottish Highlander.

All six Council Members wore the temporary metallic silver Tribunal sash chain with the emblem of the Dominion Council in a gold material hovering over their left breast.

As all six made their way to their assigned seats, they took a moment to look around before sitting down.

All currently in the Chamber save for the guards followed taking their seats.

"As agreed upon by my fellow Tribunals, I shall begin the proceedings," Marcus Salt announced. "A reminder, we will be speaking in the accused's native tongue during the duration of this inquiry. For those that are not accustomed to the tongue, please have your translators properly set. Defender Oozaru, please stand with Sophia Dennison of Earth."

Freedom rose the same as Oozaru taking a poised, respectful stance.

"Before this inquiry officially begins, is the accused aware of the charges against her?"

Oozaru turned to Sophia, who nodded.

"Yes, she does, Tribunal Marcus Salt."

"The accused has a final chance to change her claim in exchange for a lesser sentence. Does she wish to change stance, or does she maintain her original position?"

Oozaru answered on Sophia's behalf without turning to ask her.

"Sophia Dennison maintains her stance of innocence, Tribunal Marcus Salt."

A soft smile grew on her face as faint grumbling was a wave over the hall before returning to the ocean whence it came.

"Very well," Salt nodded. "Head Accuser Novtia, you may begin with your opening remarks."

Novtia used her feet to float her seat back before rising with a smile of confidence as Oozaru and Sophia sat back down.

As she walked to stand in the circular disk in the center of the hall, her expression transformed to solemn sternness.

She turned, giving the Assistant Accuser aiding her a nod. With a few taps from his tablet, he activated a projection video for all to see.

Sophia massaged her nose in frustration as she bore witness to a projected history of human violence.

"From the beginning of their existence," Novtia began her speech. "The human species has been drawn to violence and conflict."

Her eyes glanced over in Freedom's direction, looking for a reaction. It did not penetrate Sophia's professional courtroom face as she continued.

"In fairness, their history is similar or almost identical to many here. But we are not here to judge the actions of their past. We're here to judge their actions in the present, and what it means to the future."

The video projections switched to the attacks of a lone assassin dressed in an identical attire to Freedom obliterating Dominion Council's diplomatic ships in various assaults.

"Three attacks on seven-star ships resulting in eight thousand four hundred and seventy-three deaths, including three diplomats. Colleagues, friends, and family members, known by many in this very hall …all tragically lost forever due to an unprovoked attack by the individual sitting over there at the table of the defense."

Novtia made sure to point the finger at Sophia.

"Defender Oozaru, a highly respected Council Member, selected for this inquiry will have you believe that Sophia Dennison of Earth is not the assailant. That someone else was responsible for these horrific acts. But in these very halls, we believe in unwavering scientific facts and the truth."

Novtia walked to the edge of the circle, making sure not to step out. Her eyes stayed locked onto Sophia, who made sure to keep eye contact with her.

"Through the recorders that we retrieved from wreckages of the vessels, and the scans taken of the accused physiology will prove that Sophia Dennison of Earth is without a doubt the only one guilty of these crimes. And the only one that must be held accountable and punished."

She lingered for a while with her staring match with Sophia before strolling away back to her desk.

Oozaru took a moment to collect his thoughts before standing up on his disk seating. With two taps of his feet, the disk carried him to the center of the circle to begin his opening statement.

Holographic video projections once again filled the hall of news reports and feeds of Sophia Dennison performing acts of heroism on Earth.

"Head Accuser Novtia speaks the truth, this Council does deal in facts."

Oozaru began his opening statement fixated on Sophia.

"And the fact is that through several studies, an individual's habits determines their character eighty to ninety percent of the time. On her home planet, Sophia Dennison is defined as a superhero. One who uses her extraordinary physical abilities to aide and protect the lesser and weaker of her kind. She created an island and turned it into a sanctuary. A place of refuge for those under tyranny, a place of healing for those who are ill or broken. Dr. Dennison has been on this path for almost a decade."

Oozaru turned to make eye contact with Novtia.

"The facts are Dr. Dennison biologically is the strongest and most powerful of her species. She could have razed nations, toppled governments, and bent her world to her will by force. A repetitious tactic etched into many a Council Member's histories to achieve the ultimate peace and unity amongst their species. A path that Dr. Dennison has chosen not to take; instead, she allows her lesser evolved kin to stumble and find their way on their own terms.

Through multiple studies, it has been proven that a sane individual's habits are a marker for their character.

Dr. Dennison's habits prove that she is not an assassin or a mass murderer.

That, along with the evidence that we shall submit, will prove that Dr. Dennison was not involved in these nefarious attacks, and as much as the Accused refuses to believe is most likely a pawn in something far more sinister."

Oozaru humbly bowed before giving the disk a double-tap. It silently returned him to the desk.

"Impressive opening," Sophia subtly whispered. "Wish I knew you during my first trial."

"You may thank me when we have proven your innocence," Oozaru whispered back. "Now, the true battle begins."

~ ~

Several light-years away back on Earth, the clone children of Horus and Sekhmet were finally birthed.

Like Sekhmet's awakening, all four clones awoke the second the amniotic fluid was drained from each of their chambers, and fresh air was pumped in.

Just like infants, each clone let out a brief cry of discomfort from the harshness of fresh air entering their lungs for the very first time.

As the pod doors opened, the enslaved staff went into action. They gently helped all four sit up to examine them while the loving parents stood off to the side with the faces of pride as Dr. Alexander stood next to them. Though physically and mentally drained, he too was still slightly amazed at the successful birth of the additional clones.

It was short-lived as the doctor jumped from screams coming from one of his staff members. Apparently, while using his light pen to examine one of the females, the smallest of the two. She curiously reached out, grasping his wrist. Not knowing her strength, she ended up crushing it. As he dropped the penlight, she released him, catching it during mid-fall. Everyone in her vicinity stepped back from her as she sat there examining the device.

A second after that, a male technician went flying savagely across the room, meeting his bone-crushing end against the wall on the other side.

"Away from me mortals! You can do nothing for me."

The order came from the taller of the two male clones. His skin was an onyx color with oil colored brillo hair. His face and demeanor were his genetic father's, while his blackhole eyes emitted a flickering cauldron red glow.

"Father."

His words brought his siblings to their senses. Along with the pen-thief was her sister, who was an inch taller than her with a lighter complexion, and the same faint blue glow emitting from her matching eyes.

The last of them was their brother, who resembled the girls. He was smaller than his brother, wrapped in caramel skin with a short napped up afro. His hazel eyes produced a faint yellow glow.

Unlike his short-tempered brother, he used his hand to a shooing gesture causing the staff attending to him to quickly back away.

All four slid off their individual pods, gently getting to their feet. They each steadied themselves as their legs found their strength, allowing them to stand. All of them searched the room zeroing in on their waiting parents.

Like flies drawn to light, the quadruplets started with literal baby steps heading in their direction. Halfway to them, their strides became stronger.

With a foot of distance between them and their genetic parents, the siblings simultaneously took a knee bowing their heads.

"Mother…father…we have returned to you."

Horus walked over to one of his daughters, while Sekhmet made her way to the tallest male. They both placed a hand on their heads, caressingly running their fingers through their thick locks.

Their lips became flourishing ominous smiles as the loving parents turned to make eye contact with one another.

Sekhmet bit her bottom lip as Horus said the most romantic thing he ever spoke to her.

"Now, …the war begins."

CHAPTER 16

The Hall of Elders, the main capital building of Atticala,

Laurence stood once again on the steps outside the main doors in full armor. As he watched his cousins Anubis and Bastet ascend the steps to approach him, his mind wandered back to his time at home before his departure.

~ ~

Warmness filled his insides as he treasured the fleeting family time as he bathed, ate, and played with his children until they were tired of him. As he and Neith laid them to rest in their bed and crib, they departed to their own room to play with one another.

Laurence, however, could not rest as he gazed up at the ceiling of his home while Neith lay on top of him, nuzzling her head close to his chest.

"Lay thy troubled yoke upon me, my husband, so that I may carry it with you."

He turned to her with a saddened smile laying a soft kiss upon her forehead.

"My thoughts go to the orchestration of recent events."

"The Volorions dropping their shield letting you go?" Neith inquired.

"High Prime Vbzarma would have sacrificed his entire War Machine to have our heads on pikes," Laurence grumbled. "What bothers me more is the complexity of the energy shielding. Volorions have always perfected offense weaponry …this shield was way beyond their capability."

"So, if this technology is as advanced as you say, why go to Earth?"

Laurence made a face that made her sit up in bed. The look on the hardened female Annunaki warrior was one of fretful concern.

"You are not proposing that someone on Earth created this technology for the Volorions?"

"Within one short decade, the humans of Earth have made an evolutionary jump where people fly via their own propulsion and can lift objects with just a thought."

"You know…what this means, Laurence …if what you are implying… If it is true…"

"I am implying nothing, my love," Laurence said to her with a calming tone. "What I do know is my first home is the focal point. I pray that what I find if I find anything, will lead me elsewhere. If not …I can get ahead of it."

Neith placed a gentle hand on her husband's chest.

"I pray to the elders; it is not so."

"At times, that is all we can do, my love," Laurence whispered.

He stayed in bed with her for an extra hour discussing everything else aside from work, until they mustered up the strength to play again.

Their second rest session was shorter as Sol slithered into the room, reminding him that it was time to depart to Earth for his mission.

The face of reluctance was brief upon both of their visages as Neith sat up in the bed, covering herself in the bedsheets while Laurence slid out, getting to his feet.

She called forth the servants of the house to bring out her husband's armor and dressed him herself as they watched while handing her each piece at a time.

Laurence then quietly entered his children's room to give them each soft departing kisses as they slept.

Neith, followed by Butch, walked with him to the front of his home. She gave him his commands as she held his hand.

"Complete your mission, and then return to us, no matter who stands in your way."

"As you wish," Laurence agreed as he bowed his head.

Neith reached up, clasping his face with her hands to plant a deep kiss upon his lips. Laurence drunk in more as he wrapped his arms around her waist, pulling her as close to him as physically possible.

The years had not lessened the sweetness.

~ ~

His focus quickly returned as his elder cousins stood before him.

"You depart for Earth now?" Anubis asked.

"I do," Laurence nodded. "What will you be up to?"

Anubis gruffed with irritation before he answered.

"Unfortunately, nothing, mother has departed for Alvion Prime, she has been chosen to be one of the Tribunals in the inquiry of Sophia Dennison of Earth."

"Which means as the next in line of the Head of the House of Set, you must remain here at home."

Anubis nodded with fluttered eyes of disgust.

"Wretched laws and traditions."

"What will you be up to, Bast?" Laurence inquired.

"My punishment," Bastet muttered. "Mother has elected me to train new recruits on the art of becoming a proper Annunaki warrior."

"She's placed you in the lecture halls," Laurence shook his head.

Bastet nodded with a snarled face.

"Knowing how much I detest public speaking."

"Where will you begin with this investigation of yours?" Anubis asked.

"I shall begin with a discussion with the Regulators," Laurence answered. "Confirm with their take on events that have passed on Earth, and corollate them with what I suspect."

"The identity of this alleged puppet master," Bastet answered.

"Hopefully, yes." Laurence nodded.

"Then be off with you boy, the faster you bear fruit, the quicker my sentence shall end, and I can kill something or someone."

"Safe travels, cousin," Anubis said while extending his arm.

Laurence extended his hand, grasping him by his forearm as Anubis did the same. They connected their third eyes as a sign of affection and respect amongst warriors.

They released each other for Laurence to do the same with Bastet; she stayed with her forehead pressed longer to him than Anubis before releasing him.

"Sol."

From the housing in the back of his armor, Sol activated a portal. Laurence walked through returning to his first homeworld.

~ ~

The Grand Canyon National Park, Colorado, the Project EVOlution base,

Graves and Alexander stood off to the side, watching powerless at the final assembly of universal powers that would change everything on Earth as they knew it forever.

Horus, Sekhmet, and their Heralds stood once again, speaking to five of the most powerful warlords of the universe.

High Prime Vbzarma once against sat with passive irritation written on his face as his sons Volker and Nofarrzo flanked either side of his throne. On another screen sat a stoned faced Grand Kan Fatra Kumzi next to his daughter, Mefita Kumzi. She attempted to mimic her father's demeanor, only to fail as the memories of the last meeting cracked her mettle. On the third screen sat the Regent Maleen on her throne without her daughter Syrtria or her slave. On the fourth screen sat the Imperial Lord Hoovii Omni without his council, in a room fashioned to look like a Presidential Oval office.

The last person on the final screen was the newly crowned Grand Emperor Togar. Unlike the other rulers, Togar humbly bowed on one knee showing his respect and fidelity to his new gods that placed him upon the throne.

"Father Horus and Mother Sekhmet, your humble servant is blessed to be before your presence once again."

Horus turned to his wife, waiting for her to command her new pet.

"Rise my child and take your rightful place upon your throne."

Togar did as commanded, sitting upon his throne with a face of obedience, while the earthly mortal gods turned their attention to the other warlords. Horus stepped forward to begin the meeting.

"Lords and Ladies, it is truly wonderful to see that you all returned for this second meeting."

He noticed that their eyes were not entirely focused upon him, but the new elephants in the room.

The newly resurrected clone children of Horus and Sekhmet created a new ranking system. It sent the Heralds one step back as they proudly stood at ferocious attention behind their mother and father.

Although they were biological quadruplets, each wore a different demeanor, revealing that they each possessed their own unique personality.

"But before we begin, allow me to introduce you to our children." Horus gestured.

A confident, subtle smirk formed on the god of sky's lips as he watched the warlords' organ or organs that pumped blood or bodily fluid through each of their veins plummet to the darkest crevice of their guts never to return.

It was bad enough that the self-proclaimed gods of Earth were handing out ultimatums to them and possessed immense physical or supernatural power to back it up that none of the rulers had ever seen before.

Now they had offspring, powerful and loyal offspring.

"From left to right is our son Apedemak."

The male clone with near midnight skin with blue tints and red lips glared at the screen with unrivaled hatred and disgust at those he deemed lesser than him. The red pulsating glow from his domino eyes reflected the unbridled power slowly growing within him and matched the metallic red piping and material added to his black bodysuit and bracers. The only other color was the golden image of a lion laser-etched into the suit from his left shoulder down to his left breast.

His hair was no longer a short curly afro. Instead, his head was shaven save for a long-stranded braided ponytail similar to Egyptian males of ancient times.

"Our lovely daughter, Mekhit."

Horus motioned to the tallest of the two females. Like her brother, her hazel eyes pulsated a steady deep-sea blue glow. Her black bodysuit was similar to her brother's, except with gold piping. The only other color was bright white laser etching that created the lioness image from her right shoulder to her right breast.

Unlike her brother, her demeanor was less anger and hatred, more disgust and irritation.

Mekhit chose to shave half of her head while braiding the other half into thick braids.

"Our other son, Montu."

Opposite his brother and sister, the smaller male clone wore a sly smile upon his lips. Coupled with his eyes, which pulsated a sky green energy hue, was a mixture of tactical sadistic deviousness.

His outfit consisted of an ice blue and black color scheme. A bright silver etching of a perched hawk began at his left hip to his right breast. His hairstyle of choice was a modern low-cut Caesar, with a finely trimmed hairline, and a thinly braided ponytail position at the base of his neck.

"And last but never least, our other lovely daughter, Nekhbet."

The smallest of the two girls with caramel skin wore all of her auburn hair shoulder length and curly.

The color scheme of her outfit was black and purple. A copper-red symbol of a vulture was laser etched on the suit, starting from her right hip to her left breast.

She, too, bore a smile upon her face. However, unlike her siblings, there was truly little focus. The answer lay in her eyes, which pulsate a bright blue star color with flickers of white.

In her eyes was unhinged madness and insanity barely under control.

"Aren't they just lovely?" Horus innocently inquired.

Each ruler's eyes met the other wondering, which would speak on their behalf. Lord Hoovii Omni chose to take one for the team.

"Yes, Lord Horus …they are …quite lovely."

"Thank you, and now let us dispatch with the small talk and come to the heart of the matter. Have you all made your decision on where you stand?"

"I'm pretty sure you know what our answer is," Grand Kan Fatra Kumzi gruffed.

"That we do," Horus nodded. "But verbal clarification assures that all cards are upon the table."

As Fatra Kumzi's trunk began pulsating from the air being blown out of it, Regent Maleen took over speaking on behalf of herself and the other rulers, minus Vbzarma and Togar.

"We agree to your terms, Lord Horus."

"Thank you, Regent," Horus said with a sly head tilt. "But, I would prefer to hear it from the lips of Lord Hoovii and the Grand Kan."

Horus's request caused Hoovii to shift uncomfortably in his seat, while Fatra narrowed his eyes in vexation.

"I agree to your terms," Lord Hoovii said with a lump in his throat. "The Nowaru nation will support your war campaign."

"I also agree to terms," Grand Kan Fatra gruffed. "The Tinra Oa empire will fight alongside you."

"Of course, you will," Horus smiled. "On behalf of my family, I welcome you all into our fold."

"So now that our 'alliance' is confirmed ...," Grand Kan Fatra scoffed.

"The next steps for all of you is to prepare your forces for imminent war," Horus ordered. "And then wait to be summoned. For now, rejoice amongst yourselves for the future spoils of victory to come."

Horus's words of conquest did nothing to change the unpleasant expressions of the universal warlords now under his thumb. His visage revealed that he did not care.

"Good day to you all, except for our newly appointed Grand Emperor Togar. Please stay a while so that we may have words."

As the other screens swiftly cut to black, Togar's own expanded to full view. The Grand Emperor sat straighter upon his throne, waiting to receive instruction from Horus.

"Grand Emperor Togar, I will be sending my daughter Mekhit to your homeworld. Upon her arrival, she will take control of half of your warships and troops."

"Children from your blood are also my and my people's gods, Lord Horus and Lady Sekhmet," Togar answered. "She shall be worshipped and obeyed."

"And you child shall be rewarded for your obedience and fidelity with a long reign, endless wealth, and a strong bloodline that will last longer than the stars," Sekhmet smiled. "Long after your body has turned back to dust, and you are welcomed into the House of Horus."

As she spoke, her eyes emitted a brighter white glow.

On the opposite side of the screen, Togar's eyes widened, filling with tears. He fell once again to his knees with his head hung low weeping.

"Thank you, my beautiful goddess, …thank you …I swear … to thee …that I shall not fail you."

"What did you show him?" Horus mentally whispered to her.

"My words made images in his mind," she coyly whispered back.

With a wave of Horus's hand, Togar's screen went black, ending the conference.

"Mother, father, may I speak?"

Both parents turned to a vocal Apedemak, curious with what the clone who had been awake for a day had to say. The ominous death glare never left his face as he folded his arms.

"Speak, child," Sekhmet gestured. "What is on your mind?"

"Why are we debasing ourselves by enlisting mortals?"

Horus gave Sekhmet a side-eye look that told her Apedemak was definitely her offspring despite being a clone.

"We are the children of the god of sky and goddess of war," he continued. "Surely, the four of us can bring the Dominion Council to heel by ourselves."

"It is because we are gods, my son," Horus answered. "Our profession is to command and rule mortals. Theirs is to serve, obey, and, if need be, perish on our behalf. As a god of war like your mother, you must learn to inspire legions to topple empires in your name. That is the true power of a god."

"Yes, father," Apedemak said with a respectful nod.

A smile grew on Horus's lips as he walked over, placing a reassuring hand on Apedemak's shoulder.

"But now and then, we must show the mortals why they must tremble before us."

A sinister grin formed on Apedemak's lips as Horus strolled up to his daughter, who stood proudly gazing into his eyes.

"When do I depart, father?"

He placed a fatherly hand on her shoulder.

"Shortly, you shall also be our eyes and ears on Gregor, weed out any threats to our pawn publicly and with extreme prejudice. The people must know that Togar has the power of the gods behind him."

"It shall be done, father."

"Good child," Horus said while rubbing her shoulder with a smile.

Horus then turned his attention to his heralds within the room.

"Return to your positions, continue to build your following until the time you are summoned again."

They all bowed and answered in unison.

"We shall obey, lord Horus."

"Use the portals Meskhenet shall prepare for you to leave this base," Horus instructed. "Ken Shiro, stay awhile."

"Please follow the illuminating lights strips outside on the floor to the transport room," Meskhenet instructed.

The five members of Vitruvian Absolute nervously glanced at each other, wondering why they were not leaving the same way they came: Ken Shiro's private helicopter. They then bowed, paying their respects to Sekhmet and the new children of Horus before departing.

Ken Shiro confidently approached Horus waiting for instruction. Horus, with a finger and a mentally projected thought, instructed for Graves to come out of his corner.

"After the second event that will soon take place, you and this slave shall introduce the world to my serum. With his and your influence, politicians shall put forth legislation to recruit every capable man, woman, and, if necessary, child for the war to come. Other nations shall follow soon after that."

"It shall be done, Lord Horus." Ken Shiro answered with a bow.

"One more matter to discuss before you depart, Meskhenet."

Upon Horus's command, the screen lit up again, revealing a view of the outside Colorado Canyon riverbed. Ken Shiro's eyes narrowed a bit, wondering what Horus wanted him to see. It brought a smile to the Ancient's face.

"Commencing cellular imaging," Meskhenet announced.

The screen changed to a black and green outline of the canyon and revealed a multicolor shape of a female figure.

Ken Shiro's visage never changed, even when the ancient immortal moved closer, towering over him.

"There's a reason why I have not killed you, Ken Shiro; even before I introduced you to the serum, your mind for the science was unparalleled …for a mortal."

Horus turned to block the screen standing his arms folded in front of Shiro. Sekhmet wearing a face of displeasure, strolled over standing by his side with her hands at her hips.

"She's been here since your arrival attempting to gain entrance into this facility; she has also attempted to contact the Regulators. Fortunately, Meskhenet has blocked her attempts at communication and is impersonating their A.I. system. Once again, your family has become an annoyance to me. An annoyance I thought remedied when I had you deliver onto me your younger brother's head."

Ken Shiro's visage still did not crack as he slowly looked up at Horus.

"Nekhbet."

"Yes, mother."

The fourth clone with an eerily chirpy voice walked over while flipping the pen she took from the lab technician in between her fingers.

"Go outside and deal with our little intruder with extreme prejudice. Be sure to remember to mask your power. We're still maintaining our anonymity for the time being."

"Yes, mother."

Nekhbet turned to skip away to do her mother's bidding.

"I get to play outside! I get to play outside!"

~ ~

Outside against one of the walls of the Colorado Canyon, Shintobe, masked by her suit's camouflage capabilities, crouched down while attempting to get a communication out.

"For the umpteenth time, Maxine, I don't give a flying fuck what meeting they're in! Fucking interrupt it, I need to speak to them ASA fucking P!"

"Apologies, Yuku Shiro, but Sergeant Rogers and Dr. Champion are in an urgent Joint

Staff meeting with the President of the United States, it cannot be…"

"Fuck the President! This is bigger …"

Shintobe paused as a cold chill ran down her spine.

"That's the third time you've called me by my full name. You usually call me …Ms. Shiro."

The chill became more intense as dead silence filled the other end.

"You're not … Maxine …are you?"

The question was never answered, Shintobe dived evading the projectile that nearly embedded her into the canyon. She had to keep moving as chunks of stone that had not been disturbed in centuries came crashing down, breaking into extra pieces.

As the dust slowly dissipated, Shintobe was able to see that the projectile that targeted her was still moving.

"Wow…you're pretty quick for a mortal. No matter, I'll just put a little more effort into killing you."

"Oh yeah, and who might you be?"

"My name is Nekhbet… a goddess of old and your executioner."

"Interesting …never fought a goddess before."

Nekhbet let out an insane chuckle with a long sigh.

"You believe this to be a fight? I just said I am your executioner."

"You talk a lot of smack for someone who couldn't touch me." Shintobe shot back.

Her retort brought a soft smile to Nekhbet's lips. It was the only sign she got before the super-powered clone exploded from where she stood and was on her.

"Fuck, she's fast!"

Were Shintobe's thoughts as she barely ducked the right flying superwoman punch meant to separate her head from her body. It was a feint for the low cutting roundhouse kick intended to break her in half.

Shintobe's only option was to use speed to move with the kick to lessen the blow. It did not make it any less painful as she was launched across the riverbed creating small drag strips as she bounced.

After the third bounce, Shintobe rolled, getting her feet underneath her, slid, and then broke into a run as Nekhbet giving chase, landed seconds from where she stood.

"Wow, she's **really** swift for a mortal."

"Nekhbet."

She shuddered from the authoritative stern tone of her mother within her head.

"Sorry, mother, I shall do better."

Shintobe blocked out the pain as she ran at top speed, putting much distance between her and the white vulture goddess.

"Bitch almost broke me in half with that kick!" She thought to herself. *"Got to get out of here!"*

Nearly clearing the canyon, within the seconds she ran, Shintobe used her speed to scale the wall for a flat out run to the West Coast.

She never made it.

Even though she heard the rattling of the multiple sonic booms, her speed and senses could not help her evade or defend against the crushing aerial sack from her blindside.

Shintobe was sure her back was shattered as she flopped around in midair, plummeting back down to the river below. Her body never hit the water as Nekhbet making a quick bank, dived and caught her in mid descent.

Shintobe weakly fought back as Nekhbet draped her up, latching onto her throat with one hand hanging her in midair like a side of beef.

"You made my mother mad at me." Nekhbet hissed at her. "I shall remedy that by bringing her your heart!"

Nekhbet made her free hand into the shape of a knife. There was no hesitation as she struck to pierce Shintobe's chest plate.

"Nekhbet, hold!" Sekhmet whispered her command.

She did as instructed, stopping her impaling blow inches from Shintobe's chest. Shiro groaned nonetheless as she felt the wind pressure generated by her moved, which vibrated her sternum.

~ ~

Inside the base, Sekhmet and Horus looked upon Ken Shiro, who showed frostbite emotion as he watched his youngest sister savagely attacked and battered by Nekhbet. His eyes never closed, nor did he turn away as she prepared to run Yuku through with her bare hand.

"Care you not for your sister, who is about to die by my child's hand?" Horus inquired. "Nor for your only niece who will be orphaned by this act?"

"God over country and family every time. I care only for the glory of the House of Horus," Ken Shiro said with a consistent tone. "I shall also ensure that my niece is cared for should you allow me to live."

Shiro fell to a knee with his head bowed.

"My life is always in your hand, my lord."

Sekhmet and Horus turned to one another, nodding with approval.

"Nekhbet, bring the intruder in and restrain her," Horus commanded his daughter.

~ ~

There was a slight pout on the clone's face before she answered.

"As you command, father."

She glared at Shintobe, who began to choke as she increased her grip on her throat.

"Thank my father that he has need of you."

~ ~

Horus turned his attention back to Ken Shiro, still down on one knee.

"I am deeply interested in bringing the demi-gods of this world to heel and to our cause without needed bloodshed," Horus deduced. "I shall take your sister as one of our test subjects."

"As you command, my lord."

"Rise and take your leave until I have need of you."

Shiro did as commanded.

"My Lord, Goddess Sekhmet, Children of Horus."

"One more thing," Horus commanded as Ken Shiro turned. "Say farewell to your sister before you go."

It was the only time Ken Shiro paused.

"As you command, my lord."

As he finally departed, Horus pointed a finger in his direction.

"Take note, my children, men of faith like Shiro is who you want in your staple."

"But you knew that already, father," Montu rebuffed with a sly tone. "So why test him?"

"Because he's still a mortal, my son," Sekhmet answered on Horus's behalf. "Still capable of breaking, so now and then those with the greatest of faith must also be tested."

~ ~

Ken Shiro made sure to keep his stride heading for the elevator that would take him to a concealed helicopter hanger built within the canyon hiding his private chopper.

Coming down the opposite side of the hallway toward him was Nekhbet following a staff member pushing a modified gurney housed with thick metallic restraints for the arms, legs, waist, and neck capable of holding an EVO.

On it was his sister Yuku minus her high-tech mask. The daze and pain she felt from the damage done to her by the bio-engineered goddess went away thanks to her regenerative healing.

"Hold slave, father wants the two loving siblings to say their farewells."

The staff member did as he was instructed. Ken Shiro looked down at his baby sister, who looked back at him with a sardonic smile and a trembling lower lip.

"Hey, big bro …I'd be spitting in your fucking face right now, but I can't angle my head to get a good shot."

"Why did you follow me here, Yuku?" Shiro asked in Japanese.

"Why the fuck are you here, brother?" Yuku shot back. "What the fuck have you done? Who the fuck are these people?"

"These 'people' are the true gods of this world returned, my dear sister. And what I have done is for their glory and the benefit of the human species."

"What type of gods need a fucking military research facility, Ken?"

"The type that know that science and the supernatural go hand in hand, my dear sister," Ken Shiro fiercely answered back. "The type that I can believe in and stand behind."

"Now I can answer your question, with a question," Yuku said with a quivering tone. "What happened to Jagi, Ken. What did you do to our brother?"

Her question put a lump in Shiro's throat, preventing him from answering.

"I've been searching for him everywhere, ever since he sent that bullshit text saying he needed time away to figure some shit out," Yuku said with a shaky mousey voice. "He wouldn't just leave without talking to his baby sister, he would never do that. And you with limitless resources weren't too concerned with finding him…so what the fuck happened to him?"

Shiro leaned in, giving his sister his answer.

"Jagi was always weak, you knew that. The women, the drinking, the drugs, the scandals that never ended. That I had to clean up. Even when I bestowed upon him, the power of the gods, …it was only a matter of time."

Yuku found her target as she shot a wad of saliva into his face. She did not need to hear anymore. She knew from his eyes the rest of the story, what he had done.

"Oooooh! Grossy gross!" Nekhbet said from the sidelines.

Shiro removed a handkerchief from the inside of his jacket to wipe his face.

"Your fate is now in the hands of the gods little sister. Do as they command, and you might just survive to see the better new world they are creating. In the meantime, I shall fulfill your duties and take care of Sakura."

His word ignited rage within Yuku as she fought to use her enhanced strength to break through her bonds.

"Fuck you, Ken! Stay away from my daughter! You piece of shit mother fucker! Stay the fuck away from my daughter!"

"Goodbye, Yuku."

Ken Shiro turned, walking away with a new focus in his eyes as his little sister howled and scream, cursing him in their native tongue while struggling to get free.

Nekhbet flicked the ear of the technician, causing him to jump forward. He quickly took the cue, pushing the gurney wheeling a wailing Shintobe away as she followed behind him.

CHAPTER 17

Messer Prime, located in Sector 0015, also known as the Mustavar system in the universe, the metallic artificial moon space station was the outpost for mercenaries, organized criminals, skin traders, pimps, narcotics traffickers, and every other being of ill-repute in the known universe.

No one, however, could do any type of business or set up permanent operations on the space station without first paying respects and scheduled financial restitution to the Mulcov Organization, headed by Enuc Mulcov.

Enuc Mulcov from Tanger sat in a large deep black plush chair with gold metallic hardware held up by a gravitational propulsion system in his office that was the disturbing amalgamation of an old detective's office from Earth meshed with alien tech.

The dim sun yellow artificial light played off of the sleek metallic walls and desk that had the look of worn tan wood.

Two slated grey chairs with withered brown upholstery similar to leather hovered in front of the desk via gravitational propulsion technology, while tan colored metal file cabinets with a beaten look gave the office the feel of a 1960's Mod Squad meets Star Trek Next Generation.

Enuc, like all Tangerians, were similar to humans, save for his sky-blue feline eyes, frosted glittery hairless pale white skin, and a thick black coat of quills similar to porcupines that he wore short on the top of his head.

His attire, much like his office, gave him the appearance of a 1950's Earth mobster decked out in a yellow linen shirt with rolled-up sleeves, brown suspenders with silver metallic fittings, and the texture of leather attached to dark brown slacks with a soft wet rubbery feel to it.

On the desk sat a pyramid of stacked dense translucent golden crystalline bars, each with a faint glow as if sunshine were trapped in each of them. Enuc's attention was focused on the holographic image of a male Nowarun with tan and white fur.

His midnight blue eyes, devoid of irises, revealed his frustration as he wore a vibrant gold and blue robe similar to that of a Catholic Cardinal with markings from his homeworld showing a station of authority.

"As I said again, Grand Marquise Borvador, Princess Eleaze's compensation is not the issue," Enuc sighed. "It is the risk. No one is going to risk the possible wrath of the Dominion Council by skin trading a well-known, especially from the planet Earth, which is currently on reported quarantine."

"But is this not the ideal time," Grand Marquise Borvador protested. "Based on the Intel we are receiving, the humans may soon be extinct."

"It's still too great of a risk. No one will abduct this …Chris Evans, especially after the ramifications of the Earhart deal that almost shut this station down for good. However, if it does appear that the humans are on the outs as a species, I will take the contract, but for four times the original price."

"Would you be willing to throw in the human Rihanna for six times the original compensation?" Grand Marquise Borvador inquired with a narrowed, devious gaze.

"Now you're getting greedy," Enuc smirked. "But it will be considered. Be well, Grand Marquise Borvador."

"Be well, Enuc."

Enuc waved off the holographic image transmission of Bishop Borvador in time to receive an incoming message.

With another wave of his hand, an image of a male Tangerian with frost white skin and dirty blonde quills that reached the back of his neck with green feline eyes and an effeminate disposition stood before him dawned in a grey outfit that screamed mobster meets imperial officer.

The long flowing dark leathery tan coat covering the two-piece grey suit with a mandarin collar that fit the onyx colored tie with the texture of shiny rubber that fits into the groove of the jacket like a puzzle piece along with the battered brown fedora hat was meant to give the young

Tangerian male the look and feel of criminal intimidation.

However, the exact opposite was displayed on the image before Enuc.

"Namol, how goes the Jurtarian rebellion?"

The visage on Namol's face before he answered was disturbing horror.

"It is over …he single-handily crushed the rebellion."

"Really now?" Enuc asked, leaning back with impressed delight. "That was fast, barely a full day's work, what is the death toll?"

"The probe is still counting," Namol swallowed. "But we're currently over twenty-five hundred."

"Let us hope we hit that four zero mark," Enuc smirked, "Emperor Qlibrud will have to cough up that bonus."

Enuc's face changed to semi-concern at Namol's distressed demeanor.

"Namol, what troubles you? Did you eat something with Chuka berries again? You know what they do to your digestive system. I keep stressing to you to read the labels."

"Enuc …he's doing it again," Namol answered with a rattled whisper.

"What's he doing again?"

Namol, close to tears, leaned into the visual commlink, praying not to be heard.

"He's eating people …again. He is eating the mortally wounded, desecrating the dead, and he has a stack of bodies he wants to take back with him. Enuc, this is madness, I cannot continue to do this."

Enuc leaned back in his chair, letting out a calmed sigh as he stared back at Namol with a blunt businessman stare.

"Namol, as you very well know, people within my organization feel that the salary I pay you is quite unfair based on your subpar productivity. They feel that I am playing favoritism because you are my brother-in-law, which I am because I adore my baby sister and want the best for her even though I felt being coupled with you was the worst decision she ever made."

Namol dropped his head, wearing a distressed look as Enuc continued.

"You should be ecstatic to have this workload. Considering that he has killed three of the previous handlers I assigned to him, no one is disputing anymore the income which I pay you. Not to mention, he clearly likes you. This should be the easiest job ever. You see to his needs, take him to his assignments, and you get paid. What is the problem?"

"You know why he likes me, Enuc," Namol choked on his words.

"Again, failing to see the downside of your situation," Enuc shrugged his shoulders. "Would you prefer him wanting to eat you like he's done to his previous handlers?"

"He says the vilest things to me …makes these horrific gestures," Namol whimpered. "Things that haunt me when I sleep."

Enuc drew out a deep sigh and raised a hand to calm his brother-in-law down.

"Let us not get ahead of ourselves; he has not acted on his impulses toward you, yet. But, when and if the time comes that he does, I will assure you that Vluri will never, ever get wind of it."

Namol gasped, almost collapsing at what was just said to him.

"Enuc!"

"Namol, let me just be blunt right now," Enuc said with a stern ice-cold tone. "If it comes down to the cannibalistic human wrecking machine that has been making me a fortune. Whose only requirements are to feed, scrag, and kill for compensation against your worthless hide, I will be picking him over you every single time. And if it takes your sweet tight little orifice to keep him happy, I will joyously serve you on a platter to him myself. Now, please reframe from contacting me on trivial things such as this, finish up the job, and do make sure Emperor Qlibrud transfers the remaining funds, additional fees, and bonuses we picked up before the end of the business day, or our tremendously powerful, and sadistic friend will be visiting him to do what the resistance failed to do."

Enuc swiped away the face of a mortified Namol, shutting off his communicator. His eyes fluttered in disgust as sound from another incoming call emitted, with a holographic portrait of his secretary outside.

With a wave of his hand, he answered the call to a live image of a female Norkarian. Like others from her species, she had the appearance of a humanoid pig showing mostly within the nose and ears. Her skin was a shiny lime green color with a brown mud pattern mostly revealed on her head, neck, shoulders, and possibly other parts of her body.

Her red and blonde streak hair was pulled back into a bun, while her outfit consisted of a red blouse and pencil skirt similar to what women wore on Earth during the 1950s only with a gleaming sheer material.

Enuc's brows furrowed with concern as she looked at him with a visage of fear mostly detected within her sea-green eyes.

"What is it, Zela? Do not tell me you are expecting again, because you will be on your own with this one. As I told you, my mate will only allow me to support the first one you had for me, no more. And don't expect a salary increase …"

"The High General of the Thracian Regime is here, you vulking idiot!" She whispered, her irritation cutting him off. "She wants an audience with you now."

Enuc's reaction became the exact opposite of what she expected as his face lit up with anticipation.

"The Princess is here?" he grinned. "Well, bring her in woman, bring her in."

Enuc shot up to his feet, sending his chair floating away. As it slowly drifted back lining up behind him and the desk, he quickly smoothed out his attire and ran his hands through his quills. Before the door slid open, Enuc quickly did the breath check, huffing into his palm and taking a quick whiff.

Zela walked in first, balancing on red stiletto shoes with daggers for heels. Although she evicted the irritation she had for Enuc, fear had remained a resident on her face as Attea followed close behind her entering his office.

The Thracian High General bore a look as if she smelled something foul as her eyes moved about in her head, examining Enuc's office, which she had been to only once before accompanying her brother. She gave him a dismissive glance catching his salivating smile and eyes that refused to stop undressing her.

"Introducing the High Thracian Gen ..."

"The Princess and I are very well acquainted, Zela," Enuc cut off her introduction. "You may return to your desk. Hold all of my communications and ensure that we are not interrupted, please."

A sinister smile finally replaced the fear on Zela's face as she quickly approached his desk with defiance.

"Let it be recorded that I'd soon kill myself before I let you touch me again," she whispered. "Much less bare another one of your seeds, especially with your subpar breeding methods."

Her insult molded Enuc's face to one of irritation as she let out a snort similar to an Earth pig before spinning on her heels and sashaying out of the office, closing the door behind her. Enuc, with a headshake, remembered to discuss with her later about her disrespectful comment in front of a guest. The smile returned to his lips as his eyes fell once again on Attea, who glared back at him with a dull disgusted gaze underneath her war helm.

"Princess Attea," Enuc subtly licked his lips. "To what do I owe the pleasure of this meeting?"

Attea removed her helm, setting it down on a nearby table before dryly addressing him.

"You gave my brother information on the whereabouts of a female human within a sink vortex in the Ominaro quadrant."

"Which I assume has proven quite useful to him," he smiled.

"I want the source of this information now."

Unbeknownst to Enuc, Attea caught the fear that slipped onto his face, which he covered with a poker smile.

"Now, Princess Attea, you more than anyone should know it is the kiss of death for me to reveal one of my sources without their consent."

"Then get their consent," she ordered, finally looking up at him.

"I don't think that is possible," Enuc nervously swallowed. "This source has expressed to me to ensure their anonymity at all costs."

Attea turned to him with a blank innocent stare as she deactivated the magnetic scabbard housing her sword, which was attached to the metallic part of her dress. Enuc's eyes slightly widened as she placed it on the table next to her helm.

"Apologies, " she said, "It appears as if I am giving off the impression that I either care about the damage to your reputation or that I am prepared to accept and walk away with any answer you give me other than what I want."

A jittery Enuc washed with sweat leaned back in his seat, knowing full well what the Thracian General was capable of as Attea sauntered over to him. She sat, crossing her legs on his desk.

"Tangerians …I loathe your species more than humans," she sighed while looking at her claws for nails.

Her remark slapped an off-putting expression on Enuc's face.

"The only thing that fascinates me about your putrid species is your remarkable healing capabilities. You are feeble in every other way, but extremely hard to kill. The only way to dispatch one of you is to destroy both your major and minor brains along with your heart. Am I correct?"

"More or less," he gulped.

"Which means if I shatter every bone in your body with my bare hands, I just have to sit here and wait for a couple of minutes while you regenerate to do it all over again."

Attea's underline threat caused Enuc to shift in his seat.

"I shall ask my question one final time. Know that I shall not ask it again. During that time, you need to decide whether you will answer my question with a quivering voice, or blood-curdling screams and squeals."

Enuc, fighting to control the independent muscle spasms Attea's ultimatum brought on, forced the bulging lump stuck in his throat before he carefully spoke.

"Unfortunately, my princess …there is no fear in your arsenal that can surpass the terror my source …has instilled in me."

For a split second, Enuc's words stunned Attea. What followed was a subtle smirk on her lips that read "Challenge accepted."

"Really? Then let us put that to the test."

~ ~

Minutes later, in Enuc's waiting room, Zela shuddered to the jolting sound of breaking furniture and her boss screaming and pleading inside his office.

Two of Attea's guards waiting outside positioned themselves in front of Enuc's office door to ensure the High General would not be disturbed.

As their eyes glanced at Zela's way, she timidly sunk in her seat, fixating her eyes onto her translucent screen, pretending to do office and billing work.

Zela also quickly placed earbuds lying on her desk into her big floppy ears.

"Maximum volume," she whispered.

Her verbal command turned up the music drowning out the horrendous sounds coming from within the office.

CHAPTER 18

Regulator Base, the Ranch,

After Sister Sledge's return from Sanctuary Island and her debriefing on what occurred there, the base remained on high alert.

Rogers, in full gear along with Lady Tech, stood in front of several monitors conversing with the Joint Chief of Staff for the second time in days after the alien attack on Earth.

"We've taken your report under serious advisement Sergeant Rogers," General Joseph Francis Dunford Jr. said with a gruff voice, "And began coordination with all of our allied forces and their superhuman units to begin the process of a unified defensive response should the alien invaders return. However, any discussion of coordinating with the Russians, North Korea, or Iran will have to be put on hold. The political climate we're in right now is too hostile to begin those talks."

"Respectfully general, we might not have a political climate if and when these extraterrestrial hostiles choose to return," Rogers responded with a professional steel tone. "Two of our most powerful assets are no longer on the planet. I advise again that we must get all hands-on deck, and I mean people we currently have bad blood with. This is now bigger than a rigged election, or who's making nukes behind our backs."

"With all due respect Sergeant Rogers, neither Ms. Dennison nor her daughter fought or stood for the interests of the United States, or its allies," General Mark A. Milley reminded him.

"No, sir, she fought for the world," Rogers retorted. "The only side she took was for what was good against what was evil. Now we can debate her allegiance all day, but we all know that's nonproductive. Ms. Dennison was a **universal deterrent** for the planet, and with her not here, we are at a major disadvantage. The entire planet needs to fight as a unified front, and that means **everyone**, sir. Powered and non-powered humans, together."

"The Eye of Ra is here," Lady Tech sent a mental whisper to Rogers's mind.

"Where?" Rogers thought back.

"He's standing in the main hanger. Waiting."

"So, you don't believe this threat to the planet is over, Sergeant Rogers?" General Robert B. Neller grimly inquired.

"Sir, you wouldn't be speaking to me if you thought this was over."

Each member of the Joint Chief of Staff made bleak eye contact with one another as both Rogers and Lady Tech read the room, understanding that Rogers's words held a weight of validity to each of them.

"Sergeant Rogers, we will take your report and your words into **serious** consideration," General Joseph Francis Dunford Jr. gave his final answer.

"Sir," Rogers nodded.

"Ms. Champion," General Dunford Jr. acknowledged her.

"General."

As the transmission came to an end, Lady Tech turned to Rogers.

"We better get down there. Your girlfriend just got wind, and she's making a beeline to him to tear his head off."

Rogers muttered a curse under his breath while breaking into a stride to get to the hanger with Lady Tech trotting behind following him.

~ ~

Rogers entered the hanger filled with verbal threats, profanity, and growing chaos.

The Eye of Ra stood calm as an enraged Sister Sledge being held back by both Heavy Element and Merge in metallic form, attempted to get at him, while Oliver, Cyclone, and Nitro stood in between them.

"Where are they, Ra?! What have you done to them?! Where the hell are, they?!"

"Sister Sledge! Come on! Now's not the time to be a comic book cliché!" Nitro yelled.

"Shut the fuck up, Aashif!" She barked him down.

"How's it taking **both** of us to hold her back?!" Heavy Element asked his sister in perplexed disbelief.

Rogers used his fingers to make a high-pitched whistle getting everyone's attention.

"Alright! Knock this shit the fuck off! Sister Sledge, stand down **now**!"

A flustered Sister Sledge glared at him while shrugging both siblings off of her as they held up their hands backing away. Rogers then took up where she left off, making a beeline to get into the Eye of Ra's personal space.

"**You** need to start talking and telling us what the **fuck** is going on! Now!"

An unintimidated Laurence calmly responded.

"I would not be here if that was not my intention, Sergeant Rogers."

"Alright, then." Rogers huffed, calming down a bit. "Let's go."

~ ~

Twenty minutes later, Laurence stood in the middle of the Regulators' central command running down to them on who attacked Sophia, why, what happened to Kimberly, where they were taken, and what was each of their fate before he returned to Earth.

He was unfazed by the mixture of emotions that choked the room backed by hostile glares. Sister Sledge sucked in some air, further calming herself while taking a step forward.

"Right."

She exhaled the air before continuing.

"You, sir, will be taking me to your homeworld now."

Her stern request caused several of her team members except for Rogers, the Eye of Ra, and Lady Tech to widen their eyes or disengage their lower jaws.

"That will not be possible," Laurence calmly answered.

"You have my **goddaughter** on your planet comatose in a pod!" Sister Sledge snapped at him while pointing a finger.

"She is both well protected and cared for, you have my word."

"I don't give a damn about your word. I give a damn that Kimberly's there by herself while her mother faces some bullshit trial on some trumped-up charges! I need to **be there** when she wakes up!"

"You do know this allegation is the most asinine thing I have ever heard," an irritated Lady Tech spoke up. "You're talking about a woman who hasn't been past Mars being accused of traveling to other solar systems billions of light-years away enacting universal war crimes. If that's a term, you people use."

"I am in agreement with you, Dr. Champion," Laurence said while turning to her.

"So, you mean to tell me a network of advance alien races can't figure out that they have the wrong woman?"

Lady Tech began waving her hand around, giving proposals.

"No energy signature or trajectory scans, facial recognition that you guys can use to figure this out?"

"As technologically advanced as other worlds are, there are still limitations to their capabilities, especially against the vastness of space," Laurence responded with a furrowed brow. "The ships and crew that were destroyed and massacred were struck by long-range energy attacks that disabled most of the ships' functions. The assailant, whose face was covered by a hood similar to Dennison's uniform, stayed a safe distance away and emitted a pulse that prevented proper identity detection. The only evidence was the attire and the Fawohodie Adinkra symbol on the assassin's outfit, which only Ms. Dennison wears. No other species in the universe has this symbol aside from Earth, which originated in Ghana."

"But you still believe she's innocent," Rogers stepped in expecting confirmation.

The Eye of Ra turned to Rogers, giving him a nod.

"Someone knew where those ships would be. They wanted it to appear as if Freedom attacked and destroyed those vessels."

"It wouldn't happen to be the same alien species that came for Freedom?" Heavy Element speculated. "Based on the damage they caused, it didn't seem like they were interested in taking Dennison alive."

"I have been wondering that as well, considering they have the most to gain from this incident." The Eye of Ra grimly answered.

Unified scowls grew on everyone's faces in the room from his answer, as Rogers stepped up, asking the question, they all thought.

"What do you **mean** they have the most to gain?"

"If the Dominion Council finds Dennison guilty of these crimes, they may also conclude that she did not act alone."

"You're saying they'd believe she was acting on behalf of the human race?" Lady Tech filled in the blanks.

"Yes."

"Which would be perceived as an act of war." Rogers impatiently followed up. "What do these Thracians get out of it?"

"An act of war means the probable swift extermination of the human species. Because the Thracian Empire is the current shepherds of this quadrant, they will be awarded possession of the Earth, and the six other viable planets that technically belong to the human species."

The Eye of Ra's blunt answer delivered the effect of a Deantay Wilder punch without the real knockout for everyone.

"Holy shit," a floored Cyclone uttered.

"Six …**we** the human race own …**six** fucking planets?" Merge gasped.

"Six including this planet capable of sustaining human life within this quadrant totaling three galaxies," the Eye of Ra elaborated. "If and when humans are deemed worthy of joining the fold of the Dominion Council, they would be informed of this revelation and provided with the necessary technology to travel and occupy these worlds."

"This Dominion Council would freely aide us humans in doing this?" Blitz skeptically inquired. "Why?"

"To forge the bond between species and fortify the strength of the Council." The Eye of Ra turned to him with an iron tone. "It is why the Dominion Council has maintained peace and prosperity throughout the universe since its formation for eons."

Laurence made stern eye contact with each Regulator member as he continued to speak.

"Otherworlds, including the human species, owe their existence and current progression to the Dominion Council. From the shadows, they protected countless lives from those whose intentions varied from subjugation to extermination."

"Excuse us if we're not more appreciative," Nitro snidely jumped into the conversation. "You just told us that we're on this Dominion Council's chopping block."

The Eye of Ra gave him a subtle nod before unleashing his retort.

"Let us have understanding. Humankind will not survive a war with the Dominion Council. If the Council renders a judgment that humans are a threat to this universe, they will wipe this planet clean, and it will come as quickly as a summer breeze. You will be fortunate if they elect to spare the younglings, which will be removed from here, adopted and integrated into other species."

"Younglings meaning children, right?" Heavy Element whispered his question to his sister.

Merge, wearing a soldier's poker face, nodded that he was correct.

Lady Tech, with her arms folded, had a face that read she was processing everything. She took a step forward, drawing Laurence's attention. She raised her head, locking eyes with him before she spoke.

"So why tell us? If we're as powerless as you say and the fate of mankind rests on a murder trial several light-years from here, what do you want from us aside from filling in some blanks which we **do** appreciate?"

"Can you confirm the exact time Dennison tapped into her reserve power?"

"Yesterday at exactly 3:45 PM."

"Sol."

On command, Sol popped out of the back housing within Laurence's armor, becoming animated and slithered sitting across his shoulders.

"Exactly ten Earth minutes after that, the Volorions dropped the shielding on their planet."

"Oh shit! He's got a talking King Cobra in his back!" Nitro jumped.

"Its form is called a Seni, a creature similar to a King Cobra on Anu," Lady Tech corrected him. "Sol is a cybernetic machine."

"I am a familiar," Sol corrected Lady Tech.

"Why are we comparing time frames?" Rogers asked, demanding to know.

"My team and I were on a diplomatic mission to a planet outside of the Dominion Council to negotiate terms for compliance. Unfortunately, the line of communication broke down in a hostile manner." The Eye of Ra began to explain.

"Means they were trying to kill one another," Cyclone whispered to Nitro.

He nodded in agreement as Laurence continued.

"They deployed a planetary shielding that prevented us from leaving. During the battle, Sol informed me about what was happening here on Earth. To get here, I began disabling the shield when the Volorions chose to drop it on their own. We immediately came here."

"You think someone was watching what was going on here, and ordered these Volorions to let you and your team go?" Sister Sledge asked, filling in the pieces.

The Eye of Ra nodded.

"Yes, I believe so."

"Seems to me these Thracians might be working with the Volorions," Rogers deduced. "And when shit went south, they herded you guys here to calm things down."

"It would be a plausible theory if I did not know that a Thracian would rather eviscerate a Volorion than converse much less work for them. A Volorion would also do the same. The hatred between the two species is oceans wide and deep for them to even consider working together."

"Still doesn't mean it's not plausible," Heavy Element backed Rogers's idea up.

"The risk of consorting with the Volorion Regime that stands for everything that the Dominion Council is against would be cripplingly damaging to the Thracian Empire. It is not a risk the High Region or anyone in his government would dare take."

"Would anyone responsible have knowledge of creating this?" Lady Tech asked. "Maxine, bring up the formula, please."

On command, Maxine displayed a holographic image of the red serum formula capable of turning humans into EVOs permanently. Sol instantly began to analyze it.

"This is a reverse-engineered altered version of Aten," Sol answered.

"Are you sure?" Laurence grimly asked.

"The base of the formula is Aten. Slight modifications entail targeting Dennison's genetic material and behavioral change."

The Eye of Ra turned to Lady Tech with a stern right eyebrow lifted.

"Where did you get this formula?"

"**We** got **several** cases of it off of insurgents in Iraq, who bought it off a Mexican Cartel," Rogers said while stepping in between the two of them. "They purchased it from an elusive superhuman group selling the stuff to select criminal organizations. One capable of waltzing into our own base when we weren't home, boosting the shipment we confiscated from our vaults, and then erasing all traces of the formula from our database and Maxine."

"All traces except for me," Lady Tech informed him.

"What else has taken place?" Laurence inquired with narrowed eyes.

"You're MI-6's prime suspect for the murder of Sir Knight Light," Merge bluntly answered.

"What is the basis of this accusation?"

Lady Tech sighed before giving him the rundown.

"Major Henry Butcher was found dead within his home on September 8th, 2016, at eleven A.M. His internal organs, muscle tissue, and bones displayed severe burn marks. The assailant, who appears to be extremely powerful and capable of leaving no DNA traces, was identified as a male due to the large burn mark print of his hand around the front and side of the Major's throat. The only evidence left at the crime scene was grains of sand on the Major's fingertips, which trace back to Luxor, Egypt. A local superhero here in the U.S. known as Flaming Jay was murdered by the same M.O., except her death was made to look like a suicide when the killer dropped her from several miles up onto a parked car. Both victims had every single cell within each of their bodies burnt to a crisp."

"Let's not forget that this same individual was able to impersonate the Major for several months before his actual body was found," Blitz threw in. "So, we're uncertain if the suspect is **actually** a man or woman."

"You said the sand came from Luxor, Egypt?"

Lady Tech nodded while answering Laurence's question.

"Yep, we went down and scanned the area looking for clues ourselves. All we found was an empty tomb approximately twenty miles from the Valley of the Kings."

"What are the exact coordinates to this tomb?"

Lady Tech's spine vibrated from Laurence's voice, the unnerving glare that was not intended to be hostile toward her.

"Maxine …pull them up."

On Lady Tech's command, Maxine pulled up a holographic display pinpointing the tomb they found in Egypt.

"Sol?"

"They are the exact coordinates where he was imprisoned."

"Where **who** was imprisoned?" Rogers demanded to know.

"And you are certain the tomb was empty?" Laurence pressed Lady Tech while ignoring Rogers.

"It was empty," She quickly answered. "Although the ground appeared to have been disturbed and …"

"Eye of Ra, I am still receiving the original signal from the Bleed Casket within Horus's tomb that contradicts Dr. Champion's answer."

"Horus's tomb?" Rogers asked a second question with irritation in his voice.

"Did you're familiar, just call me a liar?" Lady Tech inquired, taking a defensive tone.

"On the contrary, Dr. Champion, I detect that you are telling the truth based on your vital signs," Sol spoke up for himself. "However, I am still detecting a signal from the tomb, which indicates that Horus's Bleed casket should be there."

"What the hell is a Bleed Casket?" Heavy Element asked.

"Sol, open a portal into Horus's tomb immediately," Laurence ordered.

"As you command."

Sol's eyes blazed as he opened up a portal in the middle of the Regulators' command deck. He then transformed into staff mode while slithering down into Laurence's right hand as the Eye of Ra walked through the portal. Erica nervously glanced at Rogers before darting into the gateway after him.

"Erica, wait! Dammit!"

Rogers quickly turned to the rest of his team to give commands.

"Blitz and Merge with me! Heavy Element, you're in command until we get back!"

"Yes, sir!" Heavy Element acknowledged.

Blitz and Merge followed the Sarge diving into the portal before it closed. On the other side, they found Erica standing behind the Eye of Ra, slowly looking around an empty tomb.

"Sol, are you still detecting the false signal indicating that the Bleed Casket is here?"

"Negative," Sol answered. "The signal stopped transmitting the moment we entered the tomb."

Laurence clutched Sol tighter as the hair stood on the back of his neck, knowing that there was a strong possibility they had walked into a trap.

"You should not have followed me here," He said without looking in the direction of the Regulators.

Laurence's weighted statement brought mixed reactions from the team. Lady Tech wore a face of nervousness, while Blitz's own was that of confusion. Merge chose to pull out the sidearm in her right holster, check the clip, reload, and remove the safety preparing for anything.

The Sarge donned his mask of irritation as he stepped into the Eye of Ra's personal space.

"Enough with this cryptic one-liner bullshit!" Rogers spat. "**Who** the hell was down here?"

Laurence paid no attention to Rogers as he narrowed his eyes, staring straight ahead at the wall on the other side of the empty tomb. It did not take long for the air to crackle forcing Rogers to turn his head along with the rest of his team to the interdimensional commotion before them.

A portal opened and expanded out of thin air allowing for Apedemak to step out into the tomb that once housed his father with Seker perched on his shoulder.

He dismissively scanned the room before zeroing in on Laurence and spoke.

"The descendant of Amun-Ra, I presume …I pictured you to be much **larger**."

Rogers pointed to the lion god of war, asking the Eye of Ra a question.

"Is that Horus?"

"No," Laurence answered. "That is not Horus."

"Descendant of Amun-Ra…remove your armor and familiar," Apedemak commanded. "Prostrate yourself before me, and I may allow you to breathe air a little while longer before delivering you to my father."

"I take it your father is Horus," Laurence calmly guessed.

Rogers answered for the Eye of Ra by pulling out his sidearm taking aim. Merge also had sights on Apedemak from her vantage point, while

Blitz powered up, taking his electrical plasma form.

"Leave it to me to run into a portal without my toys," Lady Tech muttered.

Erica tapped the side of her visors, which activated her bodysuit and the nanotechnology within it, causing the sleeves to expand, coating her hands becoming form-fitting gauntlets. The upper part of her suit began to form a malleable helm covering her entire head while connecting to her visor.

The act of aggression brought a scoffing smirk to Apedemak, with his eyes still focused solely on the Eye of Ra.

"Detecting a temporal displacement," Sol announced.

"Where?" Laurence asked.

"All around us," Sol answered.

The walls, ceiling, and floor all around the tomb began to crack and crumble, bringing in cosmic light.

"Sol."

Laurence's familiar immediately created individual golden sphere constructs enclosing all of the members of the Regulators, while the Eye of Ra's faceplate to his helm came down.

"Combatant before us is a Cosmivorse with red supergiant star energy output," Sol confirmed.

"What of his familiar?"

"Detecting it was constructed from components of the original Bleed Casket. Its AI system appears to be on par with me; it's mirroring my attempt to confirm its combat capabilities."

"Once we have confirmed our destination, send the Regulators back to Earth," Laurence instructed.

"Understood."

As expected, each Regulator reacted differently to the tomb being torn apart and dissolving before their eyes as they were whisked through an interdimensional tunnel to an unknown destination.

"Rogers."

He turned to Lady Tech, looking back at him from her own sphere.

"I can hear you, everyone else?"

"I'm here, sir," Merge confirmed.

"Also here, sir," Blitz acknowledged. "What is the plan?"

"The second we reach where ever this son of a bitch is taking us, everyone form up on my location if and when the Eye of Ra drops his shielding on each of us. Is that understood?"

"Yes, sir!" the trio rang out.

As predicted, Seker brought Apedemak and everyone else to the destination it plotted out. A desolate, war-torn planet possessing very little water and a red and green spikey fern vegetation that dominated the world as it orbited a red star making the sky a blood red with a splash of orange.

"Planet Otra located in the Mustavar system," Sol confirmed. "And we are not alone, detecting two warships in orbit belonging to Volori and Gregor."

Laurence's eyes narrowed under his visor as the subtle grin on Apedemak's lips grew broader.

"Send the Regulators …"

"Unable to attempt portal initiation," Sol reported.

"His familiar is preventing it?"

"Affirmative, which should not be probable."

"The interference is similar to the shielding system on Volori," Laurence growled.

"Affirmative."

"Is that fear I smell under your helm, descendant of Amun-Ra?" Apedemak villainously inquired. "Should I be the one to tell your mortals this world is where their flesh will rot? Where their bones will revert back to dust, and no markers for their graves? Worry not, you shall witness each of their deaths, final memories you can take with you to the afterlife."

Laurence's answer was not for Apedemak.

"Sergeant Rogers, I am transmitting this to you and your team. I will be releasing my shielding constructs, an assault will be coming from above shortly, be ready for it."

"Confirm the type of assault?" Rogers asked with an ice-cold tone.

"Fighter ships, high powered armor, possible assault vehicles."

Merge mimicked Blitz's abilities as they both powered up, preparing for an attack from the sky. Rogers checked his sidearm once more, preparing for combat.

"Uh, Rogers," Lady Tech swallowed while looking up. "You're going to need a **lot** more firepower."

Her visor readings picked up what the Eye of Ra and Sol already knew was coming. Death meant for them that blotted out the red sky.

CHAPTER 19

Planet Gregor, located outside the Oongova system, a territory outside of the Dominion Council rule. A planet close to the size of Jupiter with a star similar to that of Earth. Because of its size and proximity to the sun, days and nights are longer, and each season lasts a full six months on each side of the planet.

A planet ruled by an iron-fisted patriarchal system, Gregorian society was a highly advanced amalgamation similar to the old Soviet Union with philosophy and belief mirroring the Islamic State of Iraq.

From the steps of the central capital of Othollo, an anxious Grand Emperor Togar stood with his personal guard and emissaries behind him. At the bottom of the steps were a sea of his new subjects. Many of them were forced to travel from the far reaches of the planet by his decree.

The reason for the grand audience was the dimensional portal that finally opened up. Mekhit, the lion goddess of war, stepped through. Togar willingly took the knee with his head bowed, prostrating himself before her. Following suit were his emissaries, personal guards, and eventually, everyone else attending wishing to avoid the penalty of death.

"Goddess Mekhit, daughter of Horus, god of kingship and sky, and Mother Sekhmet, goddess of war," Togar recited. "The Empire of Gregor is blessed for you to finally stand on our soil."

"Rise, faithful servant," Mekhit motioned. "Witness as I converse with your people on my father's behalf."

Togar rose as the rest of his subjects remained where they knelt. Mekhit took a couple of steps to gaze out into the capital at the sea of worn and skeptical Gregorians waiting to hear from a self-proclaimed goddess from another world.

Mekhit began her address to the nation with a soft voice projecting into the capital vibrating the bones of the citizens while causing buildings and massive military vehicles to quake.

"Children of Gregor…because rulers of old chose to turn their backs on your gods…your gods decided to turn their backs on you. A fatal error that has left your world in misery and left them feeble and powerless never to return. As you can see and feel…power runs through me, and even greater power through my father and mother who sent me here to bring blessings and guide you to a golden age of prosperity never imagined in your wildest of dreams."

Mekhit paused, allowing the citizens of Gregor to process her power and her words. They turned to one another, trembling yet amazed by a being capable of causing a nation to tremble with just her voice.

"Your former Grand Emperor was slain like cattle by my mother Sekhmet for offending her, giving you the ruler, you deserve," Mekhit said while motioning to Togar. "One who will return your traditions to you, as well as your right to worship your original gods."

Her words brought whispers of shock and surprise to the people, including Togar himself.

"Only this time, you will decide where your offerings flow," Mekhit's gentle voice boomed.

"To your cowardice gods who watched your suffering from afar and feebly hid refusing to answer the call of their people, who begged them to intervene, or to the House of Horus, who has heard your words, your crying whispers, blessed you with justice, and will continue to reign blessings that will cause the universe to tremble. Tis for you the people to decide."

Mekhit's thundering voice spoken in clear Gregorian dialect brought the masses to life with waves of cheers, rejoice, and adulation all laid at the feet of the House of Horus.

A satisfied Mekhit turned to Grand Emperor Togar, who stood waiting for instructions from her.

"Per my father's orders, you will send one-fourth of your warships to Earth for him to command," Mekhit instructed.

"I will gladly send all of my warships to Lord Horus and mother Sekhmet if they desire," Togar answered, placing a hand over his left breast.

"One-fourth will be sufficient at this time," Mekhit answered. "They will be rendezvousing with a portion of the Volorion War Machine that is also en route to Earth."

"May I ask the objective of this mission, my goddess?" Togar respectfully inquired.

Mekhit devilishly smirked before she answered.

"One requires hounds to bring down the kill once the trap has been sprung."

~ ~

Alvion Prime, Capital Planet of the Dominion Council,

Sophia tentatively sat listening to experts selected by the accused. One gave authenticity to the assailant in the footage, although she could not confirm the individual's identity due to the massive about of radiation feedback the assailant was emitting.

The second expert was a biologist and geneticist specializing in Cosmivorses. The male Averan Al'Kraz from Avsolar gave detailed insights on the destructive capabilities of Cosmivorses, how they correlated to the attacks on the diplomatic ships. He then explained how the current readings were differentiated from other Cosmivorses and similar to the defendant.

Information Sophia already knew the Accusation would bring during her discussion with Oozaru. Two things that did take her off guard was seeing the updated chart of known Cosmivorses. Kimberly's name was officially on the list. It was further down, preventing her from being a suspect, but her name was on the list nonetheless. After a discussion with Oozaru, Sophia gave permission as her parent to release her medical records from Anu to ensure she was never targeted as a suspect.

It still unnerved her to see her name listed.

The other thing that caught her by surprise was that Al'Kraz was also a Cosmivorse, ranked two levels below Kimberly.

Oozaru reiterated with the first specialist that since facial recognition failed, there was inconclusive evidence that Sophia was the actual assassin. With Al'Kraz, Oozaru argued that the list of current Cosmivorses accounted for was also uncertain, that it was possible for another assailant with equivalent power level to her own to perpetrate the attacks.

Head Accuser Novtia did not counter-argue Oozaru's first refute. She did stand to speak for his second.

"Teacher Al'Kraz," Novtia formally addressed him. "Given the footage that you have seen with your own eyes, what is the possibility of another assailant matching Sophia Dennison's ability level?"

Teacher Al'Kraz glanced at Freedom, then back at Novtia before he answered.

"Because the human species are the latest to evolve to the level of Cosmivorses, we are still not privy to the extent of their capabilities, or their limitations. However, to the best of my expertise and studies, and after reviewing records of Sophia Dennison's physiology, she is on a level of the spectrum few Cosmivorses will ascend to in their lifetime. The plausibility of an assailant equivalent to Sophia Dennison is highly improbable."

"Thank you, Teacher Al'Kraz, no further questions," Novtia said with a smile.

As Teacher Al'Kraz left the inquiry stand, Novtia rose to address the Inquiry Tribunal.

"The Accusation calls upon Sophia Dennison of Earth to stand before the Inquiry."

Members of the Tribunal glanced at one another and nodded in agreement. Nephthys spoke on their behalf.

"We recognize the Accusation's request and call Sophia Dennison to the Inquiry stand."

Sophia glanced at Oozaru, who nodded, giving her authorization to rise and head to the Inquiry stand.

The hairs on her body became needles feeling all eyes upon her once again. She stood in the circle sitting in the backless cushiony disc-shaped seat with self-propulsion.

Sophia calmly clasped her hands and mentally blocked out the eyes, focusing on Novtia leaving her desk to approach her.

"Sophia Dennison of Earth, do you pledge before the Tribunal and the Council to answer my inquiries truthfully?"

"I do," Sophia nodded.

"Given the evidence presented, do you still maintain your innocence in the attacks at the border of your territory?"

"Yes, I do, considering I have no knowledge of where Earth's territory begins or ends."

"What do you know, Sophia Dennison, about us?"

Sophia narrowed her eyes slightly while reminding herself not to look menacing.

"Are you implying before the attack on my homeworld?"

"Detainment for inquiry," Novtia calmly corrected her.

"The Eye of Ra mentioned the name Dominion Council in passing," Sophia said bluntly. "He never went into further detail, and I never asked for any additional information."

"Just to be accurate, you are referring to Laurence Danjuma, the second Eye of Ra of Anu?" Novtia asked.

"I did not know that was his name, nor that he was the second," Sophia answered. "But yes, that same Eye of Ra."

Accuser Novtia strolled up to her with an attorney swagger that was apparently universal. A pleasant sardonic smile formed on her face before she spoke.

"You must realize that your defense is filling up with holes, Sophia Dennison. Diplomatic ships attacked within Earth's territory by a female assassin dressed in your uniform, operating on your power level. Yet you had a conversation with the only person with privy knowledge of this Council, and you stand here and say before us that there was no extensive talk?"

"If you believe that Laurence Danjuma allegedly conspired and divulged information in a plot to destroy those ships," Sophia carefully said with a sprinkle of sternness. "Why not bring him before this Inquiry to defend himself?"

An impressed smirk formed on Novtia's lips at Freedom's counter; it disappeared as quickly as it came as she got serious again.

"There is currently no compounding evidence against the Eye of Ra that would warrant him standing before this Inquiry. As your Council most likely informed you, that or a credible accusation is the only thing that can legally compel a member of the House of Ra to stand before this Inquiry. Is there a credible accusation for you to make, Sophia Dennison?"

"No," Sophia answered bluntly.

"No further questions for the accused," Novtia said, turning to the Tribunal.

"Permission to redirect," Oozaru stood up, addressing the Tribunal.

The members of the Tribunal once again quickly conferred, nodding with one another in agreement. Sashal, the Vice Prime Minister of Femado, spoke on their behalf.

"You may proceed, Defender Oozaru."

Oozaru turned to Sophia.

"Sophia Dennison of Earth, in your own words, why are you not the assassin in these images?"

"Aside from my oath to do no harm, anyone with half an intellect would know that committing an act, this egregious, could only be defined as suicidal genocide for myself and my people. No Earthbound government would be insane enough to sign off on such an attack, nor would I willingly carry out such a monstrous and despicable act of violence. I have no doubt that this Council has extensive knowledge of the barbarous history of my people, but if you examine further, you will see that we have evolved past stupidity. Please ask yourselves what the people of Earth could possibly gain from these attacks, aside from ensuring our annihilation? I assure you as I sit here before this Inquiry, we do not have the technology to defend, the numbers to fight, nor the alliances needed to back us.

And I say this not for you to take my words as truth but to use your vast, limitless resources and examine for yourselves. Morally I am not capable of this. Strategically my people would not dare attempt such an attack."

Freedom's words brought softly whispered conversations amongst the Council members.

"No further questions," Oozaru said to the Tribunal.

"Request to redirect," Accuser Novtia requested.

Although her lips remained pleasant and sensual, her eyes were that of a predator aiming for Sophia's jugular.

The members of the Tribunal nodded to one another in agreement, Shogonite Faustra of the Sar Republic answered.

"Proceed, Accuser Novtia."

"Thank you, Tribunal Faustra."

She turned to Sophia to verbally pounce on her.

"Sophia Dennison of Earth, you just said before this Council and Tribunal that your sworn oath to do no harm would not allow you to do this."

Sophia's eyes instinctively narrowed, remembering what she had said and knowing what Novtia's next words would be. She had slipped up, and the Accuser smelled the blood in the water.

"I know where …"

"Please answer the question," Novtia sternly pressed, cutting her off.

"Yes, but…"

"But you have broken your oath," Novtia steamrolled through Sophia's chance to defend. "You have done harm."

Knowing the longer it took to answer, the more damage she brought to her defense, Sophia reluctantly answered.

"Yes, I have."

"Can we go as far as to say, you not only harmed but killed?"

"Yes, I have."

"And you have killed to defend your world."

"Yes," Sophia solemnly nodded.

"No further questions for the accused, Tribunal," Novtia triumphantly said.

"Permission to redirect, again," Oozaru defiantly spoke up.

Once again, the members of the Tribunal agreed, Tribunal Mulfus Siral answered on their behalf.

"Proceed, Defender Oozaru."

"Sophia Dennison, please elaborate on why you were forced to break your oath."

Freedom took a slow, sad breath before she raised her head, looking at the Council to answer.

"I killed to defend my child from being taken away from me and used as a weapon. I killed to avenge a mother who was forced to watch her son torn apart by a warlord's men before they raped her, and I killed to protect my world against a terrorist and her operatives from subjugating it through bloodshed."

Sophia's head fell in shame, as she allowed the condemnatory sentence to leave her lips.

"But…Accuser Novtia is correct…I have broken my oath …to do no harm. Regardless of the justification …I am guilty of that."

Freedom's words brought soft whispers amongst Council members for a second time. Sophia's eyes remained to the ground, filled with her regrets, unable to see the subtle frown on Novtia's lips, not the satisfied smirk on Oozaru's beak.

Novtia did not count on Sophia, not defending her actions and showing genuine regret.

Something the Dominion Council who championed civility and accountability, would take into consideration.

"No further questions for the accused," Oozaru said, resting his case.

The Tribunal waited for Novtia to redirect again. She remained silent, taking her defeat for now.

"Sophia Dennison may step down and return to the side of the defense," Tribunal Fenian Dayra decreed.

Fenian's words snapped Freedom out of her poignant self-assessment of her life and actions. She rose quietly, returning to her seat, while Novtia and her team regrouped.

Head Accuser Novtia, after confirming with her staff, rose to her feet.

"Members of the Tribunal, we wish to bring forth a new witness for testimony, a human named Mildred Humphries from Earth."

At the mere mention of that name, a cold chill shot up and down Sophia's spine. She never knew her name, never bothered to learn it.

However, it was clear to her who the owner of the name was.

"What is the relevance of this witness?" Tribunal Mulfus Siral asked.

"As stated by the accused to her defense, there is only one other human with her capabilities that could execute these horrendous acts," Head Accuser Novtia answered. "We need to officially get on the record and establish the whereabouts of this witness."

Tribunal Mulfus Siral glanced at the other members. As each of them nodded in agreement, Mulfus spoke for them.

"Very well, we approve the testimony of this witness after a pause for fifteen minutes of Earth time."

~ ~

Several light-years from Alvion Prime, Princess Attea's warship, which was a similar design to her brother's only dark purple with glowing pink undertones, moved at hyperspeed.

Sitting in her command seat with parts of her skin and attire covered in dried blue blood,

Attea anxiously waited for an answer from her communications officer.

"What word from my brother?!" She snapped.

Her communications officer, a Thracian male with red scale skin, black spots, and dreaded purple hair styled into a mohawk, turned to her.

"His command ship has indicated that they are at Alvion Prime, High General. He is attending the Inquiry on Lord Nelron's behalf."

"Change course for Alvion Prime, notify security of our arrival, I must have words with him immediately."

"As you command, High General," the communication officer acknowledged.

Attea leaned back in her seat. With instinctive rage, she hammered the armrest to her chair, damaging it while slightly drawing the attention of her crew. Her ears twitched while her eyes became narrowed slants as she fought to control her anger as her mind processed the information she retrieved from Enuc.

CHAPTER 20

Alvion Prime,

Back within the Chamber Halls of the Dominion Council, soft rumbling and small talk began amongst the other Council members as they waited for the witness to be escorted into the Chambers.

At the sound of footsteps, Sophia held her breath as her eyes went in the direction of Peace entering the hall escorted by two guards.

Peace's wrists were restrained in the same deceivingly thin golden claspers placed on her on Anu.

Like an ominous magnetic attraction, the two of them eventually locked eyes with one another.

Sophia's right foot began to shake with the desire to leap over the table and get at her.

The desire came from what no one else in the room saw but her.

Although Peace appeared as a woman brought back from the seventh level of hell after spending time grounded and chewed up within Lucifer's jaw, the subtle wrinkle in her nose that Sophia caught read that she knew something no one in the entire universe knew.

Once again, she eagerly looked forward to blowing up Sophia's life.

Her eyes stayed on Peace as they led her down to the center of the Council Chamber, placing her on the inquiry stand. The two guards repositioned themselves flanking her as Head Accuser Novtia left her desk, approaching her to begin the examination.

"Please state your name on record for the Council."

"Peace."

"Please state your official human name, which is on record on your homeworld."

"I don't recognize my slave name."

Low grumbling vibrated through the Council Chamber as Head Accuser Novtia, with narrowed irritated eyes, moved closer to the inquiry stand.

"Unless you wish to be treated as a hostile witness, I advise you to remember where you sit and comply with my requests."

Peace leered at her with the desire to bite out vast chunks of her face and neck with her teeth.

"Mildred … Humphries."

Head Accuser Novtia took a leisurely little stroll purposely, stopping in front of the defense desk as she continued her questioning.

"Can you please tell the Council where you were retrieved from?"

"Yawl yanked me out of the center of a fucking black hole."

"How long have you been confined in this black hole?"

"Too fucking long."

"Can you be more specific?"

"Summer of 2015, I think."

A faint rumbling of conversation filled the Chamber hall again.

"Almost four of your human years, most beings with your capability would expire after less than a year," Head Accuser Novtia said with a nod. "Quite impressive."

"I have a bit of a roach mentality," Peace explained while locking eyes again with Freedom.

"Can you tell us how you came to end up there?"

Freedom's nose began to flair, activating the grinding of her teeth as Peace slowly raised her cuffed hands, pointing in her direction with her middle finger.

"That bitch right over there."

"Let the record state that the witness is pointing to the accused."

Head Accuser Novtia quickly turned to face Freedom before asking her next question.

"Now, Mildred Humphries of Earth, to your knowledge, aside from you and the defendant, is there anyone else from your world with your abilities, or on your power level?"

"Aside from maybe that brat of hers," Peace scoffed. "From as far as I know, nope. But things could have changed during the time I was trapped in the middle of a collapsing star."

"Thank you, Mildred Humphries, of Earth, I have no further questions for this witness," Head Accuser Novtia announced. "The defense is free to question her."

Head Accuser Novtia returned to her desk as Defender Oozaru began to rise approaching the inquiry stand. During the transition, Peace's eyes subtly moved to Prince Merc, who sat in his father's seat on the Head Council, representing Thrace's interests. True to form, his demeanor was as frigid as dry ice, disavowing any knowledge or contact with her.

She returned the sentiment, becoming emotionally dead as she harnessed the space itself; she was trapped in.

"Mildred Humphries of Earth, what was the reason Sophia Dennison of Earth placed you within the center of that collapsing star?"

Peace shrugged before she answered.

"Because she's a miserable cunt."

"Wasn't the reason for your imprisonment because you attempted to murder in cold blood every leader on your world, and take control of the planet? That you intended to subjugate the weaker part of your species for your own means once you took control of the planet?"

Peace's upper lip curled on the right side of her mouth as she leaned in for a retort.

"Trust me, Gizmo, if you knew anything about my species, and their fucked-up history, then you'd agree a little bloodletting mass murder was the only way of saving my planet. And the subjugation of the lesser masses of my species was a necessary and temporary evil meant to strengthen the roots of our malnourished foundation. See, I can talk like an intellect too."

Her eyes began to move about the Chamber in an accusatory manner.

"How much horrors and atrocities were committed in benefit of your worlds, for the greater good? You look down from your seats in judgment of me knowing damn well many if not all of your climb up the evolutionary tree was soaked in blood."

"Well, I stand here before you and can say that my species' historic growth was not one of blood and oppression," Defender Oozaru calmly retorted. "The fact that Sophia Dennison prevented you from taking your species down such a horrific path speaks to her character of a protector and defender, not a cold-blooded murderer such as yourself."

Peace hunched over, letting loose a cackle that echoed throughout the Chamber. She lifted her head, giving him an insane hysterical face with her fangs as the cherry.

"Good for you Furby, can I get you a cookie?"

Her expression switched to that of rage as she pointed the finger at Freedom.

"And that bitch is no fucking hero! Her hands are soaked with blood, just like me! She just ties her so-called 'good deeds' up in a pretty pink little bow of screwed moralism so that she can sleep at night."

Although Sophia kept her composure, the rage said it all in her eyes.

"I am nothing like you!"

During the exchange on the floor below, a granite-faced Merc sat watching while nervous relief slowly stripped away from him. It was witnessing his father's grand scheme unfold before his very eyes.

As mortally embarrassing as it was to have his father clean up his mess, his only fear was what his father had planned for him once all the deception and subterfuge were completed.

So long as Peace played her part, it would be the least of his worries.

In the middle of him focusing on the trial, Merc's ear twitched as one of his guards quietly leaned in, whispering to him.

"Apologies, my Prince, your sister, Princess Attea, is here, she wishes an audience with you. She said it was a matter of urgency."

"Can you not see I am representing Thrace in the middle of an inquiry?" Merc rumbled his question.

"She instructed me to inform you that if you did not excuse yourself to converse with her, she would enter the chamber and speak with you in front of the entire Council."

Merc grunted and snorted his frustration. Gingerly he stood up, quietly excusing himself to fellow Council members before he followed the guard back into the aisle exiting the Council chamber.

He turned to see Attea waiting for him alone with her arms folded. Once again, she had a look on her face that read, she had the desire to behead him.

"Leave us."

The guard, following his command, fell to one knee while smacking his left breast. He rose again, taking his leave as Merc walked up to his sister. With his arms folded, he stood glaring unintimidated back at her.

"You do realize I am in the middle of an inquiry that I must be present for. What is it?"

Attea snarled at her brother, stepping into his personal space.

"You damned fool! You have undone us! You have undone **all of us**!"

"What are you ranting about this time?" Merc impatiently snapped at her.

"I had an in-depth conversation with Enuc on how he came upon the information about the human's location within the sinkhole. He honestly did not know who the informant was, but he knew where the informant hailed from. The filthy Tangerian betrayed you brother."

Attea's revelation forced one of the most powerful beings in the universe to lean back with an unnerved visage on his face.

"I don't understand," Merc swallowed. "What do you mean? Betrayed me? Why? For who?"

"The 'who' has apparently instilled a greater fear in Enuc than you could ever inspire," Attea answered, shaking her head. "The 'where' is the cosmic joke for the ages; it came from the very planet you hoped to acquire for the 'glory' of Thrace."

"Earth …," Merc choked. "The information …came from …Earth."

Merc covered his mouth as a sick feeling washed all over him. Before Attea could ask him what he was thinking, both of their ears picked up a considerable commotion within the Council Chambers.

Without a word, they both rushed back in to see the cause of it.

In the middle of the trial, energy began to crackle and pop, startling everyone within the Council Chamber.

Tribunal Member Salt slowly rose to his feet in disbelief.

"A portal within the Chamber? Impossible; guards!"

As the Council Chamber guards made their way down the aisle to the floor of the central chamber room where the portal sat, someone stepped out.

It caused Freedom to rise to her feet while she felt a massive gut punch. It came from the man who slowly stepped out of the portal, wearing a male version of Freedom's outfit in a blue and white color scheme and the Fawohodie symbol in bright silver affixed to the shoulders of the suit.

The hood on the copycat attire covered the top part of his face and forced two words out of her mouth.

"Oh… shit."

As fast as Freedom's perception was, everything in the next three seconds went in slow motion for her.

A calm devious smile spread across his face as the intruder's entire body began to pulsate a green burning glow. While he stretched out his balled fists, the energy within him elevated his body three feet off the ground.

As this took place, the portal behind him dissipated.

Sheer utter chaos ensued within the Chamber Hall as the guards leaped down flights of steps with their rifles drawn, opening fire on the assailant to no avail. Their energy rounds were absorbed into the field of wild energy he produced.

Attea, already upon him with her sword drawn, was shocked as she slammed right into the energy barrier, he created preventing her from cutting him in half. Nephthys stepping in, used her power, going another route to launch him into the void of space.

The mother of Anubis was not fast enough as he unclenched his fists dripping with untold cosmic power and performed a thunderclap on a near supernova level.

As her world quickly went bright green before her very eyes with destructive energy, Freedom's eyes instinctively gazed upon the last person in her world.

What she didn't expect was that same person to be looking back at her.

Peace's eyes, which were drenched with an emotional mixture of rage, fear, and frustration, spoke back to her.

"We are so fucked!"

In a flash, the capital of Alvion Prime, the cornerstone of the formation of the Dominion Council along with almost fifty percent of the surface of the planet, went up in a destructive flash, symbolizing the catastrophic foreshadowing of change for everything to come in the known universe.

~ ~

Back on Anu, word had not reached the homeworld yet of the planetary attack on the Dominion Council.

Instead, Thoth was preoccupied with another smaller explosion that took place within the Halls of Healing.

A female healer met him en route there.

"The youngling human patient is awake and quite anxious."

Thoth nodded as he entered the Hall of Healing with her where there were four armored Annunaki warriors and several other healers.

They all respectfully parted out of the way, allowing him to witness what they were seeing.

Standing outside of an obliterated pod was Sophia's daughter, disorientated and sheepishly covering herself from the crowd staring back at her.

"Oh, dear," Thoth slowly swallowed.

Kimberly's face had the written expression of a terrified little girl, while her bright golden glowing eyes revealed she had the destructive power of energies that birthed the universe coursing through her veins.

With the child's mother off-planet, Thoth gingerly held his hands up, ordering both guards and healers present to not make any sudden moves. He stepped forward, attempting to handle this situation as one would carefully fold wet tissue paper.

Kimberly uttered six words from a cracked voice as she scanned the room.

"Where am I? Where's my mom?"

To be continued in Book 2

ABOUT THE AUTHOR

Kipjo K. Ewers was born on July 1, 1975. At an early age, he had an active imagination. By the time he started kindergarten, he would make up fictitious stories, one of his favorites was about a character named "Old Man Norris," who hated everyone in the world except for him.

When he attended our Lady of Victory Elementary School in Mount Vernon, he continued writing and reading stories to his classmates. His teacher, Mrs. Green, told him the children would laugh, but she would remind them that that is how some of the great stories that they read came about.

After elementary school, he went to Salesian High School in New Rochelle, NY, then on to Iona College.

He would go on to work for several major firms and companies within the New York area, but his passion was about wanting to become a journalist/writer. Therefore, it is not surprising he decided to write his first book/novel.

Kipjo began working and creating a new superhuman universe, finding inspiration and solace in losing his first daughter due to an unfortunate miscarriage that devastated both his loving wife and him; he began writing a hero origin story now titled "The First."

After publishing "The First" in 2013, Kipjo wrote two more follow up novels to the series, a spin-off novel titled the Eye of Ra, and a romantic supernature novel titled "Fred & Mary."

Now known as the EVO Universe, Kipjo continues to write to expand the series and create new projects for the foreseeable future.

Thank you for reading and your support.